BEING
BLACK 'N
CHICKEN,
& CHIPS

BEING BLACK 'N CHICKEN, & CHIPS

Caroline,

Missed you at the laundromat more than I missed the spelling of your name!!. sorry!!.

MATT OKINE

hachette
AUSTRALIA

hachette
AUSTRALIA

Published in Australia and New Zealand in 2019
by Hachette Australia
(an imprint of Hachette Australia Pty Limited)
Level 17, 207 Kent Street, Sydney NSW 2000
www.hachette.com.au

10 9 8 7 6 5 4 3 2 1

NATIONAL
LIBRARY
OF AUSTRALIA
A catalogue record for this
book is available from the
National Library of Australia

ISBN: 978 0 7336 4168 8 (paperback)

Cover design by Design by Committee
Cover image by Dreamstime
Author photograph courtesy of Anneliese Nappa
Typeset in Adobe Garamond Pro by Kirby Jones
Printed and bound in Australia by McPherson's Printing Group

MIX
Paper from
responsible sources
FSC® C001695

The paper this book is printed on is certified against the
Forest Stewardship Council® Standards. McPherson's Printing
Group holds FSC® chain of custody certification SA-COC-005379.
FSC® promotes environmentally responsible, socially beneficial
and economically viable management of the world's forests.

Dedicated to my daughter, Sofia Atswei Okine.
Your grandmother was strong, smart, caring and
hilarious. I see more and more of her in you each day.
I love you more than anything in this world.
– Dad

PROLOGUE

As you might imagine, lying on the sand, half-naked, begging your own mum to wee on you, is not the best way to start a new year. It does little for the self-esteem, and – as it turns out – even less for a jellyfish sting.

I'd planned to start my first year of high school with a bang, but Mum had extinguished those hopes with a crisp number one, and if that wasn't bad enough, somehow – as far as my year's turn of events would go – that parental golden shower would turn out to be one of the highlights.

·

It was 1998.

Year of the Tiger.

Year of the French soccer World Cup, and England hating David Beckham.

A year that four brightly coloured blobs, called Teletubbies, would debut on Australian TV, dancing around each other in a green field, muttering an indecipherable language, captivating every baby in the country.

It was the year that rugby league was getting its shit back together after a disastrous breakaway competition called Super League, which broke the patience of fans, and the pockets of clubs, so that it could finally go back to making headlines for all the regular reasons: drug possession and assault charges. Our prime minister, John Howard, was making headlines of his own, proving he had little taste by refusing to meet the Spice Girls.

It was the year of the Winter Olympics in Nagano, Commonwealth Games in Kuala Lumpur, and US President, Bill Clinton, having quite a bit to answer for.

It was the year of Britney, and Buffy, and dorks stampeding at dawn to install the ground-breaking operating system, Windows 98, on their lightning-fast Pentium IIs.

It was also the year, in a city called Brindlewood, two thirds up the East Coast of Australia, three months after the pissing incident, that I found myself sitting on the edge of a jetty, with the wind howling across the nearby mudflats and all those damn mosquitoes.

For every mosquito I slapped on my arm, it seemed there were seven more on my legs. Some sort of kamikaze mosquito mission; one taunting my top half, sacrificing herself so that the masses could feast below. I could see Dad's torchlight way off in the distance, flickering across the moonlit waters, disappearing briefly behind thick mangroves and re-appearing again.

This was 'The Swamp'. A small cove of mud and mangroves, at the base of Jenkins' Reserve, where the Burnett Creek met the curved banks of the Brindlewood River. This was my backyard. Not in a literal sense, but I'd grown up here long enough to own it. Five square kilometres of bushland, sprawled across the southern base of Brindlewood's biggest peak, Mt Kartha. To the east was the fancy side of town, home to posh shops spruiking smelly candles, my high school, and a prestigious golf course that cushioned the yards of all the rich kids. To the west was the cheap side of town, where my house (of course) was bordered by the unkempt nature of 'The Reserve'. Splitting the Reserve down the middle, like a prawn's poop shoot, was 'The Creek', that ran from the top of Mt Kartha, down to where I was sitting right now. The Swamp. The asshole of it all. Sometimes you could sit in this spot of an afternoon; the murky water lapping sullenly at the wooden frame of 'The Jetty', the occasional guppy ducking its head up and out of the water to capture little gasps of air, like a dog lapping at freshness from the yawning window of a car. Other times, in low tide, like now – the muddy riverbed exposed – you could see all sorts of sea life scampering across the muck, darting in between the short, stubby mangrove roots that jut out of the earth, each about the size of a cigarette; they looked sole-slicing, but would actually crackle and crunch quite easily under the thick rubber of a damp Dunlop.

'Mike!' I heard Dad yelling to me, his voice thin and faint as it dispersed around the huge open marshland; only ten per cent of it reaching me, the other ninety per cent filling the open sky and disappearing up into space.

'What?' I screamed at the top of my lungs; my voice echoing across the stillness of the creek mouth.

'Just checking!' he screamed back.

God, Dad was so annoying. He was always giving me oily eyes; I mean, anything he said would make my eyeballs roll.

'You asked me to stand here with the torch, so I'm standing here with the torch!'

'I'm coming back now!' he screamed again. 'Stay there!'

Where did he think I was going? Did he think that I would just disappear?

It'd been in the mid-twenties most of the day, and I'd had no problems rocking my fave get-up all afternoon, but now I was shivering in my black shorts and striped purple polo. Tully had really ripped me hard when I'd come home from Tassie wearing it for the first time. She said it looked like I was wearing a sleeved stained-glass window. She'd asked whether I'd spewed on myself cos it was so technicoloured.

But I didn't care.

I'd had the best time in Tasmania with Mum. She'd taken me there as a graduation present during the summer holidays between finishing primary school and starting high school. That once-in-a-lifetime month of happiness that sees you leave childhood behind, before puberty and profession start presenting you life's problems.

This shirt reminded me of that.

I would never forget it, even though – now – I was cold, wet, and itchy, sitting on the edge of the Jetty.

Slap.

Tasmania.

What I'd do to be back there.

Just me and Mum.

Before the pissing incident, of course.

·

We'd been sitting on the shores of a spot called Friendly Beaches, watching the timid Tasmanian waves crawl towards us as the sun gradually dipped below the treetops; that beach soundtrack of a thousand analogue TVs without reception, engulfing us.

We'd been to Cadbury's Chocolate Factory in Hobart, and while the colours and gadgets weren't quite up to Wonka's standards, it was pretty rad seeing the birthplace of my Friday night snacks. From there, we'd driven up along the south-east coast of the island, before making a pit stop at Friendly Beaches.

Mum and I were lying amongst the sparse tufts of grass that acted as a fringe between the beach's carpark and the sandy slope leading down to the sea. She was scribbling away furiously in her smart, black faux-leather diary, and I was practicing my triple jump.

'What's a sonic boom gun?' I asked as I drew a line in the sand with my toe and took a few steps back for a run-up.

'I'd say it's a good indication that you play too many video games,' Mum replied, barely looking up from her writing.

'Uncle Greg told me at your fortieth that if I ever hear the floorboards creaking in the middle of the night, it's not the floorboards, it's sonic boom guns. That they're "listening to us".'

Mum lowered her diary. 'This. This is why I *never* have parties.'

'We've never had floorboards,' I said.

'What else did he say?' she asked, one eyebrow cocked.

'He said he's been trying to contact the Queen, but she won't answer, and that he's sixteenth in line to the throne, which makes me thirty-second in line to the throne,' I shrugged.

'Well, you're not,' Mum said, matter-of-fact. 'You're not even in the line. It's like Disneyland. You need to be "this tall" to go on the ride, except "this tall" is an incestuous bloodline, and "the ride" is a horribly outdated and colonial sense of supremacy.'

'Oh man,' I said, spitting little particles of sand out of my mouth, 'I already told Tully I'd make her a duchess.'

I dusted off my legs, stood up and went back to my mark for another jump.

'Why isn't Uncle Greg a patient at Woolvin Park?' I asked. 'Don't you want to help him?'

'Mike, I'm an Aquarius. It's basically my cosmic duty to help others, but my job is to help people get out of that place, not send them in.' She sighed. 'Plus, you should never work with family.'

She flicked over the page of her diary and kept scribbling as I hop-step-and-jumped away from her, landing with a thud, the wind kicking sand back into my eyes and mouth.

'Jesus, Mike, do you mind?' she said, waving her hand around her face like she was swatting flies.

'I'm sorry,' I said, spitting sand out of my lips again. 'I need to practice. I really want to make the team for the Dobson Dash.' The Brindlewood All-Schools Cup – more commonly known as the 'Dobson Dash' – was a massive, interschool track and field event named after some guy called Gary Dobson, an ex-Commonwealth Games runner from Brindlewood who apparently won lots of gold medals back in a time when metres were still yards and Aboriginal people couldn't vote. The event was designed to bring all the kids together from the high schools right around the Brindy region to raise money for a charity of your school's choice. Every metre jumped or thrown was a dollar towards the kitty, and every first, second, and third in the races earned ten, five, and two dollars respectively. At the end of the day, a team from each school – two boys and two girls – ran a 4 x 100-metre mixed relay, and the winning school would score an additional $1000 for their charity of choice, paid for by the local newspaper, *The Brindlewood Chronicle*, who would also chuck you on the front page of the sports section to boot. You can bet your boulders I was keen to get amongst it. I could picture the flashes of the paparazzi cameras already.

Mum's voice brought me back to reality. 'Don't be too disappointed if you don't, Mike. You've been a big fish in a small pond for too long. It's good to be challenged.'

A big fish in a small pond was an understatement. I'd won every single event at the Ironbark Primary School athletics carnival, from the shot-put to the sprints. I wasn't a big fish in a small pond, I was a shark in a bathtub. A goddamn blue whale in a tear drop.

'I know, Mum. That's why I've got to practice. I'm going to be at the same school as Skon Helpmann now. He wins everything at States. The guy is a monster.'

I remember the first time I saw Skon compete. He had the swagger of an athlete who knew no-one could touch him. But I was sure as hell going to try.

I crawled over to Mum and put my head on her chest. It was nice and warm, offsetting the cool coastal breeze that was blowing around us. The moment felt right, and even though my nerves were tingling and my heart was pounding, I took a plunge.

'Mum.'

'Yes, Mike?'

'Can we get the internet?'

Mum laughed and rolled her eyes. She put a full stop at the end of the sentence she was writing, snapped her diary closed, and stood up, dusting off her backside and gathering her things.

'Oh, I love you, my little chook. Now let's go, I need to use the ladies and my squatting days are over.' She wrapped her arms around me and ruffled my curly hair.

'Stop it,' I said, wriggling out of her grasp. 'I'm serious. I'm in high school now. I need the internet to study!'

'That's what the library is for, Mike.'

I was scrambling, 'Or I could use it to learn an instrument, or … or for workout techniques! So I can be big enough to beat Skon. I'm sitting on "zero from nine" from every meet we've ever done together. If I let him get to ten, I may as well wear a tombstone to school because my athletics career will be as good as dead.'

Mum laughed again.

'Mike, don't be silly. The internet is expensive. Plus, you're too young to be working out.'

'Just because *you* never work out,' I said.

She stared at me, laser beams. 'Go wash yourself off.'

'I'm sorry. I didn't mean it like that, promise,' I said, looking sulkily out at the ocean as it welcomed the rich navy of night. 'It's just … you can't treat me like a kid anymore. I'll be a grown-up soon.'

Mum's eyes softened. 'Fine, but there's no need to be rude. Now go wash off. You're not getting in the rental car looking like that, unless you want to walk all the way to Coles Bay?'

'But Mum. It's too cold.'

'No whingeing, Mike. You'll be a grown-up soon, so act like it.'

I felt really bad. I didn't mean it like that.

So I took my shirt off and started running.

Running towards the cold.

CHAPTER ONE

SATURDAY, 28TH MARCH 1998

You'll be a grown-up soon.

I certainly wasn't a grown-up yet, sitting out on this stupid jetty, waiting for Dad.

There were guys at Brindlewood High with facial hair, and I don't mean whiskers, I mean full-blown, crumb-catching beards. The senior girls all wore bras and shaved their legs and armpits and had hips and cellulite. High school was no place for a kid like me.

I had a high-pitched, whiny voice that sent dogs into panic whenever I piped up. I had a pokey little pigeon chest with scrawny arms like chicken wings, and legs that resembled two bendy, brown chopsticks. I hadn't so much as grown a single strand of bumfluff on my top lip, and my downstairs region had as many thick-and-curlies as a Sphynx cat.

I needed to grow up.

I got to my feet and cautiously walked up the jetty towards where Dad's car was parked. Each step was an uneven gamble for my ankles, as the occasional wayward nail head poked the rubber of my thongs firmly against the soles of my feet. Each footstep, a chance for fate to send me straight through those rickety boards and plunging into the water below.

But I knew what was down there.

The Irukandji.

Dad always took me on crabbing trips, ever since I was a little kid, and I hated it. I mean, it's kinda fun when you're eight or nine, but not when you're almost thirteen. I wanted to be hanging out with Zoe Ingham, my crush from school. I wanted to be lazing about in the Reserve with her. I wanted to be holding her hand as we walked across the small bridge that crossed over the Creek. I wanted her to stop and look down at some guppies, and for me to stand behind her, put my arms around her waist and then kiss her neck. I wanted to lie down on the grass somewhere, or maybe even on a high jump mat, and I wanted to make out with her, and feel her boobs and ass.

Instead, I was standing on a creaky old jetty in the middle of nowhere, stinking of fish guts, while my dad looked for goddamn mud crabs.

'Hey Zo, I was just wondering if –' I had to stop myself. Was it weird to call her 'Zo'? I cleared my throat and tried again.

'Hey, Zoe. You, me, and a picnic in the park. Whatya say?' Jesus, was I a waiter at a rock-n-roll diner in the sixties?

'Can I kiss you?'

OK, now I was jumping ahead. It's not like we'd ever talked. I was only in a couple of classes with Zoe, and high school had only been going for two months, so everything I knew, I knew from overhearing conversations in class, but I liked what I'd heard. She'd told a story in English one day about how she'd beaten up her sister for 'accidentally' kicking the Sega plug out of the wall when they were neck-and-neck, coming out the final bend of the beginner track in Daytona, and it really cracked me up. I'd thought about her beating me up a few times, and it always made me smile.

I imagined myself standing next to her in the parklands, looking over the pond. Arms around her waist. I tried again, 'Can I kiss you?'

'Of course,' she would say. And then we'd go at it. Our tongues lashing across each other like silicone brushes oiling a hot BBQ grill. Opening and closing our mouths like goldfish.

By now, I'd stopped in the middle of the Jetty.

Dad was still at least five minutes away, which I figured was enough time for this freak show to hit second base. I curled my right hand into an oval, up against my chapped, windblown lips and started really going for it; slowly at first – small, soft pecks – but soon enough I was sticking my tongue in and everything. I could taste the salty remnants of fish bait that I'd been helping Dad with earlier.

It was disgusting. I'd turned into a monster, but I couldn't help it. I kept going. I'd seen people kiss their hand in movies as a joke, but I wasn't joking. It's as close as I could get to the real thing, and I needed the practice. It's embarrassing to admit – and trust me, I've lied about it plenty before – but Zoe would be the first person I ever kissed.

At least, I hoped she would be.

That's when I heard the footstep.

A stick breaking. Thick, and hard, under the weight of something.

Or someone.

I dropped my hand to my side, embarrassed, and quickly wiped the saliva onto my shorts, looking up. God, there was a lot of slobber. Is kissing really that messy?

I stared back towards the bushes flanking the narrow dirt path that led to Dad's car that was parked forty metres away.

Was it a person?

Standing there. On the left of the path. Still, but breathing. I could see their chest moving from the single orange light that barely illuminated the mostly dirt carpark of the Reserve.

Ours was the only car when we arrived, and I'd been sitting alone for twenty damn minutes. I would've heard someone else turn up.

Unless they didn't want me to.

The figure took a step closer, and it suddenly occurred to me what was going on. It was Dad! Trying to scare me. I almost let out a chuckle too, when –

'Mike!' Dad's voice, cracking the night air. But Dad's voice was coming from deep inside the mangroves.

My head snapped to my right to check, and, sure enough, there was Dad's torchlight flickering within the thick foliage, all the way across the bay.

This person wasn't Dad.

This person had been watching me. Watching me get my pash on with my dirty stinking fish hand.

I wanted to point my torch right at them, but I was frozen.

'Help!' I tried to yell for Dad, but it didn't come out nearly loud enough.

I felt my stomach lodging up next to my heart.

'Please, don't yell,' the figure rasped.

I couldn't help it.

'Help!' This time I was louder. Much louder.

I snapped my torch up and shone it directly into the bushes where the stranger was standing.

That's when he stepped forward. The old man. Not rough-looking, but not clean. He looked the way Dad looked after a Saturday in the garden. Not clean enough for a meal at the pub, but clean enough for the pokies room. The type of body fat percentage you could only get in prison, he had a dog by his side – and at this distance I couldn't tell if the dog was friendly or not.

'I said – stop yelling,' he croaked. He was now blocking the top of the Jetty; my only way out, unless I went the other way. Into the river. Into –

The Irukandji.

'I'm sorry,' I mumbled. And that's when I saw the gun. Held by his waist; its long barrel running against his thigh.

He stepped forward, walking towards me, marching, urgent and gruff as though he'd caught me keying his car.

That's when I ran, feeling –

The cool rush of sun-setting wind.

I dropped the torch and sprinted as fast as I could towards the end of the Jetty.

Running away from Mum, towards the cold of the Tasmanian ocean.

I could hear footsteps behind me. Speeding up.

Promising that as soon as I hit the waves, I'd be a man. All grown up.

The closer I got to the edge of the Jetty, the more I realised I was going to have to face my biggest fear.

I'd stood at the edge of the Jetty that afternoon, twelve hours earlier, when Dad was setting up his crab pots, still dreaming of Zoe Ingham, and how we might one day even get married, and how my next-door neighbour Tully would be my best woman, and I'd look out into the front row of the chapel and I'd see Mum and Dad sitting there. In the same room again. For once.

And as my foot hit the edge of the ocean, I took off, hopping over the first line of whitewash, stepping across the waves.

No looking back.

Jumping into the sea, to clean my body of sand and sins.

Standing at the edge of the Jetty that afternoon, cutting my curls off.

Unaware of the swarm. The Bloom brought by the North-Easterly winds.

Jellyfish. So many jellyfish.

'No, don't!' The man's voice bellowed past me, but it was too late.

I hit the last board on the edge of the Jetty, and like a jumper at the Olympics, I put everything into my calves, dipped my quads, and took a breath.

And I thought about how I might never see Mum again.

And that made me sad and mad, at the same time.

Because I really loved her, more than anything in the world.

But this was all her fault.

And then I jumped.

CHAPTER TWO

SUNDAY, 8TH MARCH 1998

Suddenly I was cold.

The squelching, and the swooshing, and the schlucking of water, surrounding me. Unsure of which way was up, my head hitting the bottom – or was it the top?

My face, smooshed up against tiles, like a frog looking out of a fish tank.

I pushed off against the surface and felt my hands pressing down on small round disks. All different sizes. Metal. Coins.

Wet. Panic. What. The. Fuck?

A hand gripping around my bicep, yanking, pulling me up.

And suddenly I was out. Standing. Soaked.

The sobering lights of department stores. Couples canoodling as they ascended the escalator. Two old ladies sitting on benches outside Myer who both sported tight perms; nothing to buy except time between visits from their now-grown children. The clinical whiteness of Brindlewood Shopping Centre.

'Brindy' Shopping Centre.

I knew this place well. I'd seen shops come and go, carparks extended, cinema screens expanded, and awkward teens trying to hide their acne as they flirted with each other at the bus interchange. If the Reserve was my backyard, then this was my second home. Not far from my Dad's place, it was the centre I would catch the bus to every day with Tully after school before walking home through the Reserve to our houses. Most of the action revolved around the food court and the bus stop. Some days we'd hop off the bus at the interchange and walk straight home, no looking back. Other days, if I had a buck or two, we'd brave the crowds and get a thirty-cent cone from Maccas for the stroll. Over the years, we'd learnt to make our cones last. One lick every twenty steps would usually see us take the last bite as we hit our driveways. But we stopped doing that after high school began. It had started to feel uncool. They say Adam and Eve felt naked and ashamed after eating the forbidden fruit, but maybe it wasn't the fruit's fault. Maybe they had just become teenagers.

A long, rectangular, three-storey concrete building, 'Brindy' wasn't the biggest or the nicest shopping centre in town, but it was always buzzing. The arctic breeze of air-conditioning was a welcome shot to the nostrils when you walked in after a stinking hot ride on an old council bus, filled with kids from rival schools.

They'd recently added something called a 'Chill Zone', which was really just a big square of carpet with a few cushions and uncomfortable seating cubes, designed to stop high-schoolers from leaving their bags strewn across the nearby food court.

It didn't work.

Every afternoon after school the food court would heave with kids of all sorts; 'Stateys' and 'Snobs', Year Eights to Senior, the big dawgs trying to figure out what size of 'alpha' suit their style, the mean girls trying to out-blush each other between brutal backstabs.

Separating both areas was a big fountain – now the nucleus of all the action. It bubbled water up towards the glass dome ceiling that provided Brindy's only natural light. A reminder of the real world. A peephole for the gods. And if the gods were looking down through that peephole in that moment, they would have seen me, smack bang in the middle of the scene, knee-deep in the fountain and soaked.

The gods must have been smiling on this particular day though – a Sunday – because I dare say if I'd fallen in the fountain on a Friday, the food court's most popular day, I doubt I'd be here to tell this tale at all, because, trust me when I say this – Brindy could make or break you.

In our first week of high school, six weeks ago, Tully and I had witnessed an absolute career-ender. It was a kid from the local Lutheran college, a dweeby-looking bloke, with high-waisted shorts, big bushy hair, and metal frame glasses. This kid got dacked in the middle of the food court, undies and all. Everyone saw it, and everyone laughed, and the mistake that poor dweebus made was that he started crying. And I don't mean a single tear or two. I mean, full-blown fire hydrant howling in the middle of the food court, and nothing feeds a bully like the salty, wet tears of a nerd. Rumour has it – that kid left town the next morning, and I've heard a few whispers that his stubby-peened ghost still haunts the food court to this day.

I drew a line in the sand that day as I realised, from the unrelenting taunts of adolescent onlookers, that men shouldn't cry. That was one line I wouldn't triple jump over. From this day forth.

'Mike, the flyers!' Dad yelped in his hybrid Afro-Australian accent. He was bent over the fountain edge, grabbing desperately around me at the small, A5 pieces of paper dispersing daintily atop the water. Flyers that, only moments before, had been firmly held in my hot little hands; each one proudly promoting

AFRO GOOD TIMES with a silhouette of a West-African figure playing the maracas.

'How could you do this? No shopkeeper is going to put wet flyers on their counter,' Dad said, snatching at floating flyers.

'No shopkeeper has put *dry* flyers on their counter!' I argued.

A warning glare from Dad.

We'd been walking around Brindy for thirty minutes asking shopkeepers to display Dad's nightclub flyers, but they all said they didn't have enough room, even the counters that had enough real estate to land a 747.

'These flyers cost money, Mike. Money doesn't grow on trees,' he scowled.

'Paper grows on trees,' I replied, scrambling to grab what I could, 'and that's what these are made of. So why you're paying for them is beyond me.'

Dad shot me a second stink-eye and went back to grabbing whatever leaflets were in reach.

'Mike, please. I'm bringing Serwaa and the Swingers out for the concert this month, and it needs to be full. She's costing me an arm and a leg. Actually, more. Three arms, four legs.'

He'd used most of the strength that his nuggety, rounded, five-foot-six-inch frame could muster to pull me out of the fountain, so was puffing by the time he eventually stood up. Soggy pamphlets clutched awkwardly against his mid-section, from his right hand to the crook of his elbow, he produced a handkerchief from his back pocket with his other hand to dab the sweat on the crescents of his tightly-curled, widow's-peaked hairline.

I finally spotted what I'd dropped in the fall and snatched it out off the floor of the fountain.

'Jellyfish,' I said, holding up my drenched science book. 'I was reading about jellyfish. Really bad jellyfish. In North

Queensland. Maybe if we had the internet, I wouldn't need these cumbersome books?'

Dad shook his head, disappointed, and went back to plucking out the remaining floating flyers from the fountain, as though they were bits of bread and his hand was a duck.

Whether he noticed the laughter and simply ignored it, I'm not sure, but when I finally turned around to face the food court, I realised we'd gained ourselves a pretty healthy audience.

The older you get, the less people laugh when you fall. I was twelve, so people were having a right proper cack. Some covered their sniggering mouths, feigning concern, others – mostly children – were quite happy to straight-up point and laugh.

I didn't mind people laughing at me though. It was something I'd gotten pretty used to. In fact, it's how I liked it most of the time. When people laugh, they let their guards down, and there's power in creating that vulnerability. Even a king needs to laugh. I'd prefer to be the clown in the court, performing gags for the king, than the farmer in the field, grumbling grievances into the dirt.

Of course, there's a big difference between people laughing *at* you, and laughing *with* you, and that difference is you. I knew what was up, so was really only left with one option.

'Thank you!' I yelled, as I held my hands up and out to the crowd. I may have milked it a little too much, but I still drew a few chuckles, followed by some half-hearted claps too. Not bad. Overall, it wasn't my best performance, and I certainly couldn't guarantee a return season, but I was happy enough with the response and looked forward to the write-up in the papers tomorrow.

Dad finally dragged me out of the fountain and onto dry ground. I continued the charade as he pulled me through the crowd, towards the carpark; all cheers, smiles and waves at the onlookers, until –

Until I saw her.

The one person in the whole world who I would've done *anything* to not see me end up, ass-over-head, in a shopping centre fountain.

Zoe. Freakin'. Ingham.

Strolling casually through the food court, next to her mum, with her bright red hair in low pigtails, wearing a loose white training singlet over a pair of short black bike pants that really highlighted how long and pale her legs were, a pair of black and red running spikes, tied at the laces, draped over her shoulder. Her freckled face looked a touch more flush than normal, the result of sunshine and sprints. She was eating chocolate ice-cream that was over-packed into a waffle cone, the type of scoop that you constantly clean up with your tongue rather than simply enjoy.

From across the mall, I locked eyes with Zoe's mum. I needed to get moving. Quickly. I tried digging my feet into the floor to make a getaway, but they wouldn't stick to the gloss tiles. I felt like Wile E Coyote, whipping my legs after I'd just run off a cliff. Too little, too late.

Zoe's mum made a beeline for Dad and me with Zoe and her little sister, Georgia, in tow. While my heart hammered in my chest, Dad and Zoe's mum started to talk about Georgia's dental work.

'The fissure sealing you gave Georgia has made her back teeth sensitive,' Mrs Ingham said, squatting in her matching activewear. 'Show Dr Amon where it started hurting last night when we were eating the Viennetta.'

I looked up from my feet – straight into Zoe's eyes.

It wasn't the normal Zoe. She was wearing those candy teeth, with the pink gums, that just barely covered her top row of incisors. Those candy teeth that have lasted the party mix test of time, not least because of novelty as opposed to actual taste.

'What do you think of my new teef?' she asked.

I checked over my shoulder, assuming there must've been some cool Year Ten jock behind me. The kind of guy who had floppy hair and a mouth that always hung a little bit open. The kind of guy that came to school without a schoolbag, their untucked shirt covering a folded exercise book jutting from the back pocket of their grass-stained shorts, always asking the kid next to them if they can borrow a pen. Zoe deserved the kind of guy who could get her invites to cool parties, not some idiot drenched in fountain juice.

Finally, I remembered I could talk.

'Have you just been training?' I asked.

'Nah, this is just how I dress now,' she smiled, pulling her gummy teeth out, exposing a little gap between her two front top teeth, about the width of a twenty-cent piece.

I'd noticed that gap since day one. Across the stinking-hot assembly hall, as the Year Eight co-ordinator Mr Bortey welcomed us all to Brindlewood High, droning on about where the school nurse's office was, and how any visitors needed to check-in at head office first, I noticed that gap. I loved that gap.

'She's going to win the Dash!' Zoe's little sister Georgia chimed in, standing next to Zoe in a small hypercolour T-shirt that lost it's 'hyper' a long time ago, and gold sequined shorts. She was cleaning up a mint choc-chip scoop of her own, catching green trails with her tongue as they dribbled down her forearm. She was seven, maybe eight, and her hair was set in the same pigtails as Zoe's, but wasn't as red.

'You know there are easier ways to make money?' Zoe said, reaching up and plucking something off my forehead. It was a coin. It had been stuck there the whole time. 'You get good luck if you throw them *in,* not take them out.'

'Can I have it?!' Georgia asked, reaching for the coin.

Zoe held it out of her reach as Georgia jumped up and down, trying to grab it, while trying to keep her ice-cream seated in its cone.

'Maybe if you ask nice, Mike will go fishing for another one for you.'

She knows my name.

I felt that feeling.

That feeling that starts from deep behind your belly button near your spine. That feeling that sits so deep within the pit of your stomach that if you were to reach in and pull it – like a loose thread on the elastic of your undies – you would turn the whole universe inside out. That feeling of hollowness and fullness all at once, like every cell in your body was doing the Macarena.

I felt that feeling.

Suddenly aware of all my limbs, how I'd crossed my arms across my chest, shivering, I let them go, dangling on either side of my body.

But they just felt so *heavy!* Do they normally just hang there like that?

I thought about what the cool, jock dudes at school do when they're talking to girls. All tossing footballs around, or rubbing their stomachs under their shirts, so I started rubbing my stomach, but it was covered with Dad's mulched up wet flyers so it just looked like I was exfoliating with pamphlets.

I felt tight in the chest.

I'd been holding my breath the whole time, in case the air that came out formed words that I'd regret for the rest of my life, so I exhaled and laughed at the same time – but water had dribbled from the mop of loosely-curled hair on my head, down over my lips, so when I suddenly laughed, it shot droplets of water all over Zoe's face.

Sweet Jesus. I considered taking another dip in the fountain and never coming back up.

Zoe laughed in shock and wiped her face with her non-ice-cream hand, and I admired her teef gap again.

We looked into each other's eyes for a second and that was all I needed.

True love.

It could be confirmed. I was in love. Call the *Brindy Chronicle*! It was official. I was *actually* in love. Deni Hines had sung about it. Leonardo Di Caprio had died grasping onto a floating door because of it.

And now I knew what it was.

Dad was counting his remaining flyers in frustration, barely looking up at Mrs Ingham. 'Oh, um. Just send a request to the school nurse, and I'll have someone see you this week.' He dug a thumb into my back and marched me forward as he said a swift goodbye.

I turned back, just for a moment. The heat in my cheeks finally cooling.

I can't be one hundred per cent sure. Because right at that moment, the movement of my head sent some droplets of water down my forehead and into my eyes, so what I saw, I saw like a driver with broken windscreen wipers driving through the rain.

But I'm pretty sure I saw Zoe turn around and look back at me too. And I saw that gap, because she was smiling.

I think.

I dunno.

Maybe.

CHAPTER THREE

I don't blame Mum for losing it. I really don't.

She'd just got home from a romantic getaway with her boyfriend, Kenny, and was probably basking in post-holiday bliss. So opening the door to see me, standing there, semi-soaked, with a big Afro Good Times poster wrapped around my shoulders and only one shoe on, must have really snapped her back to reality. At some stage during the fountain fall, I'd managed to lose my left Puma, and with all the commotion and Zoe and everything, I somehow didn't notice until Dad and I had gotten back to the car. By that point I didn't really want to bring it up because Dad was already pretty cranks with me.

Poor Mum, though. She took one look at me and her eyes glazed over like she was already imagining how she was going to justify murder to the judge.

'I'm going to kill him,' she said, matter-of-fact, as she walked past me and over to a window in the corridor of our old, 1960s brick unit block. She looked out to see Dad, standing four floors below on the garden paving outside the complex, next to the unit letter boxes, ready to see if I'd made it inside safely. That was the routine: he'd drop me at Mum's every afternoon after school, and the one-weekend-a-month that I'd actually sleep overnight at his place, then he'd wait, and, once Mum opened the door, I would wave down to let him know I could get inside. We'd had that routine for four years, but this time it was Mum waving at him, and it wasn't a happy wave.

She slid the window open, and leaned out.

Giving no care to the neighbourhood, she yelled down, over-articulating her words just to be sure he could lip-read them too. Dad had a habit of not hearing things.

'You stay right friggin' there, Marvin!'

Fucking yeh right! I'd never seen a dude scramble like Dad was scrambling. He scuttled backwards so hastily that he tripped up on the shrubbery of the garden path behind him, skittling over onto his ass and hands. He quickly jumped back onto his feet, and race-walked towards the car. Race-walked, because to run would imply guilt.

Mum race-walked too, down the hall to the unit block's lift, and bashed the button repeatedly.

'Pressing it more won't make it come faster,' I said, immediately regretting my words.

Mum stepped into the elevator, spun around, and shot me a glare that could've broken glass.

I could see why Mum was mad. She'd been planning her getaway with Kenny for months, and here were Dad and me, putting a sour little footnote at the end of it all.

No sooner had Mum disappeared behind the closing elevator doors, than I heard the low whir of a wheelchair behind me. Mum's boyfriend, Kenny, appeared in the doorway of our apartment, coming through diagonally at first, reversing, correcting his angle, and then rolling down the small, homemade wooden wedge-ramp that Mum had made to broach the gap from our unit's entrance, out into the common area corridor.

He rolled up next to me; his shoulders wide, his chest large, his belly rounded and soft. He'd had a rugby injury growing up; a collapsed scrum, and he'd broken his neck. I mean, you hear about the dangers, but he was living proof. A big, burly bloke in his youth, now in a wheelchair the past thirty-something years; and not a small wheelchair either. A big, bulky chair, with a huge battery pack underneath it that just scraped the edge of the wooden ramp as he rolled from carpet down to tiles. On its right armrest was a small joystick that made it look like he was always ready to play *Street Fighter*.

Laying in the lap of his baggy dark-blue pants was a wooden ship in a bottle, perched delicately on its tiny wooden stand.

'I had it custom made, ready to pick up on our arrival. An incredible piece to add to my collection. I'm quite delighted,' he said. 'Would you like to take a look?'

'Umm, sure,' I said, reaching out to pick it up.

'No touching, Mike!' He caught himself and cleared his throat. 'I'm sorry, but they're worth quite a lot. If you want to admire it, you'll have to crouch.'

I just nodded instead and turned to look back out the window.

Below, Mum emerged from the unit block foyer, racing towards Dad, who had just reached his car. He was fumbling for his keys, checking his pockets, then finally found them in the left pocket of his favourite leather jacket. He had to find the right key in the bundle though, and Mum was gaining ground!

'You better hope you've inherited her fight, Mike. Her passion,' he said. 'I don't know what I would have done without her this weekend. She made me very proud.'

Ugh. I felt a shiver wash over me, like it sometimes did when I stepped into Brindy Shopping Centre's freezer-like food court. I hated that he thought he knew her enough to be 'proud'.

'*Wheelchair-accessible*, they said, Mike. That's what we booked,' Kenny continued, shaking his head, disappointedly. 'And we get there to find a step leading up to their lift. Of course, your mother gave them a piece of her mind, and then some. If she hadn't, we would've been out on the street. The incompetent hotel manager called every person that worked in the entire obnoxious building, trying to hoist my chair up that step.' Kenny paused, reliving it, his eyes narrowing as he turned to me. 'The chef was there, Mike. The chef. The guy who makes scrambled eggs out of powder every morning. BBQ sauce on his whites. I could smell it. He was huffing his cigarettes all over me.'

Kenny thought about it a moment longer, stopping to take one of his long, considered, breaths.

'It was just so humiliating,' he said.

I glanced sideways at Kenny, as fragments of the setting sun pierced the unit block window and bounced a rich peach glow off the corridor's tile floor and amber brick walls.

I looked out the window and down to Mum, who was now yelling through the driver's side window at Dad, who looked shrunken in his sky-blue Corolla. He even tried to wind the window up, but Mum stuck her arm in it.

'Don't even think about it!' I heard her scream.

Dad raised his hands up, in surrender, gradually sinking lower and lower into his seat until it looked like Gary Coleman was behind the wheel. Eventually he conceded, reaching into his pocket, pulling out his wallet, and handing Mum some money. A pineapple and a lobster for ya boi's new kicks.

Mum accepted the money and shook her head. She turned back towards our building and disappeared underneath, into the lobby.

Dad shot a look up to me from the driver's seat and shook his head as he sat back upright, a wry smile reminding me it was all my fault. Then he did a pretend karate chop in my direction, a little game that we had played ever since I was a kid; Dad would pretend he was chopping me, and I'd either pretend to get hit, or block him.

This time I took the hit, clutching theatrically at my neck. Dad shot me an ever-so-slightly loving smirk.

I couldn't help but smile as he drove away, and I was laughing by the time I heard the elevator doors open, and Mum appeared in the hallway again.

'Don't you dare laugh, Mike! I'm getting Kenny into his taxi, and when I come back, you have some explaining to do. You understand?'

'Why am I in trouble?' I protested as a drip of water rolled down my calf, across my bare ankle, and onto the tiles.

Mum stormed back past me and over to Kenny and helped guide him past me as he rolled over to the lift. I stood in the doorway as the lift opened. Mum looked back at me, shaking her head. 'I can't believe that's the artwork he's using these days,' she muttered, as the lift doors closed.

I was definitely in trouble, but looking back, it was all kinda nice. Me, standing there, shivering, wrapped in Afro Good Times. Mum angry. Dad scrambling.

It all felt like home.

•

'I broke all my rules,' Mum sighed.

She was trying to lose weight.

'Every time Kenny wasn't looking, I was shovelling chips into my mouth like a seagull.'

I felt sorry for Mum. She was always a bit large. She would make jokes about it, and I knew she was just trying to be funny, but I also knew she was self-conscious. I never really understood why. Mums are supposed to be a bit big, aren't they? That's what being a Mum is. Having bits to hold and love.

I liked Mum how she was. She was my mum.

She was sitting on the lounge room floor of her apartment, playing 'Stars and Dice: the Game of Destiny'.

'Stars and Dice' was a silly game. You had to roll four weirdly shaped, eight-sided dice, and according to the combination of numbers and colours and 'elements' that came up, an accompanying booklet would somehow decide your destiny. You were only supposed to play once a day, but sometimes, if my destiny wasn't very good, I would just keep playing until I got a sweet deal.

I was lounging opposite Mum, browsing the entertainment lift-out of the paper.

My sights were set on the SBS programming column of the TV guide. In particular, the programs scheduled for after 8:30pm. It was a ritual every Sunday when the guide came out. The guide would list the name of the movie, followed by the classification, and then – in brackets – they'd tell you why it was classified. MA (for Mature Audiences only) followed by (SN), was what you were after. The 'S' stood for sex scenes. The 'N' stood for nudity. It sounds silly, but it was important to have both letters. Just an 'S' might mean there's a sex scene, but the director used some crafty movie magic to hide all the good bits. An 'N', might get you nudity, but you never knew what type. There was nothing worse than spending a whole night in front of the TV, with your thumb poised anxiously on the remote in case Mum came out of her room, only to find – after two hours of arthouse cinematics, Italian subtitles and World Cup soccer advertisements – that the so-called 'nudity' you'd been holding out for was actually just some hospital scene where an old man asked a doctor to check him for haemorrhoids.

No matter what Margaret and David gave that movie, it would be one star from me.

I loved Mum's place, more than anything in the world. The dull brick exterior paired with the most offensive olive-green trim you'd ever laid eyes to was no indication of what the inside was like.

A corner apartment, you could see all the way around the city, except behind us to Brindy Shopping Centre and to Mt Kartha beyond. It had a long hallway that stretched from my bedroom, past Mum's room, the bathroom, and then out into the living area, where you were greeted with floor to ceiling sliding glass doors that looked out over the river. I'd use the hallway to do triple jump with only a half run-up, careful to stick the two-footed landing, to stop myself cascading through the massive sliding glass doors and out onto the balcony. Thankfully, there was an old, steel balustrade that would prevent a four-storey plummet out into the Muddy Snake – mind you, I'd take a dip in the river over the roasting Mum would dish out for smashing that glass.

The bleating of our home phone rang out through the lounge room.

I looked at Mum.

'Don't,' she said.

So it kept ringing. And ringing.

'If she really wanted to talk she'd visit one of these days.'

I nodded.

'Why are you fighting this time?' I asked.

Mum sighed, tired. She went to answer, but the sound of a helicopter interrupted us, and we both looked up through the glass balcony doors as it choppered past our apartment, up along the river.

'They've been flying up and down all afternoon,' Mum said.

I stared out at the city, weirdly filling with pride and affection for Mum and her home.

'I love this apartment,' I said.

'I know you do, Mike,' Mum said. 'That's the problem.'

I kept staring out our window, pretending I hadn't heard that.

'Ahhh, Brindlewood,' Mum sighed, as we watched the helicopter turn around and fly back down the river and out of sight towards the mountain. 'What a truly unremarkable place.' Mum chucked the dice to me and I took my turn. Mum checked the booklet.

'Water,' she read. 'Well, no explanation necessary there!' She was smiling, but there was a hint of concern in her voice. 'So, what had you so distracted that you ended up in the Brindy fountain?'

'I was reading about jellyfish,' I replied, sheepish. 'Now – if only we had the internet, I wouldn't have needed a book, and I wouldn't have been so distrac—'

'Stop right there,' Mum said. 'I don't want to hear that word in this house, OK?'

Mum took her turn and noted down the number from the dice on the paper.

'Fire,' she said, referring to the booklet. She thought for a second. 'The person sitting next to us in the hotel restaurant kept blowing their cigarette into my face. Does that count? God, I hope they make that illegal one day.' She handed me the dice. 'Jellyfish, like the ones in Tasmania?'

'They're called the Irukandji,' I said excitedly, distracting myself from flashbacks of the pissing incident. 'They can be only one-centimetre big, and when they sting you, you don't even notice. You just walk back to your towel and think, *Hmm. I've got a headache. Oh well, better drink some water.* So, you pack up your towel and your beach umbrella, and – let's say you walk across the road to the fish and chip shop for some calamari.'

I stood up, and walked over to the couch, pretending I was opening up some fish and chips.

'And then, all of a sudden –' I pretended to spew everywhere '– you do a cheeky vom!'

Mum gave a smile; a small one that required effort.

'And then you collapse onto the ground, suddenly unable to move.' I rolled off the couch and onto the floor. 'And you can't breathe! And, as if that's not the worst part, you see, before you die you get completely overwhelmed by the sense of … wait for it … impending doom! As if the vomiting and paralysis wasn't enough. You now have to contend with impending doom! How are these things not a weapon of war? If North Korea gets their hands on these jellyfish, we're in big trouble.'

Mum was laughing now, big and open-mouthed, exposing her teeth. Her top ones were the exact opposite of Zoe Ingham's – crossed over at the front, with her other teeth banked up on either side like they were traffic-jammed after a prang. At the top right she had a snaggle tooth, a fang, that stood out the front of the pack like William Wallace yelling *freedom!*

'Oh dear, what am I going to do with you?' she said.

'Do you think I could be, like, an actor or something?'

'You can be anything you want, Mike. You're very talented.'

'You don't have to tell me.' I picked up the dice and rolled.

Mum checked the book. 'Well, what do we have here? Apparently "love" is in your destiny,' she read, then looked up at me. 'You can roll again if you'd like.' She stared at me as her words trailed off, narrowing her eyes.

'What?' I said, my eyes darting around.

A smile was born. 'Oh, is there *love* in Mike's future?' She reached across to tickle me.

'No, as if!' I said, trying to wriggle out of her clutches.

'Tell you what, you're obviously not *that* good at acting. Who is it?' She kept poking at me, right in my pits.

'No-one,' I stuttered. 'This is unfair. You're using torture tactics to interrogate me. Next you'll bring out the jellyfish!'

She finally stopped. 'Well, whoever it is, you just let her know that you might almost be as tall as me these days, but you'll never stop being *my little chicken!*' She started trying to kiss me all over my face.

'Please stop!' I didn't want to be laughing, but I couldn't help it. I was hot in the face from thinking about Zoe, and fending off Mum. I had tears streaming down my cheeks from laughing.

She finally let me go.

And this is where everything kinda gets awkward.

I've thought about this moment so many times since it happened, and I don't think I'll ever understand it. Because every time I think about it, I just get so damn sad.

But I'm going to try and explain.

Mum sat up, proud of the embarrassment that she'd just inflicted on me, and rolled the dice. Then she looked at the booklet.

'Struggle,' she read. Then she laughed, but it wasn't the same laugh as when I'd been pretend-vomiting and rolling around on the floor. It was forced, and there was a glimmer of sadness in her eyes. 'Well, I've certainly struggled keeping Jenny Craig happy, that's for sure. I think I put on at least three kilos this weekend alone!'

I was still wiping tears away from my face. My cheeks red. Catching my breath. I laughed at her 'joke'. More a residual laugh from the tickling than anything. I swear I only meant it as a joke.

And I think that's what hurts the most about the whole situation, because, looking back, that's the only way I could've meant it.

She'd said, 'I think I put on at least three kilos this weekend alone!'

And it was only because I'd been thinking about how much I love her, and I wanted to make her feel good about herself.

I said to her, 'Oh well. At least you still have big boobs.'

And then I reached out, with my right hand, and I grabbed her. On the boob.

On her left boob. I grabbed her.

And what happened next, happened in fast-forward and slow-motion at the same time. Because it didn't hurt at first. It took a few seconds for all my senses to figure out what happened.

She slapped me. Right on the cheek. My left cheek.

I couldn't move. I wanted to tell her that I really didn't mean it, not like that. That I was just playing along with her jokes. I don't know why I grabbed her. She'd just been tickling me so damn much.

Mum had her mouth open. She looked shocked. 'Don't ever touch a woman like that, Mike,' she said.

'I'm sorry,' I whispered. That's all I could say.

I could feel them coming. I was right on that edge. I didn't want to cry. So, I turned around and ran.

I ran out of the lounge room and down the hallway, past the bathroom, past Mum's room, and into my room.

Lying there, in the dark, in my room, with my head buried into my pillow, I managed to hold it together.

I didn't cry.

I was too old for that.

Thank god.

•

I lay on my bed, listening as Mum packed up 'Stars and Dice', and I heard the clattering of plates as she washed the dishes that we'd left in the sink after dinner. I replayed over and over again what had happened, as I heard the shower next door turn on, and then off again, and Mum going through her usual pre-bed ritual of brushing her teeth and applying seven different sleep creams.

I pretended to be asleep when I finally heard my bedroom door open later that night. The light from the hallway cast an illuminating triangle across my back and onto the wall next to my bed, which I was now curled up and staring at.

'Mike,' her voice was soft. Forgiving. Mum. 'If I ever do something like that again, you have to tell your dad, OK?'

I didn't say anything. I didn't move. I just lay there. Pretending to sleep.

'I love you, chook,' she said.

Then she closed the door, and everything fell away.

I cried. I cried as I heard Mum switch off the hallway lights, I cried as I heard the sound of her bedroom door close, and as the helicopters swept up and down the river all night. Tears sticking to my hot, embarrassed face.

I should've realised that something wasn't right.

But I was too busy crying like a dumb little kid.

CHAPTER FOUR

MONDAY, 9TH MARCH 1998

Brindlewood High was cut in two by City Road, the road that ran north to south from the City to Brindy Shopping Centre. The smaller junior campus, for Years Eight and Nine, sat on the east side of City Road – Mum's side – in the shadow of its senior campus counterpart. The senior school campus, on the west side – Dad's side – was bigger, older, scarier.

While Ironbark Primary had consisted of one three-level building and a few 'temporary' demountables that ended up being about as temporary as the sun itself, Brindlewood High was like a city in its own right. There were several multi-storey structures, within which we spent more time scaling the stairs than sitting and learning.

The school was falling apart in places. For every shiny, new building there was a crusty, old block with peeling paint, rotting timber edges, and the occasional cracked louvre – just waiting to stretch the legs of the government's liability lawyers.

But the difference between primary and high school was nowhere more evident than the tuckshop. Where the culinary highlight at Ironbark Primary came in the form of half a soggy English muffin, wearing slices of ham and cheddar like oily bedsheets, the tuckshop at Brindlewood High housed a downright smorgasbord of mouth-watering and artery-clogging delights. Stretched across three serving counters, at least seven frantic women scurried to prepare the spread before students rushed them at the first blaring of the lunchtime bell. This was food for grown-ups. There were steak and mushroom pies, Hawaiian pizza pockets, bacon-and-cheese buns from the world-famous Vietnamese bakery down the block, and Chiko Rolls jam-packed with whatever the hell is in those things. Around the back of the building was a sweet tooth's Silk Road – a separate serving area crammed wall-to-wall with chocolates and lollies, its doors always open to whichever Hansel or Gretel had change left over from lunch.

It was beside the tuckshop that Tully and I were playing handball the day after the slap. We were in between games, and Tully wedged the tennis ball in between her self-described 'chunky trunk' legs as she re-tied her frizzy, strawberry blonde hair back into a ponytail. Her cheeks were a cherry ripe hue, thanks to the uncloggable pores she'd managed to acquire during sixth grade.

'There's something not right about today, Mike,' Tully said. 'My hair tells me it's going to rain.'

A teacher walked past, an old one. One of the oldest. He approached Tully, whipped out a tape measure, and held the tape out against Tully's leg.

Tully groaned. She lifted up her white button-up blouse and unravelled the rolled-up waistband of her navy school skirt.

I watched the bottom hem of her skirt drop from mid-thigh to just-below-knee.

'Rules are rules, Ms Maxwell,' he said, before moving on to terrorise a young Asian boy for wearing the wrong hat.

'See?' Tully said, eventually serving the ball to me with some spin, out the back of her hand. 'Today is weird already.'

'How are things with Danny?' I asked, returning serve. Danny was Tully's boyfriend from primary school. The fact that she was already 'taken' instantly gave her a social advantage at Brindy High. It was like a membership card to the cool bench. Singles need not apply.

'Terrible! Mum has banned me from using the telephone after I spilled dinner in bed last week, and I haven't been able to talk to him since.'

She waited until the ball was super low to the ground, then slapped it deep into the left side of my court.

'Is he liking boarding school?' I asked, only just getting the ball back with my outstretched right hand.

'He reckons the supervisors are nice, and they get fed all the time, which sounds awesome. I just wish he wasn't going to a school on the coast. I don't trust those beach bitches. It's like, put some clothes on.'

'Do you think you guys will get married one day?'

Tully thought about this. 'Maybe. It's so different going from a primary school relationship to a high school one, you know? We're both becoming a lot more mature.'

'Do you think he's been playing soggy SAO?' I asked, trying to hit the ball between my legs.

Tully slammed the ball back past me. 'See that? Immaturity. You're really showing your age there, mate.'

'You're only three months older than me!' I said.

'Three months is twenty in high school years.'

I scrambled to get the ball before it rolled under some nearby port racks, and started the next game. 'When do you see him next?'

'That's why I'm stressed! His parents won't let him come back here any time during term, and I'd go visit him, but bus tickets to the coast are fifteen bucks each way, and Mum would never give me that much money.' She hit the ball back, and I dived to reach it.

'I need a job.'

'What?' I asked, body stretched out on the concrete, genuinely in shock. 'How? What job?'

'Any job.' She shrugged. 'Delivering papers, whatever.'

She gave me an easy one so I could get back on my feet.

'If Danny's at a rich private boarding school, can't he lend you some money for bus tickets?' I asked.

'Yeh, but I don't want him to know that I'm coming.'

'You're going to get a job just to surprise him at the coast one day?'

'I'm going to spy on him,' she whispered. 'I'm telling you, I don't trust those coasties. I don't trust any of them.'

She slapped the ball low and hard to my left. It went flying off the edge of my thumb and out of bounds. Game over.

'What about you, mister? We've been coming here for six weeks now. Anyone caught your eye?' Tully asked, giving me a sly.

Suddenly, my watch alarm went off. I grabbed my tennis ball and packed it in my bag.

'Dude, what the hell? You can't hack getting beaten by a girl?'

'Sorry, I want to get to assembly early,' I said, zipping up my backpack.

'Mike, this is high school. Getting to anything early is the lamest thing you could ever do. You might as well have "bash me" tattooed on your neck.'

'My dad says tattoos give you Hep C,' I replied.

'You already get Cs in everything. At least you'd be maintaining your standard!' she yelled, as I bolted ahead.

•

Year Eight assemblies happened every Tuesday morning in the junior school gymnasium block that housed all of Brindlewood High's indoor sports. A multi-sport hardwood court lay underneath a large, steel-raftered ceiling with a number of exhaust fans that, if the sun was right, would cast hypnotic spinning shadows across the inside walls of the building. If the weekly updates about the debating teams and whichever nerd was excelling in the Duke of Edinburgh program wasn't enough to send you to sleep, those spinning shadows would get you every time.

I'd been summoned early to help announce our school's hosting of the Dobson Dash. The Dash moved from school to school each year, so to be in Year Eight and get to be a part of the hosting team was a thrill. From the rich kids at Stables Grammar on the Greater Brindle Tableland, whose parents owned farms so big you'd mistake their size in acres with a mobile phone number, to the uptight kids at St Joseph's on the coast (the same school Tully's boyfriend Danny called home), and every high school in between, knew how big this event was.

Just being asked to announce it was a kick. When I arrived, Mr Bortey – our Year Eight co-ordinator, was already setting up in the gymnasium.

He was the go-to man for anything Year Eight-related, he was my English teacher, and he also coached the school's athletics team. Mr Bortey loved spreading himself thinner than Nutella.

A similar chocolate complexion to my own, Mr Bortey had a prominent nose that bumped at the ridge, large brown eyes, and pretty unforgiving acne scars that were usually hidden under a carpet of stubble. He smelled like an unemptied vacuum cleaner bag – not bad, just dusty – and obviously graduated from the Seinfeld school of fashion; sneakers, jeans, T-shirt, jacket. That was Mr Bortey's uniform. Every damn day.

Skon Helpmann was there too. He basically followed where ever Mr Bortey went, not out of will but necessity, punishment. His wisecracks and bullying would see him in a never-ending cycle of community service sentences; no sooner had he finished one, he'd find himself in another for dropping chewing gum in the hair of a passerby from the City Road bypass, or trying to steal a tray of chicken burgers from the tuckshop.

Skon stood at the back of the room, kicking a soccer ball against a wall, his short black hair spiked up at the front, his blue shirt untucked at the back with the top two buttons undone, and his long grey socks falling down to his ankles, exposing calves like frenched lamb shanks. The pocket of his dark-blue and maroon pinstriped blazer already boasted gold insignia for his involvement with the school's rowing team at the very start of term; but if they gave out gold pockets for being an asshole, Rumpelstiltskin would be hard-pressed weaving enough shiny thread for Skon's achievements.

I, on the other hand, was wearing a big dog costume. It was the mascot for our high school athletics team. It had long, flappy ears and a top hat, and it wore the school colours and had thick, white cursive font on the front that read 'Brindy High Harriers'. On the back it said, 'Top dogs of Track & Field!'

'Does it fit?' Mr Bortey asked, zipping me up at the back like Tully did for her mum whenever she was going on a date.

'Too well. You only chose me because I'm tall, didn't you? This would have folded in half on someone shorter.'

'I chose you because you're the best for the job, Mike. I reward based on merit, both in class, and as the athletics coach,' he said with a smirk. 'Now, do you remember the plan?'

I nodded.

'Remind me,' Mr Bortey said.

'I'll be in the supplies storeroom at the back of the hall. When you announce that "we're hosting the Dobson Dash right here at our brand-new oval on the last day of term", Skon and Zoe will give me the signal, and I'll burst out of the storeroom and start dancing.'

Mr Bortey listened. 'I trust you.' He turned to Skon, 'Now, where's Zoe?' he asked, as he cranked a handle on the gym block's wall, drawing the basketball hoops up towards the ceiling and out of the reach of hats, empty milk cartons, or any other potential projectile that might tempt the arm of a fidgety, inattentive student.

'How would I know where she is? We're not married,' Skon said, sauntering over to us, his baby-making baritone voice bouncing around the room, almost rumbling the lino basketball court apart underneath my feet.

'No, you're not married, but you are Athletics captains, and part of that role is maintaining adequate communication or else your co-captain will turn around one day and tell you over breakfast that your communication has broken down to a point of no salvage, that counselling would only be a band-aid solution, and that there was no hope for your future together.'

Mr Bortey gave the handle one final crank through gritted teeth, and it could be cranked no more.

'She was supposed to select what charity we are competing for. We'll just have to go without her.' He wiped the sweat off his brow. 'Skon, when I announce that we're hosting the

Dobson Dash, you give Mike the thumps-up, and he'll come out dancing.'

He shoved me into the hall storeroom and slammed the door.

It re-opened.

'Quick, what's a charity?' Mr Bortey asked, panicked.

'RSPCA?' I said, muffled through the mouth of my dog head.

'That'll do, dog, that'll do.' He slammed the door.

It opened again.

Mr Bortey lifted the head off my dog costume, reached into the top, and flicked a switch. A little fan started whizzing away inside. He plonked the head back on me and patted me on the shoulder.

'That's so you don't die in the cupboard.' He winked.

Then he slammed the storeroom door closed again.

Just in time, too. I stood in the storeroom, listening to the ruckus of Year Eighters still on their sugar highs from eating sweet breakfast cereals in front of Cheez TV, filtering into the gymnasium, taking their seats on the basketball court. So many kids. That was another thing that stuck out when I got to Brindy. At Ironbark Primary, the classes only went up to 'C'. I had been in 7B. At Brindlewood High, the classes went all the way up to 'N', with almost thirty kids a class. I did the math and realised I was about to dance in front of about four hundred kids. I should've charged one dollar per head.

Mr Bortey blabbered away at a lectern in front. The stupid little fan in the dog's head was so loud that I couldn't hear a thing Mr Bortey was saying. I could just see him talking to all the kids, his back to me, gesturing excitedly.

Skon was standing next to him, and I could see everyone clap when he stepped forward and waved his hands in the air like a gold medallist at the Olympics. They were welcoming their captain. I would be up next.

I saw our principal, Mrs Tamer, walk into the hall, right when Mr Bortey was about to make the announcement.

I watched him nod as Mrs Tamer took to the stage, talking to the grade. This wasn't the plan.

I was waiting for ages, waiting for the signal, waiting as Skon kept looking back towards me as if everything was still set.

As Mrs Tamer spoke, I could see the kids weren't smiling so much anymore. Then I saw mouths drop, and it looked like people were gasping. Mrs Tamer must have stolen Mr Bortey's thunder.

Skon turned around and gave me the signal, and it was my time to shine. Just like we'd planned.

I burst into the auditorium. Dancing. Like a stupid dancing dog. Doing the hula. In my big dog costume. But instead of laughter there was a stillness in the air. All I could hear was the fan in the head of my dog suit, whizzing away.

The only difference between people laughing with you or laughing at you, is you. But I had no idea how to react when people weren't laughing at all.

So I danced harder. Faster. Like a dog possessed.

I hula'd like no Hawaiian ever could.

I did the sprinkler. The shopping trolley. The lawnmower. Moves that had raised the roof at my Year Seven graduation dance, but were barely raising a titter here and now.

I jumped. I boogied. I used the space. Until eventually I could boogie no more.

I stopped dancing and stood for a moment in my suit, staring at Mr Bortey, who shook his head and looked away.

I took off the head of my suit and stood in front of the whole grade, silent.

'Mike, I'm sorry,' Mr Bortey said, quietly. 'Something terrible has happened.'

It wasn't until I spotted Tully that I realised something was really wrong.

She was crying.

Then I realised Mr Bortey was crying.

Everyone was crying.

Except for Skon. He had his head down, hands over his face, peeking at me through a gap in his fingers.

I got so mad, because I saw his eyes.

The asshole was laughing.

·

The Reserve began its colonial life as an old sheep station in the late 1800s. Approximately twenty hectares of natural bushland, set at the foot of the settlement's biggest peak, Mt Kartha.

Dad moved there in the eighties. The scrub, thick. The Creek, deep and swimmable. The residents kept awake at night by the sound of koalas spreading chlamydia.

Over the years, the surrounding houses and developments would gradually encroach, suffocating its veins, cutting off the main artery that flowed through the parklands, and turning the Creek from a strong, gushing waterway, into a dribbling stream. Easily crossable by foot.

When Tully and I were young, a single downpour would deem the Creek uncrossable, lest you risk losing your sneakers in the drool of its torrent. On those afternoons you'd curse the glands of heaven. If it seemed like it would only be a short burst, you could play creekside for an hour or two, waiting for the gush to ease before crossing. Otherwise, you'd have to backtrack.

Fifteen minutes back towards Brindy Shopping Centre, and then an hour around the park.

These days, to stop you from crossing the Creek at our favourite spot, it took a downright hurricane.

Or the death of a seven-year-old girl.

It was a ferry that killed her. Zoe's sister, Georgia. Just at the crossing at the Swamp. Down where Dad catches crabs and where Tully and I walk to get home every day. 'A bizarre accident' was how the radio described it, and police believed there were 'no suspicious circumstances'.

'It means she wasn't pushed,' Tully said, as we made the trek down the Goat Track – a steep, rocky, bush trail that started on the main road opposite Brindy Shopping Centre, and led down through the east side of the Reserve towards the Swamp. Mum had called it the Goat Track because she reckoned it resembled the rocky, death-defying incline that you'd find a mountain goat happily grazing upon.

Mrs Tamer had announced to our grade there might be disruptions getting home. That they were still officially considering Georgia a missing person because no body had been located, so if anybody saw anything on their way home they needed to notify the school immediately.

'So fucked up.' Tully sighed. 'I don't know what I'd do if someone in my family died.'

Tully was one of three kids. Her and two younger brothers. To two different fathers. Tully's Mum had got a job at our high school tuckshop, and finished by 2pm. And when you finish work early, you start drinking early. That's why she made us walk home from school. One day, really early on – maybe Grade One – Tully's mum had come to pick us both up, and our teacher had gotten into a huge argument with her and told us we weren't allowed to get into the car. Tully's mum was fuming, and she had to leave her car on the side of the road, and we had to wait to get a taxi home and she swore the whole time in the back of the cab about how our teachers didn't know what the fuck they were doing.

So now we caught the bus and walked home. Every day. Together.

'You didn't answer my question this morning,' Tully said, jumping down the small, rocky embankment to the dirt path lined with bush that lead through to the Swamp.

'Which question?' I asked, jumping down behind her.

'You know which question. Who do you like?'

'Nobody,' I said.

'You're brown, but you're not that brown. I can see you're going red. Just tell me who you like.'

I stopped dead in my tracks. 'Zoe.'

'I knew it!' Tully yelled, victorious.

'No, look.' I pointed ahead. 'It's Zoe. She's with the police.'

The usual path to the Swamp was cordoned off with police tape. At the base of the Jetty, near the dirt carpark, there was a white gazebo set up. There were police officers and workers in hi-vis teeming through it like bees in a hive, standing around desks, scribbling across maps. In the water, a diver came to the surface, mask on, dressed in full-body black like a ninja, and then disappeared beneath the surface again. At the end of the Jetty, I saw Zoe, hands wrapped around her dad's tall, lean frame, head dug into his chest.

Tully stared ahead. 'Poor thing.'

'No suspicious circumstances,' I whispered, as we approached the cut-off point.

An officer was standing guard. 'The Reserve is closed from here, kids. You'll have to go around.' He had fair skin.

Completely bald. Intense blue eyes that made me think he liked starting fires. A softer, less gaunt Peter Garrett type in his late thirties.

'We just want to get home,' Tully said.

'We all want to get home, kid. Go around.'

Tully and I both looked depressingly back up the steep Goat Track.

'Constable Dukes,' a fellow officer called out from behind him. She was standing with two hi-vis workers, and they had what looked like a town plan of sorts spread out between them. She ushered Dukes over.

'Let's just find a way through here.' Tully pointed towards the bush on her right.

'I don't know where that goes,' I said. 'We'll get lost.'

'Where's your sense of adventure?' She grabbed my arm and dragged me in.

'My sense of adventure is halfway up the Goat Track. My sense of adventure gets home late, but alive. My sense of adventure doesn't die in the bush trying to survive on wild berries.'

'The later I get home, the more wine Mum's had,' she said quietly. She let go of my arm and started walking into the thick scrub alone. 'And I'm not in a fighting mood.'

•

We walked, beating our own track, the scrub getting denser and denser; the closer we traipsed towards the mountain, the further away the opportunity to cross the Creek seemed.

'Where are we going?' Tully asked.

'The Creek has to be down there, I think. I don't know where, exactly,' I said, pointing vaguely to our left.

'Are we lost, Mike?'

'Where's your sense of adventure?' I said, sarcastically. 'Let's just keep going.'

I wish we hadn't.

About ten metres ahead, we stepped out into a small clearing, and I felt a pit of discomfort form in my stomach. The first thing I noticed was the makeshift canopy; fashioned from dirty, white tarpaulin, crudely soiled with fallen, wet leaves, drooping over a thick, upright branch that was jutting about head-high out of the earth. And then we noticed the mattress, sitting, not underneath the tarp, but under the natural ceiling of the trees touching above us. And there was a milk crate next to it, too. Surrounded by some empty cigarette packets, their coloured labels now browning like the teeth of their smokers.

'Is this a cubby house?' Tully asked.

'I don't wanna know who plays here,' I replied.

'This is dirtier than my dog's bed,' she said, poking at the mattress with the stick in her hand. She bent over and picked up a magazine that was lying next to the mattress.

'Ugh, gross!'

It was a porno mag. The picture she'd opened to was of two bikies, really going at it. They were covered in tattoos.

It was the first time I had ever seen an actual penis going into a vagina.

'They look like animals,' I said.

'It's what grown-ups do, Mike. You'll get there one day.'

I didn't know what to say. A million feelings flashing through my stomach. A call to action, with no instructions.

'This doesn't feel right,' I said quietly.

I stepped away from Tully, discreetly tucking my boner into my waistband, and noticed a small, square, navy-blue cool-bag, covered in dirt near the edge of the clearing. We stood over the bag on the ground, and I felt a cold chill wash over my sweaty body as the afternoon breeze swept through the trees.

'What do you reckon's inside?' Tully asked. 'My guess is condoms.'

'Danny can put them over his fingers when you guys decide to hit second base,' I said.

Tully whacked me on the arm with the magazine.

I knelt down to open the bag, and, like a bad game of pass the parcel, inside the bag was a box. It was black, white and yellow; designed like it were No Frills. About the size of a VHS. It's label reading JOYCE'S SELECT GRADE; FULL METAL JACKET.

'What is it?' Tully asked, stepping next to me to have a look.

'I think they're bullets,' I said, kicking them, lightly. Just to get some movement.

'Maybe they're chocolates?' Tully suggested. 'Mum's always partial to a "bullet".'

'I don't think these are chocolates.' I was starting to feel a bit numb.

'Fuck me,' Tully gasped, as she heard the rattle and clanking from inside the box.

She looked at me, anxiously. 'Mike, I feel sick.'

I knelt down towards the box.

'What are you doing?' Tully asked.

I poised my finger on the bottom of its lid.

'Mike, leave it alone. Let's just get out of here.'

But I couldn't just go.

I lifted the lid of the box that proudly stated QUANTITY: 100 BULLETS in small print, with the considered pace that one lifts an old scab off their finally-repaired skin.

Five rows of twenty. All there, bar six. Ninety-four bullets in a box in the park.

'Jesus,' Tully whispered.

'I know,' I said. I was shaking.

That's when the man's voice boomed through the trees.

'Oi!'

Our heads snapped up to spot the police officer, Constable Dukes, walking towards us, through the thick bush, about fifty metres away.

'Stay right there!' Dukes yelled again.

'Quick, cover it,' she said, and kicked some dirt and leaves over the bag and bullets.

'What are you doing?' Dukes said, getting closer, until he finally charged into the clearing and made a beeline for me. I barely had time to think, before he grabbed me by the arm and twisted it around my back.

I felt lightning shoot up through my shoulder. Suddenly, my whole body, was on the ground, my face pressed up against the leaves and the dirt.

'Help!' I tried yelling, but my face was too smooshed.

'Jesus, stop it!' Tully screamed.

'Do you have drugs on you?' The police officer said harshly into my ear, looking around the clearing, 'Have you been smoking marijuana?'

'No!' Tully screamed, 'We've never been here before.'

'If you've got drugs, I'll find them,' the police officer said, his hand patting all down my back.

'Please stop, it hurts,' I said.

'Roll over,' he said.

'I didn't do anything,' I said.

'Just do what he says, Mike!'

I rolled, he patted, reaching into my left pocket, then reaching into my right. He grabbed.

'Argh!' I squealed. 'That's my –'

He stared angrily into my eyes, and then finally pulled his hand out of my pocket.

'Sit up against that tree, and don't move,' he barked.

I sat up and scooted back to the tree, my groin aching, my shoulder burning from the twisting.

I could feel tears coming too, but desperately didn't want to cry in front of Tully.

'I told you to go around the Reserve,' he growled, turning between both of us.

I tried to answer, but I couldn't. I just started crying.

I set Tully off to, and she started crying.

'We were just trying to get home,' Tully said.

'We didn't want to get home late, that's all.'

The police officer stared at both of us, and then finally nodded.

'Get up,' he said, kicking at my legs.

I dragged my sniffling, sorry ass up off the ground, my chest convulsing as I tried to control myself.

Then, the police officer walked real close to me, his chest almost pressed right up against mine, the air from his nostrils hitting me on the forehead.

'Stop crying. You look pathetic,' he whispered, leaning into my ear. 'Real men don't cry, understand?'

He stepped back and looked at the whole area, then his walkie-talkie let off a screech.

'Officers, we have found a body. Presumed to be the missing. Six kilometres downstream. Please report back to base immediately.'

He took the radio off his belt and spoke into it. 'Copy.'

He turned back to us.

'By the looks of it, this isn't a place you want to be, day or night. If I see you here again, I'll take you to the station and call your parents,' he said. 'Now, get out of here.'

He turned back and walked out the way he came just as the sky opened up, and it started to rain.

'I think I just beat you to second base,' I joked. Joking was all I could do. I was rocked.

'See?!' Tully said, as the rain fell around us. 'I told you. The hair never lies.'

•

When I got home, Dad was in the backyard, with a beer sitting on a rock, tending to his plants.

I sat on my bed and played *Street Fighter* for a bit, but I kept dying. I wasn't focusing on the game. I kept thinking about the porno we'd found in the Reserve.

I'd spent six weeks just desperately wanting to kiss Zoe Ingham, and now I realised that kissing was only the beginning.

Life was already raising the bar, and I hadn't even taken my first jump yet.

I needed to make a move fast, or else get left behind.

When Dad was done with the garden, he dropped me at Mum's.

'How did your shirt get ripped?' he asked, when we were in the car.

I looked down and realised you could spot my hairless little armpit through a large tear under the sleeve.

I hesitated. 'I was reaching for a book on the top shelf in the library. See? This is why we need the internet. Think how much we'll save on stitching!'

Dad nodded calmly, and then pulled the car over.

'Here's a tip, Mike. Your mum can smell lies from ten miles away, so I suggest you tell me the truth so we can come up with a better story before I drop you off. Understand?'

I nodded.

'A police officer tackled me to the ground because he thought I was doing drugs in the Reserve,' I said quietly, eyes to my lap.

'Be honest, Mike. Were you doing drugs?' He asked.

'No! Tully and I were just playing.'

He looked out his window for a moment. 'Bastards,' he whispered under breath, then he turned to me with a serious gaze. 'People like us are targets for them. You'll realise this more, the older you get. They squeeze me, Mike, for putting up my posters. I fight back but they tighten their grip. They must know you're my son and are taking it out on you. I'm sorry, Mike.'

'It's not your fault,' I said.

'No, but I can't help you either. That's what's frustrating. Just don't do the wrong thing, and stay out of their way, even when you've done nothing wrong. They like to find things, Mike. Understand?'

I nodded.

'And don't tell your mother, OK? She'll storm right into that station and start calling for blood, but that blood will come from the mark on your back.' Dad whispered, as he pulled back onto the road. 'Fucking bastards.'

•

When I got home, Mum was already in bed, and the dishes hadn't been done. I tried to sneak past Mum's room to get changed before she could spot the damage, but sneaking was never my strong point.

'Mike, what are you doing there?' her voice came through her closed bedroom door.

Dammit.

I opened the door.

Mum was lying in her giant white bed T-shirt with a Rastafarian Bugs Bunny on the front, writing in her diary.

'Oh Mike, what on earth have you done to your shirt?' she said.

'Dad had me working in the garden and I caught it on a branch. You can call him if you want?'

Mum's eyes narrowed. Then she nodded, satisfied.

Damn. Now I owed Dad another shift putting up Afro Good Times posters.

'How come you didn't go to work?' I asked.

'Did you hear about what happened in the Reserve?' She sounded tired. 'That poor girl.'

I wiped my suddenly clammy hands on my grey school shorts. 'Why didn't you go to work?'

Mum took a sip of water from her bedside glass; a tiny little sip that she concentrated on for too long before swallowing, all the cords in her neck unusually activated, a few dribbles escaping out the sides of her lips. She awkwardly wiped her mouth on Rasta Bugs' face.

'I've had a headache all day,' she said, closing her eyes and leaning back. I took her glass into the bathroom and replaced it with fresh water.

'How was your performance?' she asked when I came back in.

'It wasn't a performance, it was an announcement, and it went terribly,' I said, placing the glass back on her bedside table.

'They told the whole grade about what happened to Georgia, so nobody laughed or anything.'

'Mike, don't be so egotistical. A girl is dead,' Mum snapped.

My jaw dropped.

'I know a girl is dead. I actually *know* the girl!'

Mum rubbed her temple, let out a big, heavy breath. 'I don't think I could live if something like that happened to you,' she said, sounding right on the brink of sleep. 'Oh, and can you please clean up all your dishes from breakfast, Mike. The kitchen is starting to stink.'

Your attitude is starting to stink, I thought.

I didn't know why Mum was being so mean all of a sudden. She'd slapped me last night and I thought she'd at least apologise again today, but instead she was calling me egotistical and making me do all these stupid chores. I walked into my room, feeling heavy about Georgia, the bullets, the policeman and Mum's moods.

'Do you have any other washing?' Mum asked through the door.

There in the corner was a pile of almost all of my school clothes, dirty, not to mention the one I was wearing.

'No!' I yelled back. I didn't need her help right now.

I lay down on my bed, looked up at the ceiling and sighed.

CHAPTER FIVE

MONDAY, 16TH MARCH 1998

A week later Tully and I were hanging out after school, walking through the Franklins supermarket inside Brindy Shopping Centre. As we passed each aisle, I would stop to look under the shelves to see if anyone had dropped any coins. This was a pretty regular ritual. If we were lucky, we'd find a dollar and be able to go halves in a packet of Maltesers or something. It was a pretty povo thing to do, but I'd already spent all my pocket money and Tully never had pocket money in the first place.

'You hear John Howard wants to bring in the GST?'

'Geriatric Scrotum Tickler?' I guessed.

She rolled her eyes. 'I don't know what it stands for, but it means that everything's going to cost ten per cent more than it does now.' She picked up a packet of M&Ms. 'These M&Ms, instead of being one dollar, they're going to be one dollar and ten cents.'

'Oh man, it's hard enough finding one dollar under these shelves, let alone one dollar *and* ten cents.'

'Mate, you think you've got it tough. Mum reckons it'll apply to tampons too.'

There was no treasure under the shelf I was checking, but I kept my head at ground level and pretended to search, giving my suddenly flushed cheeks a moment to cool.

We moved on to the next aisle.

'I applied for a job,' Tully said, crouching down.

'What do you need a job for?' I asked, crouching next to her, spotting the silhouette of a dollar coin. I reached out.

'I put you down as a referee,' she said.

'What's that?' I asked as my fingers recognised the ridged edges of a bottle cap. Dammit. A fool's coin.

'If they call you, just pretend you own the newsagency and tell them I've been delivering papers for you and how awesome I am.'

'I'll do anything you want if ...' I trailed off, as I started rummaging through my school bag.

'If ...?' Tully asked, single eyebrow raised.

I found what I was after and handed it to Tully.

A small, palm-sized bouquet of origami flowers. All different shapes and colours.

'If, you give these to Zoe ...'

'Oh mister, you've got no chance!' For someone so blunt, Tully's words certainly cut deep. 'I know Zoe, she's smart, and funny, and raw. Plus she's not exactly in a dating mood at the moment.'

'I know all this,' I said. 'They're just a present, to say I hope she's ... you know ... doing OK.'

Tully rolled her eyes and took the bouquet. 'It's sweet, Mike. Probably too sweet. Girls like a guy with edge. You're too much of a mummy's boy. Always playing by the rules.'

'Isn't that what referees do?' I quipped. 'Don't tell her they're from me, OK? Just leave it in her bag when she's not looking.'

I knelt down to check under the next shelf and did a double take.

'Any luck?' Tully asked, spotting my curiosity.

'I think someone dropped an M&M. A peanut one. Green.'

'Dare you to eat it.'

'You always dare me to do gross things like that. No, I will not eat an M&M off the ground. No, I will not lick the rubber escalator handrail. No, I will not wear your stinky spikes as an oxygen mask. Stop asking.'

She sighed. 'See, *that's* the kind of boring behaviour that puts you out of Zoe's league.'

'Zoe would want a guy who will take her out to a restaurant, not eat M&Ms off the floor.'

'You're so safe, Mike. You need to take more risks! Look at Skon. All the girls love him because he doesn't give a crap about anyone. It's super sexy.'

I paused to think.

'Go on.' Tully egged me on, smelling weakness like a neighbourhood dog sniffing out a park picnic.

'It's too far away,' I groaned, reaching out underneath the shelving.

'What's too far away?' Footsteps approached.

I stopped immediately. And my heart began to pound. That wasn't Tully's voice.

'Zoe, my chica, what's up!' *That* was Tully's voice.

Oh. My. God.

Zoe Ingham was right behind me. 'How's the view down there, Mike?'

I was suddenly too scared to speak.

I looked up and saw Zoe smiling at me. It wasn't a full smile, there was something off about it, like an error fixed with white-out. But you could tell she was trying.

She was with her mum again, who was there, but she wasn't. She was vacant. A black hole of energy hanging around her that I imagined would be an inky shade of purple. I wondered if she would ever shake that colour off her.

'Hi Zoe. Hi Mrs Ingham,' I said, still kneeling, face close enough to smooch their socks.

Tully reached down and yanked me up, and – as was always the case when I was near Zoe – my common sense shut-down, and I went into idiotic autopilot.

'Mrs Ingham, I believe you're wearing the wrong shoes on the wrong feet,' I said.

Mrs Ingham shifted her gaze slowly towards her toes, as if she were watching a balloon drop from the shelf in front of her.

'Oh gosh. Well, that explains a lot,' she said, before kneeling down to make the appropriate switch.

'What else was down there?' Zoe asked, pointing to below the shelves.

'Oh! It was just some money, that's all.' I hoped she couldn't hear my heart pounding.

'Oh really? I'll get it! I've got smaller arms than you.' She quickly ducked down onto the floor and reached under the shelves.

'No, don't!' I yelled.

Tully covered her mouth to stifle laughter.

Zoe stopped when she realised what she was reaching for. There was no money. Just an old M&M, covered in dust. I watched as she slowly grabbed it.

She got back to her feet and held the M&M out to me.

I was frozen.

'Do you still want this *delicious* M&M?' Zoe asked. The false smile she'd shown before had now turned into a very real one. 'Which has been lying on the floor for god knows how long.'

'No … thanks.' It was barely a whisper. I couldn't look at her.

She shrugged, then she popped the M&M into her mouth, chewed it for a second, then brought her forefinger and thumb to her lips like a TV chef. 'Mmmmm, hairy!'

Mrs Ingham stood up, admiring her own feet. 'That's better,' she said. 'What's your name, dear?'

I just stared at both of them. I'd somehow forgotten.

'It's Mike,' Zoe said.

Mrs Ingham smiled 'Thank you, Mike.'

Then Zoe smiled, took her Mum's hand, and they walked on to the next aisle.

Tully took one look at me and laughed.

Suddenly I could breathe again.

Halfway home, as if reading my mind, Tully put her arm around me and said, 'Don't worry, mate. I think I'm in love with her now too.'

•

'Did anything happen at school today?'

Mum was lying on her bed, her ceiling fan flinging so full pelt that I worried it might fall off and make sashimi out of her at any moment.

'Nope,' I said.

I wanted to tell her *everything*, that I'd bumped into the love of my life, that Zoe had actually talked to me! But I was still a bit annoyed with her. She hadn't really talked to me much either, to be honest, and it made me pretty sad. For the last few days she'd still had a headache, and usually went straight to bed as soon as she'd put her plate in the sink.

'Will you take the bin out, please?'

'Why are you in bed so early? You're always in bed.'

'When you work all day and then come home and cook dinner and then clean up all your bits and pieces, then you'll be exhausted too. Now, please just take the bins out.'

'Is something happening with Kenny?'

'Kenny is a disability rights activist and top-tier lawyer. Something is always happening with Kenny.'

'I mean, between you two. You haven't talked about him since you went away.'

'I don't want to talk about this right now, Mike. I have a headache, that's all.' She motioned for me to close her door and went back to scribbling in her diary.

'Actually, something did happen at school today. I learnt all about the GST. Apparently, everything is going to cost ten per cent more, so we should probably get the internet installed now so that we don't have to pay –'

Mum slammed her diary closed. 'Mike, don't you dare say that word!' She growled.

For a second, it didn't even look like her. She was like a wolf. A wolf with laser beams.

I could feel my breath, hot in my chest. Tears bubbling away just under my throat. I nodded and walked out of her room. As I left, I turned her fan down a few notches.

'Mike, come turn that back!' I heard her yell as I walked back down our long hallway to my bedroom.

I wasn't going to do what she said. I was starting to get mad at her. The more she carried on like this, the more I thought about moving in with Dad. He never cared about anything, and certainly didn't care about whether I made my bed or did the dishes or took out the bin or anything like that.

We could be boys together. Men.

CHAPTER SIX

THURSDAY, 19TH MARCH 1998

The next two days were the same story. Dad would drop me at Mum's, I'd walk in, and Mum would already be in bed. But now there was no going to work, no asking how my day was, just more dishes in the sink, and the sound of her bedroom ceiling fan on full bore behind a closed door.

By Thursday, Mr Bortey had pulled me aside and said he needed to speak with me after class.

'Have I won something?' I asked. At Ironbark Primary, the teachers would hold you back after class if you had won an award or something.

Needless to say, I'd never been held back for that reason, but I was hopeful today, because I'd spent the whole class being super well-behaved, just sitting in the back row, staring out the window, thinking about where I might fit all my things at Dad's place. My room wasn't as big there as it was at Mum's.

Mr Bortey wouldn't match my eye. 'Just hang back after class, please.'

Everyone packed up and made their way to the exit.

'The crane has landed,' Tully whispered as she headed past me.

I looked to the back of the class, where Zoe was packing her books into her bag, when she stopped, spotting something. She reached into her bag and pulled out a small bouqet of origami flowers – albeit, they were so squashed now they looked more like a multicolour paper-mâché dinner plate.

She looked up, quizzically, at the classmates exiting around her, then over to me, and I snapped my gaze so quickly away and down to the floor, that I wondered if I was going to end up with one of Mum's headaches.

I couldn't tell if she was on to me, but I sure as hell felt self-conscious, the same way you readjust the back of your T-shirt to cover your jeans just after you pass someone you lock eyes with on the street.

Mr Bortey came over and sat down next to me at my desk on the other side of the room, but it was weird. He was looking at me funny. Almost like he pitied me.

'Mike, you know it's my job to teach you English, and coach you in athletics, right?' Mr Bortey said, quietly.

What a weird thing to say, of course that was his job.

I nodded.

He looked around to make sure there was definitely nobody else in or around the classroom. Zoe was the last to leave. She took her bag and headed out to the building's hallway, and we watched her changing from her school shoes into her sports shoes.

Mr Bortey moved his chair a bit closer to me.

Then, he put his hand on my knee.

Now I looked around too, glad that Zoe could provide solid testimonial.

'Are you going to kiss me?' I said.

He reeled back, snatching his hand away like I'd singed the curly black hairs on his slim, bony wrists with a match.

'What? No! God, no, Mike. What?' He jumped out of his chair, and straightened his oversized cheap suit jacket. 'Is everything OK at home, Mike? Are you safe?' He must have seen my face change.

'It's just – and this is hard for me to say, Mike – but you …' It was like he couldn't find the words, 'you smell, Mike. And your clothes have been noticeably dirty for the last week. I just …' He cleared his throat. 'After recent events in our community, I've been asked … we've *all* been asked … to increase our awareness for parental negligence, because when parents let their guard down, accidents happen, and then it can be too late.'

I followed his eyes which were focused outside on Zoe, as she tightened the laces on her sneakers, grabbed her bag, and jogged down the hall out of sight.

His attention snapped back to me.

'I just need to know that everything is OK and that your parents are looking after you properly, Mike.'

How dare you …

I didn't need anyone to look after me.

I was a man. Well, almost.

Sure, I hadn't washed my clothes, but that's because Mum never taught me how to use the machine. And I wasn't about to ask her because, other than when we were eating dinner, I wasn't speaking to her. I felt my stomach tying up like shoelaces, and my eyes starting to sting, but I started to laugh.

'Haha, no, our washing machine has broken, and Mum has been on the phone with Harvey Norman basically every day to see if they will deliver a new one at a time when someone's home, but they only do daytime delivery while she's at work. I'm sure we'll get a new one this weekend. I'll put in extra detergent so that I'm squeaky clean!'

It felt fake. It was fake.

Mr Bortey paused for a moment. 'There are always people you can talk to, Mike,' he said.

'Talking has never been my problem, Mr Bortey, you know that.'

Mr Bortey stared at me for a second longer, waiting for me to break. Then the alarm on his watch went off.

'It's "Coach" now, Mike. Training has just started. You head down and let the squad know I'll be a few minutes late.'

I nodded. 'Gotta get ahead of Skon. He's been on fire recently. I really want to make the team for the Dash!'

I went for the door and, as I left, I looked back at Mr Bortey. He was wearing the face of someone who felt like they had done all they could in the given moment, but had still failed. And I actually felt a bit sorry for him.

I should've told him not to worry, that things had felt a bit strange and that I was actually a bit confused about my living situation for the first time in my life. But I didn't. Instead, I laughed at him again, just to make him feel even more silly for what he'd tried to suggest.

•

I should have known something was wrong as soon as I walked in. The shower was running and Mum never had a shower until after dinner. She'd always said she didn't want to go to bed smelling like chops. I was actually glad she was in the shower though, because it meant I could quickly run to my room and spray deodorant under my pits in an attempt to somehow erase the terrible conversation I'd had with Mr Bortey.

I was running back down the hallway to let Dad know that I'd gotten in safely, when I heard Mum.

I don't think I'll ever forget that sound.

'Miiiiiiike!' she warbled through the white noise of the shower.

The first time Mum didn't sound like Mum.

I stopped and turned back towards the bathroom.

I'd been super excited because I knew there was an MA (SN) movie on SBS that night, and I'd mentally been trying to figure out which cricket highlights video I'd be willing to tape over, but suddenly I was scared.

Really scared.

I knocked on the bathroom door, knowing I didn't need to. It was slightly ajar, and I could hear Mum moaning. When I eventually stepped in, I thought I'd been pranked because I couldn't see her. I could just see the steamed-up glass of the shower screen; nobody on the other side.

Then I looked down.

Mum was sitting on the floor of the shower, completely naked. It had been a few years since I'd seen her naked. I used to hang out in her room all the time when she was getting changed or putting on creams, and it was never a problem, but then a few years ago she told me that I shouldn't see her naked anymore. That it wasn't appropriate.

Now, I was looking down at her, helpless. I turned my head and looked away. I wasn't really sure what she wanted. She had her head hung in her hand, and the shower screen was slightly open. Water was splattering all over the tiles and starting to dribble past my feet onto the carpet in the hallway. I didn't want to touch her naked, so I just quickly turned off the shower taps.

I handed her a towel from the rack and turned away from her again. My heart was racing. She didn't look good at all. Her eyes closed. Her lips blue. Slumped on the floor, now shivering.

'Is your dad still outside?' she mumbled, barely audible.

Oh, shit! I forgot he was still waiting for me to let him know that I'd made it in safely.

'Yeh, I'll give him the signal,' I said as I turned to run out the bathroom door.

'No!' she yelled, much louder this time. 'He needs to stay,' she spluttered through wet lips. 'I … I think I need to go to hospital.'

It took me a minute to compute everything. Standing there, looking at my naked mum. Her pale, plump frame slumped on the floor of the shower. Water trickling from the shower floor and out onto the carpet in the hallway. I thought about the dishes piled up in the kitchen sink. My dirty clothes in the laundry basket. And the smell. How much I smelled.

It suddenly hit me, right through the mask of the deodorant.

Mum was sick.

And so I turned around, ran outside, and called for Dad.

•

It's lucky I'd had a growth spurt recently. I'd just hit 165cm and had finally surpassed Mum; a feat I'd been chasing for a few years now.

I say it's lucky because, if I hadn't been so big, I don't know how Dad and I would've carried her out of the shower, out into the apartment building's elevator, past the letterboxes, and across the street to the car.

Dad was about to leave when I came running out, thinking that I'd forgotten to give the signal.

We'd wrapped Mum in a bedsheet because she couldn't dress herself. She said her head hurt too much, and she couldn't open her eyes. But by the time we'd made it to the car, she'd managed to lift one eyelid, and she'd started to feel self-conscious being out in public in a sheet.

'We'll just pretend you're going to the University Toga Party!' I joked, but nobody laughed.

We tried to bundle Mum into the back of Dad's car, but she started pushing back.

'I'm feeling better now,' she groaned, her arms rigid against the doorframe of the back seat, suddenly strong enough to stop us from getting her inside.

'No, Anne,' Dad said. 'We need to go to the hospital. If it's nothing, it's nothing, and we can all laugh, but this could be serious. I just want to make sure you're OK.'

My jaw almost fell off. Mum and Dad had been divorced for five years, and I could barely remember a time together when they weren't fighting. But in that one sentence, I got to see a nostalgic glimmer of love. Of caring. It made me realise that they didn't always hate each other, and that – however many moons ago – there once was a lot of love between them. I thought about times they must have spent together, watching movies or going out to Dad's nightclub, long before I came along and turned them into boring parents. They would have been young lovers once, just like me and Zoe would hopefully one day be.

Just when it looked like she wouldn't go anywhere without a fight, Mum's arm buckled, and she fell into the back seat, almost hitting her head on the opposite passenger door. She let out a moan and Dad twisted her legs so that they fully fit inside and he could close the door.

He ran around the car to the driver's side and jumped in. I stood aside as I heard his car roar into life, before speeding off, only to stop about ten metres away. Then the red reverse lights illuminated, and suddenly the car was back next to me again.

Dad opened his door and stuck his body up and out of the car. 'I'm sorry, I thought you were inside.'

'God, you're hopeless sometimes,' I said.

'Mike, get in the bloody car!'

•

We didn't talk much on the drive to the hospital. I just looked out the window as the orange street lights sped past. Mum occasionally coughing, Dad asking her if she was going to vomit. I don't think I'd ever sat in a car with Mum in the back seat. It's little things like that you remember.

When we got to the entrance of the hospital, Dad made me run inside to get a wheelchair. We helped Mum out of the car, then wheeled her into the jarring fluorescence of the emergency ward.

As we approached the desk, there was a sweaty twenty-something year old, yelling at the receptionist in charge.

'I don't know what it was, but it wasn't cocaine. I'm calling the police. These people out here are trying to kill us.'

The nurse ignored him as she saw us wheeling Mum towards her. A look of concern crossed her face. She walked around the desk and towards us. Strong and in charge.

'What's wrong?' she asked, and as Dad explained the situation, I looked around at all the sorry-sacks sitting on the cold plastic seats of the hospital waiting room: a young girl – still wearing her rollerblades and helmet – blood trickling from temple to toe, an older lady on crutches who was trying to roll a cigarette, and an older gentleman with an erection poking clearly up from his grey trackpants.

I didn't even notice when they took Mum away. I didn't expect that. I thought they would just give her some extra strong painkillers or something. But they wheeled her off, and Dad told me they needed to 'do some tests', and that it 'might take a while'. By 'a while', I thought he meant twenty minutes or so, but after an hour-and-a-half, and a few conversations with various staff, Dad came back and told me that Mum would have to stay overnight, and that I'd have to go home with him tonight.

Just for tonight.

As the streetlights flashed past, and the cool autumn wind slapped me in the face, I sat in the passenger seat of Dad's car with my head leaning on the window frame like a sad dog, and I thought about Mum getting to stay in the hospital for the night. A nice clean bed. A TV in her room. A cooked meal that would probably come with a little cake on the side.

It'd be good to stay there for now, I thought, as the wind hit my face.

After all, it was just one night.

CHAPTER SEVEN

FRIDAY, 20TH MARCH 1998

We were sitting in Biology, in our usual spot down the back-right corner of the class. The science rooms had shared seating at long benches, with gas fixtures attached and a tap and basin in the centre. I thought Biology meant hacking at dead frogs with scalpels. Instead, we got blurry diagrams of jellyfish projected onto the classroom wall, which was annoying. Jellyfish are already blurry animals.

Ms Harris, our science teacher, clopped wherever she went; a pair of black, closed-in shoes with a low block heel and a black velvet bow, permanently attached to her feet. She had a long, thin, Greek nose, big teeth, and a pair of tassel earrings constantly bashing against a line along her jaw where plenty of make-up met plenty of freckles.

'Quick quiz. What is the name given to a particular free-swimming creature that is in the Medusa stage of its life-cycle?' Ms Harris asked.

'Is it "Tully", Miss?' I yelled out.

Tully whacked me on the arm as the class laughed. I spotted Zoe laughing too and I wondered who I needed to give my address to so they could send me a Hero of the Year medallion. Ms Harris rolled her eyes and carried on.

'The answer is on the diagrams in front of you: the jellyfish. The name "Medusa", of course, comes from the ancient Greek tale, about a lady with snakes for hair.'

'Then it's true, Miss. You should see me when I've gotten out of bed,' Tully said.

The class giggled again.

'Interesting fact about jellyfish: they are asexual creatures. They each release sperm and eggs into the water. From there, a larvae is formed, and an eventual jellyfish is released from that.'

'Does that mean every time we go to the beach, we're swimming in jellyfish jizz?' Tully yelled.

Everyone laughed. Ms Harris shook her head in disappointment.

'Now, the main predator of jellyfish are other jellyfish, but they have a number of other predators. These include fish, sharks, turtles – which is why they end up choking on plastic bags – and, would you believe, certain types of diving birds, just like the ones you might see around the Brindlewood River, who spot the jellyfish from the sky and dive down to eat not just the jellyfish itself, but what's inside the jellyfish too. Imagine that. A little fish, being eaten by a jellyfish, being eaten by a bird. That's quite the turducken!'

Ms Harris gave a hearty laugh and the class stared, silently.

'That was actually pretty funny,' I whispered to Tully.

'I know, but she's a teacher. I can't laugh.'

Ms Harris cleared her throat. 'But, of course, jellyfish are best known for their ability to ruin a day at the beach. Their sting comes from tiny nematocysts, or stinging cells, on the jellyfish's bell. When triggered, the cells eject poisonous barbs that help the jellyfish catch their dinner. Now, fact or fiction: you should apply urine to a jellyfish sting?' Ms Harris asked.

'Ha!' Tully bleated. 'You should ask Mike, Miss.'

I death-stared. Mr Harris raised an eyebrow.

'Let me ask you this, Mr Amon. Do you know how acidic your urine is at any given time?' Ms Harris asked.

And now everyone was staring.

'You should be asking his Mum, Miss!' Tully yelled. 'She was the one *treating* his stings!'

I wish I could say the ensuing laughter was a gift that I 'gave' to the class. But nope. If I 'gave' them that gift, every single one of them returned to sender. So much laughter, directed 'at' me now. I locked eyes with Zoe across the room and she was doing her best to hide it, but she was laughing too.

'If you get stung by a jellyfish, use vinegar! Urine, whether it's yours *or* a very generous family member's, could make things worse. Now, class dismissed.' Her head pointed floor-bound as the whole class packed up their books. As I walked past, eyes to the floor, I could hear Ms Harris muttering, 'Mike, Mike, Mike.'

Great, I thought, *Zoe thinks I'm a freak. Tomorrow everyone will have the scalpels. I'll have a stick of playdough.*

•

The northern edge of the senior campus bordered on re-claimed Indigenous land, dubbed Golbourn Park. The land wasn't huge – just a grass city block with a few trees, a small playground in the south-east corner, and a building that looked like a soccer clubhouse to the north. How generous we are. We'll take your Country, you have a park. Mind you, you'll have to fight for it first.

'So, how long are you going to be mad?' Tully asked, as we walked through Golbourn Park.

The school had tried to buy the re-claimed land so they could build a new running track, but their bid had failed, so we had to use the track at The Showgrounds, closer to the city. To get there, we had to walk through Golbourn Park. There were always tales of close calls, thrown bottles, kids getting rolled for their money, but for the most part, you'd just stroll past people of all ages and ethnicities, drinking, sometimes at seven-thirty in the morning. An early start for a few drinks, but I wasn't judging. Hell, I'd seen Tully's mum standing by their kitchen window before school of a morning, and I'll be damned if the coffee in her mug wasn't a deep shade of ruby some days.

'You're supposed to be helping me with Zoe! Not making her think I'm a walking urinal.' I kicked a discarded XXXX beer can, and the dregs splashed up onto the ankle of my grey knee-highs.

'I am helping!' Tully said, as we walked up the small rise that split Golbourn Park and the back of The Showgrounds where the grandstand and track was. 'They say laughter is the best medicine. Wasn't your goal to cheer her up?'

The blue running track was the hallmark of The Showgrounds. A plaque at the back entry to the grounds proudly boasted that you could see the track from the sky as you fly into town; a fact Mum and I verified when we'd flown home from Tasmania only months prior. By 'state school standards', our running track was the best in the city, because it wasn't ours. A fact the snotty rich private school kids loved reminding us of.

'My dad pays for your education,' was the common line, spouted by whichever genius didn't realise that the government gave a financial contribution to *all* schools, and the private schools always got more anyway.

Most of the kids had dumped their bags in the old grandstand at the finish line, and were stretching out on the grass in the middle of the track. Skon was taking practice jumps into the nearby sand, launching casually off either foot – it didn't matter – hopping, stepping and jumping so far into the pit that I genuinely wondered whether the school might run out of tape to measure his efforts.

He even looked good, with his brand-spanking-new Nike running spikes, navy Brindy Harriers singlet, and shiny full-length compression tights. Everyone else was in daggy blue shorts and their maroon sports uniform polo.

I was sitting on the grass near Zoe who was refastening the laces on her spotless runners, her back to me, levelling her sports socks with perfection up around her freckly shins. I was lacing up a pair of ancient, dirt-clad running spikes, dried blades of grass stuck to the midsole, splotches of dirt smooshed into the fabric from heel to toe. They were the only pair I had at Dad's place.

'Woah! Brought out the old Ironbark sandals,' Tully said, sitting down next to me. 'Haven't seen those since Year Six!'

'Yeh …' I laughed, conscious of Zoe's proximity. I thought about explaining what had happened the night before. How I hadn't had the chance to get my decent shoes from Mum's, but I didn't want Zoe to overhear. My problems seemed miniscule compared to hers.

'Yeh, I thought I needed a good luck charm from my golden era,' I exclaimed with feigned cheer, squeezing my feet into their dried out, crusted interiors.

'I really want Nikes, but Mum reckons they're a waste of money. As if her seven different eye creams are a real top-notch investment,' I whinged.

'Don't even get me started,' Tully said, lacing up her grungy old sneakers. 'When we started term, I asked Mum for a pair of Doc Martens and she bought me Kmart shoes instead and suggested I paint the yellow stitching on.'

Behind us, Coach Bortey approached, in a full blue, matching tracksuit with maroon stripes down either side. Less coach, more chav. He squatted down next to Zoe.

'Zoe, you know you don't have to train if you don't want to?' he said, softly. Too softly.

'Oh, OK. So what are we all doing instead?' Zoe said, starting to unlace her shoes.

Coach cleared his throat. 'Oh, no, the tryouts are still happening, it's just ... *you* don't have to tryout, if you don't want to.'

'Why not?' Zoe asked, cocking her head, eyes narrowing.

Coach looked around and then whispered, 'If it's all a bit too tough for you at the moment ...?'

Zoe nodded, then leaned in towards Coach Bortey and spoke quietly, but with purpose.

'Coach, my sister died. Not me. I'll tryout, thanks. Just like everyone else.'

Coach Bortey looked like he'd just been dacked. His eyes darted around to the surrounding eavesdropping teammates and then cleared his throat.

He stood up. 'Alright, Year Eights! Out of the boys, who wants to trial for the triple jump spot?'

Zoe's response had inspired me. My arm almost flew out of its socket as I shot it up in anticipation. I grabbed my shoulder in pain.

'You OK?' Tully asked.

'That damn police officer.'

I looked around for any competitors. I knew that not many people had done triple jump before high school. You really had to be into little athletics, and I didn't recognise any of these people from previous meets. Except Skon, and he wasn't moving. For a second, I got excited. Then, he raised his hand, and I lowered my hopes.

'Well then, this shouldn't take long.' Coach shuffled us both over to the jumping pits and set us up for our practice jumps.

'We need to set up the board. Who wants to jump off eleven metres?'

Skon kept his hand up, while my hand and jaw dropped.

'Jesus, eleven metres?' Tully said. 'What's your PB?'

'Not eleven metres,' I whispered sotto voce.

'And who wants to jump off the nine-metre board?' Coach Bortey asked.

I sheepishly raised my hand and felt the smirks of the so-called teammates around me.

'Geez, I hope you're a grower not a shower,' Tully giggled.

And 'grow' I did not.

Where I cut a forlorn figure, gingerly shuffling down the runway before flopping into the sand like a soggy bunch of coriander, Skon leapt graciously through the air, sometimes taking sympathy jumps off his left foot, gliding so softly into the sandpit it was as though a Boeing 737 was landing on the cloudy runways of heaven.

I looked up at the sky, the sun sliding away, as each jump got out of my control.

'Alright, one more jump!' Coach Bortey screamed from the little stand next to the sandpits.

The sprinters seemed to be done too, because Tully and Zoe came over from their drills and sat down next to the pit, just in time for mine and Skon's final jumps.

'Coach, my shoulder's no good. Maybe I shouldn't jump?'

Coach Bortey ran over to me. 'Mike, I know you're worried, but this is what competition is all about. It's not about who can jump the furthest in a lifetime, it's about who can jump the furthest when it counts.'

He winked and ran back to his seat.

I stood at my mark and glanced over to where Zoe was sitting with Tully. She caught my eye and waved, and my guts filled with butterflies. Why don't they cover that in Biology? I waved back; a stupid, goofy wave – like a five-year-old would give the postman – but then she shot me a confused look.

A hand landed on my shoulder from behind. It was Skon, and he waved back to Zoe. It all made sense now. His run-up was two metres behind mine.

'Nice one, skinbag,' he whispered in my ear. 'You're up first.'

Suddenly, something swept over me. I realised that there really wasn't anything more that I could do except give it my best shot.

'Move over. I'm going off the eleven,' I said, determination shooting out of my eyes.

'Be my guest,' Skon scoffed, stepping aside and waving me through like he was a bouncer at a nightclub.

'Mike, be careful,' Coach Bortey yelled. 'I don't know whether we have insurance if you hurt yourself.'

'Mike, don't do it!' Tully shouted. 'I can't carry you through the Reserve!'

'Go for it, Mike!' That was Zoe. And that's what made me try.

I smiled at her as I took a moment. Breathed. Steadied myself. Ready.

Then I started running.

Screaming down the runway, the warm autumn breeze blasting through my loose curls as I chased my vision. My dream. A place in the team.

I hit the board perfectly.

'Yeh!' I heard Tully roar as I slammed my foot right on the thick of the white. The whole athletics team gasped as I hopped through the air, stepping gloriously with my knees at right angles, and then landed, perfectly, two feet planted together.

I'd landed perfectly, alright. Perfectly on the tartan track. About ten centimetres from the sandpit. My toes not even poking over the edge.

'Oh my god, is that sandpit deep enough for a grave because you need to bury yourself right noooooow!' Skon yelled.

He was belching with laughter, in proper fits. He laughed so hard that it turned into panic, pointing to his face, desperate for breath. It was as though he were praying for sweet death to take him because his stomach muscles ached from laughing too much. Eventually, he had to pass his final jump.

The rest of the squad didn't do much to hide their enjoyment either. Zoe was the only one with a straight face.

Calling an end to the jump trials, Coach Bortey came up to me as I packed up my gear. 'You weren't prepared today, were you, Mike?'

'It's my shoes, Coach,' I said, as I shoved my feral old runners back into their white plastic grocery bag. 'And I don't want to make excuses, but I got arrested yesterday, sir. The cop pinned me down, really ripped at my arm.'

Coach Bortey stared at me.

I looked around to make sure Zoe wasn't in earshot.

'And, Dad and I took Mum to hospital last night, and I've barely had any sleep.'

Coach Bortey kept staring as though I were telling him my dog ate my athletic ability, just as Zoe approached, red cheeked with the perfect amount of sweat across her brow and clavicle.

'The runners are ready when you are, Coach,' she panted.

Coach nodded, then turned back to me.

'Here's the thing, Mike. With the Dobson Dash, you're only supposed to compete in one event, and Skon's decided to focus on sprints, so …' He scratched his brow and let out a sigh. 'I can't believe I'm saying this, but – congratulations – you're in the team.'

Zoe smiled at me. 'Wow. Those old kicks really must be lucky.'

•

The payphones in the Chill Zone of Brindy Shopping Centre accepted coins and phonecards, but they wouldn't actually charge until the caller picked up. That meant you only needed to pay if you wanted to talk.

The code was simple. Call Dad, he picks up, phone cuts out, then call again, let it ring once, then hang up. That way he'd know the first call wasn't a prank, and that I needed a lift. Then I'd walk up to the little service road opposite the bus interchange, and I'd wait for Dad to come and pick me up.

I was still buzzing from my selection in the athletics team when Dad picked me up. I'd been waiting for him to ask how I went at trials, but he just sat in silence for a minute or so, talkback radio yabbering quietly under the air-conditioning. An old man had called in, who I suspected was having his first and only conversation for the day.

'When the authorities were conducting those searches, I had three diver birds sitting in my backyard, and I'm halfway up Mt Kartha. Imagine the ecological displacement that will happen if this ridiculous new ferry terminal goes ahead. I don't care how many guard rails or barriers you put up, nothing will ever be safer than good old-fashioned parental supervision –'

Dad flicked off the radio, took a big breath, and then asked me if I knew what cancer was.

'Cancer?' I said, as we pulled up to some traffic lights and I saw the reflection of our car in the glass door of a newsagency shopfront.

Our 'new' car. Not that it was actually new. All the cars that pulled into the pick-up zone at Brindlewood High seemed to be nice shiny new cars, but our 'new' car was second-hand. That was so like my dad to buy 'new-second-hand'.

The man was a dentist! Gabe McCormack – who I'd trained with that afternoon – his dad was a doctor, and I saw him getting picked up in a flash new Jeep. But my dad's a dentist, and we had a second-hand Corolla.

He's so African like that.

Mind you, anything was better than the rusty, red Subaru sportswagon that we used to drive around in, its seats splattered with crusted glue from the nights we'd drive around Brindlewood, sticking 'Afro Good Times' posters up on electricity boxes.

Dad had finally said goodbye to that red piece of crap after the mechanic told him he wouldn't work on it because it had too many spiders under the chassis. Apparently one had fallen on the mechanic's face, mid-oil change, and delivered a spicy peck to his cheek that had closed one of his eyes up for three days. The mechanic suggested Dad could do the next service himself down at the Reserve; all it would take was half a can of fuel and a few dozen matches.

I stared out the window while I thought about that old red piece of crap car.

'Do you know what cuncer is?' Dad asked, affording a glance as the lights turned green and we drove on.

Cancer kills people, I thought. *It's basically like –*
The Irukandji.

'No, what's cuncer?' I asked, still staring out the window.

He cleared his throat. 'You see, the cells in our body are meant to divide at a steady rate. When they divide at an abnormal rate, then it becomes cuncer.'

'Ooooh, you mean "cancer".'

'That's what I said,' Dad said.

'No, you said "cuncer" with a "u", instead of an "a". It's *cancer*.'

'Mike –'

'Just like how you pronounce it "moskwito" instead of "mosquito", and when you say "marijuana", you pronounce the "j" in it, so you say "mari-jew-ana".'

'Mike, what you're doing right now is racist.'

'Dad, I'm half you. How can I be racist?'

'Mike, please! Just listen to me.' His knuckles were almost white as he gripped the steering wheel tightly. 'It's in her breasts, but it has spread up to her brain.'

Breasts. Plural.

I thought about that for a second.

Brain.

That didn't sound good.

We drove past a small group of retail spaces that consistently housed 'For Lease' signs, and then down the hill past the veterinary clinic. We'd taken our cat, Gypsy, there a few years back. A big happy family with a sick cat. A beautiful cat. Beautiful but dumb. All white, with tips like it had stood in mud.

I was lying in bed when I heard Gypsy scream. It had sounded frantic, but cats are cats. They run around and flop and do things for the sake of it. I lay in bed that afternoon and played *Sonic 2*.

Turns out, Gypsy had been mauled by Tully's blue staffy, Cheeks, and now neither of us have pets anymore.

Dad took Gypsy to the vet that afternoon and they operated, but they found a cancer. A big one. In her liver.

An Irukandji.

Poor Gypsy had been living in pain for god knows how long and none of us knew. We just took her as being a cat. She must have felt terrible for weeks, maybe months. Intense pain some days. Maybe every day.

Was that how Mum felt?

'Is she going to lose her hair?' I asked.

Dad shrugged. 'She's getting a lot of tests done today, so we can't visit. We'll go tomorrow after school.'

'I've got more athletics trials tomorrow afternoon,' I said.

'We might need to go and pick up some of your clothes from your mother's place on the way home,' Dad kept talking.

'Why?'

'Because, obviously, you'll be staying with me for a few days. More than a weekend, this time.'

I looked out the window and thought about it. A stay at Dad's was probably just what the doctor ordered.

That wasn't necessarily a bad thing.

'I made the athletics team, by the way. Thanks for asking.'

He looked at me, then back at the road.

'That's good, Mike. Congratulations.'

•

Dad's place always smelled.

Of food. Of animals. Of difference.

He had a peanut stew bubbling away on the original eighties white electric stovetop. A small pot of thick, white, doughy semolina cooking next to it. Munched up chillies in a shallow wooden bowl on the lime-green kitchen table that he would grind down with a mortar.

I sunk into the old wicker lounge and watched TV, but my attention couldn't hold. I'd go from staring at the cobwebs that sat abandoned in the corners of the wooden rafters of the high lounge room ceiling, to watching the colourful reflections of the TV being cast onto the cork floor in front of me.

Breast cancer that's spread to her brain.

She really liked her hair too.

Before I knew it, I was sitting in the dark and Dad was changing the channel to the ABC news. The only thing he ever watched.

'What do you want for dinner? Are you going to have some of the stew?' he asked.

Trick question.

'I didn't expect you to be here, so the only other option is old chicken nuggets,' he said, as he threw the rock-hard block of god-knows-how-old nugs onto the kitchen table, shards of freezer-ice flying off it in every direction.

'I'm not really hungry,' I said. 'Can I just have Milo?'

He shrugged. 'Sure.'

I always held my breath when I went into the pantry. There were so many foreign smells and flavours in that thing that if I closed my eyes I could've been lost in a bazaar in Old Delhi.

I got my glass as Dad got the milk and popped the Milo tin with the spoon handle.

Dad watched, next to me.

I put my usual two scoops in, then looked at him.

I could feel my heart beating.

I put the spoon back in the tin for a third scoop and waited. Nothing.

Into the glass it went, which I filled with milk, and then I bounded up the dark brown wooden staircase, spilling Milo on my knuckles.

My creaky, sunken, low-set trundle bed was exactly how I'd left it in the morning; sky-blue sheet and basketball-print doona bunched to one side, three red pillows haphazardly arranged like a Chinese symbol. Mum was always at me about making my bed, but Dad didn't care.

I suddenly realised how tired I was. Being a successful athlete was draining stuff.

I opened the window and lay down underneath the faded, motorcycle-print curtains, the soft swishing of freeway traffic in the distance, a backdrop to the choir of chirping creepy-crawlies in the scrappy overgrown yard outside. I placed the glass of Milo on the carpet next to me and turned on the TV.

A movie was starting with a 'Mature Audience' rating, and a smile nearly stretched past the edges of my face when the title faded up on screen.

Sirens, starring Elle Macpherson and Katie Fischer.

It had loads of nudity.

Nudity of the good kind. I could already hear Dad snoring on the couch in the lounge room, which meant I could stay up as long as I wanted.

I felt bad about how good I felt.

I knew Mum was sick, but this was everything I really loved.

Milo, nudity and freedom.

A twelve-year-old's trifecta.

I mean, Mum was in hospital.

But I was in heaven.

CHAPTER EIGHT

SATURDAY, 21ST MARCH 1998

The following afternoon, Dad and I were doing laps of the hospital, looking for a spot on the street to park. The Royal Brindlewood Hospital – a four-storey red-brick building with terracotta tiled roofing, two giant steeples, and white window panes uniformly spaced every five metres or so – had a whole carpark dedicated to visitors, but you had to pay to use it. So here we were, scrounging for freebies.

Each lap of the hospital, we'd pass the carpark. Each pass of the carpark, my eyes would roll.

'Can we please just use the carpark?' I asked. 'What you pay in fees, you save in energy.'

'The carpark is bad luck,' he replied.

So, we kept driving.

•

I really didn't want to visit her. There was something about hospitals that scared me. They're all white and cold and smell weird – and no-one smiles. Who wants to hang out in a boring white box where everyone is so unhappy? I just wanted them to cut the cancer out and for her to be home soon.

The walls of the waiting area were white, plastered with posters reminding you to cover your sneezes, check for lumps, or tell a trusted friend if you're in an abusive relationship. The waiting area was quiet. Hospitals are full of whispers. Sickness is good at tiptoeing.

I followed Dad from the elevator. The smell of disinfectant and hand soap. The sound of newsreaders on televisions. A doctor laughing with her colleague.

People, lying around, being sick. None of them turning to look at you. I couldn't look up. Eyes focused on the shiny, sky-blue vinyl sheet floor. Dad ducked aside to chat to a nurse behind a desk and ask where 'Mrs Amon' was. She'd kept Dad's name, even after all these years. Then we were walking again, head down. I counted the doorways of rooms that we passed. One. Two. Three. On the fourth I made the mistake of looking up. An older lady, maybe mid-fifties, in a hospital gown, so gaunt you'd wonder how she could hold herself upright, stood in the middle of her room, holding her drip stand like the Grim Reaper holds his scythe.

Fuck. Head back down.

I wouldn't make that mistake again.

Keep counting. Five. Six. Then Dad turned in. This was it.

And breathe.

Mum's room was cold like Brindy Shopping Centre. About the size of a lounge room, with a connecting accessible bathroom that, through a crack in the door, I could see had a plastic chair underneath a shower with no screen. On the walk from the elevator, there'd been rooms of the same size with three or four beds, but Mum's room just had one, which sat conspicuously in the middle. It had a table with a newspaper, some chairs, a 34cm television in the corner that was switched off, and a sink in the opposite corner with a lever-style handle you could work with your elbows. It was no Sheraton Mirage, but a backpacker would've swapped it for their bunk any day of the week.

When we walked in, Mum was sitting up in her bed, wearing a white gown that matched the bed's crisp white sheets. A nurse was fiddling with the settings on the IV stand next to Mum's bed. Her name tag read Gretchen. Dad and I were at the door, and she nearly jumped out of her uniform when she saw us.

'Jiminy Crickets!' she said, clutching a set of well-manicured nails against her chest in shock, and rocking back onto the metal apparatus that held fluid bags next to Mum's bed.

'I have that effect on girls,' I said, smiling.

Gretchen laughed. 'Oh, I bet you do, little man.' She had a great big Julia Roberts smile, shoulder-length black hair, a soft, round face, and more piercings than usual. Two in each lobe, and one on the right of her nose. No earrings or studs, though. I guess sleepers could go missing in a surgery room.

'Mike!' Mum gurgled through a strained smile and cleared her throat.

'Oh, bless. Is this your little Mike?' Gretchen placed her hand firmly on my shoulder. 'Oh my, he's gorgeous!'

I couldn't help but blush. Older women always liked me.

Mum coughed. She looked bad. Real bad. Her skin so pale, her head bowed. It was almost as if she didn't want to look at me either. I'd never seen her look so fragile.

Is that shame?

'I'm sorry, chook,' she said.

I shrugged. 'It's not your fault.'

Mum's window looked east, out over Brindlewood City. A low-rise, sprawling metropolis, set on the banks of the Brindlewood River, which snaked off and away to the right, into the distance, towards the coast. They'd stopped dredging years before, but the water in the river was still a rich brown.

Mum and I used to visit my great-grandmother in a nursing home on the outskirts of town, and they would always give me a hot chocolate made with water. It was so gross. Hot chocolate should be rich and creamy, made with milk. It should hug your mouth from the inside out. A hot chocolate made with water is a criminal's drink; a drink to drown your secrets. That's what the river always looked like. A hot chocolate made with water.

Looking left, you could see the mundane suburbia of Brindlewood's northern suburbs. Looking right, you could see the very tip of Mum's apartment, one or two roofs of the high school junior campus, and the eastern edge of Brindy Shopping Centre.

Looking straight out in front, just across the road, in a cruel trick played by the city's town planners, directly opposite the sickness and death of the hospital, was the Brindlewood Showground. Home to the Royal Brindy Show. A childhood institution, the Brindy Show was the highlight of every kid's calendar. From the showbag pavilion, to the games of sideshow alley, the cake-judging to the wood-chopping, it was always good times when The Show came to town. It opened in ten days. Construction had begun.

Dad was next to Mum's bed. 'How are you feeling? What have the doctors said?'

'Oh Marvin, I really don't want to talk about it now,' she said, closing her eyes.

'He's just asking how you are,' I said. I could feel the room look to me, but I kept staring out at the city.

'The Brindy Show starts soon,' I said over my shoulder to Mum. 'Hopefully you'll be out by opening night?'

Dad looked out the window next to me. 'Just what I need, more competition.'

'Who's the next band at Afro Good Times?' Mum asked.

Dad spun around. 'Serwaa and the Swingers. Have you heard of them?'

Mum shook her head.

'Hm, you and everyone else in Brindlewood apparently.'

Behind us, footsteps were advancing up the hallway, footsteps with a purpose, until their owner entered the room, a handbag hanging from an elbow that was covered by a long-sleeved red and green floral dress, and grey hair windswept every which way.

'Oh my god, Anne, you look shocking!' That was Linda. My grandma. Mum's mum.

Mum's dad, my grandfather, was a Nazi who came out to Australia in the 1950s.

He disappeared from the family when Mum was only one year old, which is probably for the best, considering her eventual taste in men.

Meanwhile, Dad's parents died long before I was born, so Linda was the only grandparent I had.

So many nights I'd be watching *Home and Away* and Mum would be sat up the hallway in our apartment, screaming into the telephone. Asking why the person on the other end had to be so critical, why they could never just be happy for her. Any time she was doing that, I knew she was talking to Linda. After those phone calls, Mum would slump back on the couch, nails to her mouth, asking me what she'd missed, her eyes red like roses.

My only real interactions with her came in the form of a yearly birthday card, with a twenty-dollar note folded neatly into the crease, the words 'To Michael' scribbled above the card's generic, computer-printed copy, and then signed out with the same handwriting; 'From Linda'.

'So, what questions haven't you been asked yet?' Linda plopped her brown pleather bag down on the chair opposite Mum, then joined me and Dad at the big window to look at her own reflection and check her hair.

'What do you mean?' Dad asked.

'I don't want to go over old ground. What hasn't she been asked?'

We all looked at her, and she held her arms up in a *don't shoot!* pose. 'I just want new information!'

'We're discussing treatments,' Dad said.

'Jesus,' Linda went back over to Mum and put her hand on Mum's arm. 'Are they going to cut off your breasts?'

I hated hearing that. The sentence sent a sharp pain into my stomach. It made my testicles ache for some reason.

'We will do whatever it takes,' Dad said.

'No, we won't,' Mum murmured.

No, we won't.

There was a lot to say, but nobody saying it.

Beeping everywhere, in the room and in the distance. Air-con purring.

'When did you find out?' I asked.

Dad and Linda looked at me.

'Am I not allowed to ask that?'

'Oh, Mike, I don't really feel like having this conversation,' Mum replied.

'Answer your son,' Linda said.

'Anne, it's important we understand how much time we have for treatment,' Dad pitched in.

'I've been through this with all the doctors, Marvin,' Mum said. 'I don't want to talk about it now.'

'I just want to know,' I said.

Silence. Beeping. Air-con.

Mum sighed. Her eyes were red and swollen. She looked down towards her waist where the folds of the hospital sheets were turned over.

The sound of a teardrop hitting cotton.

'When we were in Tasmania. I found a lump.' She reached for a tissue from the bedside.

'Jesus, Anne, three months ago?!' Dad said.

'Please, Marvin! Just don't, OK?' Mum's eyes stayed down as she sniffed again.

I stared at her. 'Why didn't you say anything? We could've come home.'

She dabbed at her eyes. 'We had so much fun, remember, Mike? We had so much fun.'

Watching her cry made my diaphragm ache.

'It wasn't that much fun,' I replied, my voice wavering. Constriction in my chest. Heat in my face, in my cheeks.

'Didn't you have fun?' she asked.

'No, it was a stupid trip. I only went because you wanted to.' I had to lie. I couldn't tell her the truth. That I constantly thought about that trip and how much it meant to me. She'd been lying to *me* the whole time! She found the lump *while* we were *there*. I had to turn back around and look out the window. I was really starting to ache.

'Oh, I'm sorry then,' Mum whispered. Then she really started crying, her face bright red and wet, her slumped shoulders jerking back with each breath in.

Dad walked over and put his arm around her shoulders.

'I'm OK, Marvin. Please,' she said, firmly. She sniffed in her dribbles and patted down her cheeks. She let a big breath out through pursed lips and tried to sit up straight.

Dad's phone rang. He had a mobile. It was a real log; almost the size of a 600ml chocolate milk. He had a separate holder for it on his belt, like a police officer has for their weapon.

It was annoying watching Dad fumble with his phone. It was just so cumbersome, and sometimes the clip for it wouldn't release from his belt, and he'd be there tugging at it with the ringtone bleating away, until eventually the ringing would stop, the caller having given up.

'Hello?' He whipped his phone out of its holster in an uncharacteristic display of agility, firing it towards his ear. He listened for a second. 'Yes! Plenty of tickets still available,' he said, as he stepped out of the room.

I finally turned around and faced Mum. She looked at me, then looked away again quickly.

'What's been happening at school?' she asked.

'Jesus, Anne. You have tubes coming out of you. Who gives a crap what happened at school?' Linda laughed.

'I made the team for the Dobson Dash,' I whispered. 'Triple jump.'

Mum tried to smile.

'Oh, that's great, Mike. You're so talented,' she said, clearing her clogged up throat.

'The relay trials are on Monday morning. Who knows, you might see me in the paper one day.'

'Oh, I'm sure I will, Mike.' She coughed. 'Get lots of rest, and eat a nice big dinner –'

'Are you giving me health tips?' I asked.

A moment. Hurt.

'Don't be rude, Mike,' Mum whispered. 'You sound like your grandmother.'

Linda rolled her eyes. 'Yes, don't be honest, like your grandma, Mike. It hurts sick people's feelings.'

Dad re-entered, the absolute eggplant of a phone held up to his ear.

'What? No, I have no idea,' Dad was screwing up his face. He waited for a second. 'I'm sorry, but no!'

He hung up, frustrated.

We waited for an explanation.

Dad's eyes darted between me, Mum and Linda, until he finally blurted it out.

'A lady. She wanted to know if there would be any African men with big penises at the Serwaa and the Swingers concert.' He looked away. 'I mean, for god's sake, how am I supposed to know?'

Mum started laughing, or trying to at least. Linda too. Although, Linda didn't laugh, she cackled. It was a wonderful cackle, but it was so loud, you felt everyone in the world could hear it.

Then, finally, Dad joined in too.

'Well, if you find out, loop me in to that conversation, please!' Linda said.

'Oh god, now my ears have cancer,' Mum said, and we all laughed a bit more.

Lord knows, I needed a laugh.

CHAPTER NINE

The relay trials.

My chance to be on that world stage next to the love of my life.

When I arrived at the oval in the morning, Coach Bortey was there waiting for us to get started on our warm-ups. It occurred to me that Mr Bortey asked us to call him 'Coach' in track and field because he was a different person here. His eyes seemed clearer. Everything we did – he did. It's like he grew stronger with every lunge. Every sprint. Every successful jump.

In lane one was Gabe McCormack. He had qualified for the 1500m. Scrawny little Gabe. Bright red hair that matched Zoe's. You felt like Gabe could run forever. Gabe didn't talk much, but when he did, it was always something slightly unsettling. The type of guy who would win 'Most Tolerably Perverted' at the office Christmas party.

In lane two was Jon Qi. Long jump. Second-generation Chinese, Jon was the only person who ran in sneakers because he was scared of sharp things, and wearing spikes set him off. His phobia ruled him out of javelin too.

In lane three was Calvin Barnes. High jump. Calvin was freakishly tall, like a bean stalk. He had long, lanky legs and a prominent nose, and he wore coke-bottle glasses whenever he wasn't airborne.

In lane four was Tyson Brickford. Shot-put. The exact opposite of Calvin, Tyson was like a walking boulder. His neck about as absent as his brains.

In lane five was Skon Helpmann. 100m. The king. My enemy.

In lane six was Moses Matakefu. Discus. Everything except breathing was just a stopgap between him and rugby. If he could perform a walking handstand, he'd probably run faster than me, because the guy had arms like my legs and a chest like Dad's fridge.

In lane seven was Fabian Malik. Javelin. His slicked jet-black hair made him look like he was running fast, even if he was strolling leisurely down the street.

And finally, in lane eight, was little old me. Triple jump. The only thing on my side was my need to prove myself. To Mum, to Zoe. Oh, and to show Skon that he wasn't the top dog after all.

On your marks.

Get set.

I was so close. Out of the blocks just fine. Fifth became fourth, fourth became third. I prayed for someone ahead to fall over, to trip – hell I would've welcomed a ruptured Achilles.

But it was my stupid old spikes.

My not-so-good-luck-anymore charm.

The sound of the sole ripping from the Ironbark sandals wasn't dissimilar to that of passing wind.

The glue, right around the shoe, connecting fabric to sole, split right open, leaving me wearing one old, rusty left shoe, and – on my right – some sort of flapping mouth with my foot as its tongue. My sock was now hitting the track, and my shoe managed to ride right up to my shin, before clipping my left leg, causing me to trip over myself.

I ended up flat on the tartan, my mouth-shoe up around my knee, watching everybody run past.

'You OK?' Little Gabe McCormack was next to me, helping me up. 'You ate that tartan like it was ear wax.'

'I'm fine, you go.' I tried to save face. But Gabe was there, scrawny Gabe, helping me up.

We walked across the line together.

Well, technically, I actually stepped over the line ahead of him. I just had to. Sorry Gabe.

Seventh.

At least I wasn't last.

•

'Stop!'

I was standing in front of the class, handwritten papers shaking in my grips, all eyes on me. Teenagers are sadistic. They love seeing people suffer. That's what school is about. Making you suffer in front of others, to set you up for a life of suffering.

'I can't mark this, Mike. I'm not even going to bother.'

'You asked us to write a story,' I said.

'I asked you to write a tragedy,' Mr Bortey said. 'This is just silly. You're better than this,' he said, standing up and taking the pages of paper I had in my hand.

'Am I?' I asked, genuinely. 'I like "silly". I think it's the best version of me.'

'Your story is about a lifesaver who has to fart in people's mouths to save their lives,' he said, holding his hands up in frustration. The whole class erupted.

'Stop laughing! This is not funny,' Mr Bortey shouted from the front of the class

Two weeks ago, before Mum, before Georgia, before the word 'tragedy' had taken on a whole new meaning – Mr Bortey had asked us to write 500-word stories inspired by the tragic texts we'd been studying all term. Think Sophocles, Euripides. And I'd written, quite possibly, the funniest story ever: a lifesaver who ate baked beans for lunch every day, and his evil boss hated it, so the evil boss sewed the lifesaver's lips together so he couldn't eat the beans anymore. Then one day, the evil boss goes swimming, and starts to drown. And it's only the lifesaver who can save him. So the lifesaver swims out and saves him, but he can't give mouth-to-mouth because his lips have been sewn shut, and the only way to give him any air, is through his remaining open orifice so the lifesaver has to fart in his boss's mouth to resuscitate him.

'It's a tragedy when you think about it,' I protested, trying to hold in my smile. Just thinking about the strained faces pulled by the lifesaver as he huffed life-saving stink from his butt directly into the limp mouths of his drownees really made me smirk.

'I don't know why adults think you're so much better than wees and poos. You guys wee and poo, right?' Zoe said from her seat up the front, and I felt a surge of pride from her having my back.

'Sir, you should hear what my mum does every morning,' Tully said. The class laughed as Mr Bortey sighed again.

'I'm not saying this isn't a good story, Mike. All I'm saying is – this is not a tragedy. I asked you to write a tragedy. Hercules was so strong, he kicked a giant crab into the stars, but his own mother forced him to kill his own children. That is tragedy. Oedipus killed his own father and then married his own mother. That is tragedy. Can you not agree that that's all a little more dramatic than farting into someone's mouth?'

'What if the lifesaver had been really into garlic?' Skon yelled.

The class erupted, and even Mr Bortey couldn't completely keep a straight face to that one.

When the bell rang, and everyone was leaving, Mr Bortey called me to his desk.

'Mike,' he sat across from me, fingers running circles around his temples, 'given recent events that have taken place in our community, did you not stop to think that maybe a story about someone drowning could be perceived as rather insensitive?'

My heart dropped. 'I wasn't thinking about it like that, sir. I just thought it would be a funny story.'

'I know, Mike. I know. And I'm not trying to stop you from having fun,' he said. 'It's just that not everything can be treated like a joke. Trust me. I love having fun, but that's the problem. When you treat life like one big joke, you sometimes don't realise that the people closest to you aren't laughing. Go home and write me a new one, because – here's the thing – if I don't get a proper story from you by the end of term, you're not going to be able to jump in the Dobson Dash.'

'No!' I protested. 'Please. I've been staying at my dad's! He doesn't have a computer. I have to write everything out by hand.'

'Trust me, Mike. I know what it's like to not sleep in your usual bed. Academia takes precedence over athletics. Just write me a new one.' Mr Bortey handed my story back to me.

I looked at him with pathetic puppy dog eyes, but Mr Bortey matched it with his own solemn sorriness. Bags under his rusty red eyes, facial hair that was more like a nine-o'clock shadow than five, and slight staining on his brown corduroy jacket. Poor Mr Bortey, what kind of life did he have outside of school? Fart stories from his students, underperforming athletes. Was this all his life was? I felt like he could write a diary entry about his life and it'd be more depressing than any Greek tragedy.

•

I stood outside K Block with the rest of the Year Eights. All I could hear was beeping; the beeping of the big, dumb, stupid van, as it backed itself up to a nice spot on the dirt between K Block and the tennis courts.

The usual group of outcasts who ate their lunch on that dirt patch had to quickly scuttle out of the van's way, lest they be run over where they usually ate their chicken and mayo sandwiches.

When the van finally stopped, its doors opened like a spaceship's portal, and out stepped a figure from behind the dust.

'Mike,' it spoke.

All the kids turned to look at me, and I felt my face go red hot. The figure stepped forward wearing a short-sleeved, white button-up shirt. A dental badge pinned clumsily to his chest. It read: 'MARVIN AMON – Senior Dentist'.

It was my dad.

The dental van was here.

He was now working at my school. I knew this day had been coming, but it still gave me a shock to see him there in his work gear.

Hercules killed his own children, and Oedipus married his own mother, but did either of them have to share a school with their own dad?

I felt like I should save Skon time and just start teasing myself.

•

Apple and Eve.

A couple of cartoon apples stared down at me from the roof of the aging school dental van. More clinical whiteness, filled with a dense smell of fluoride that sat in the top of my head. The hum of the air-con made it sound like a big fridge. I sat back in the centrepiece of the room, the big hospital-blue dental chair, with its bulky white casing of hydraulics underneath, its single light staring down at me like a flat-faced robot. Above it was the cartoon family of fruit and veg, stuck to the ceiling. In the middle, the matriarch and patriarch of the family, Apple and Eve, two enamel-proud fruits in the crisper, holding each other's little cartoon apple hands, looking at each other from the corners of their big, googly apple eyes.

I'd grown up in this van, coming to visit Dad after classes, as he travelled around Brindlewood from school to school, like a couple of dental carnies. This was the first time the circus had come to my school.

'How long are you going to be here?' I asked, making sure all the blinds in the van were down.

'Depends how bad your teeth are,' Dad muttered. He wasn't very cheerful when he was in work mode. His spectacles dangling from a maroon cord around his neck. A thin mask over his mouth. It wasn't until after he got home from work, after he changed into one of his open-buttoned shirts and his 'home shorts', until after I heard the arctic 'psst' of a beer bottle being opened, that Dad finally loosened up.

Until that first beer of the day, Dental Dad was all business.

'I mean, working here, at the school,' I reiterated. 'How long?'

I started slowly reclining as Dad pressed the levers below me with his foot. I'd braced for the refreshing zing of a cool vinyl headrest, but the whole seat felt lukewarm when I sat down. Somebody had been lying here before me.

'I thought I was the first patient?' I asked.

'You are my first patient,' Dad said.

'Then why's the seat warm?' I asked, touching it with my hand to make sure I wasn't tripping.

Dad's assistant Sonja's eyes darted to Dad, and then down to me.

'Guilty.' She smiled, underneath her face mask. 'Can't a girl nap between shifts? You're going to get me in trouble.'

Dad pulled his face mask on and my mouth snapped open in Pavlovian response.

Dad and his face mask. It reminded me of people in China who wear masks on the train when they're sick. I've always admired the confidence that would take.

'Mike, you need to floss,' Dad said as he snapped on his signature rubber gloves.

'Everydaybeforebrushing. Yehiknow.' I rolled my eyes.

'And you need to stop drinking so much soft drink. If you're having sugary drinks, you need to eat cheese straight after.'

'Yeh, sure, Dad. I'll pack a big pack of Kraft Singles in my back pocket, shall I? Just nibble them everywhere I go. I'm sure the Year Twelve jocks won't call me "Mouse Boy".'

Sonja laughed.

I didn't like Sonja. She'd been Dad's dental assistant for years. She had a son, Peter, who went to a different school and who I'd competed in athletics against, and she would always brag to me about all the rep teams he'd managed to be selected for as if she had no idea that the competition on the south side was heaps easier than ours on the north.

Sonja was prepping her tools. 'How are the athletics going, Mike?'

Here we go.

'My Peter's really looking forward to the Dash. He hit a PB at the triple jump trials and just qualified for the big relay,' she said.

'Good for him,' I replied.

'Mike.' A stern look from Dad.

'His team's going to have to be in red hot form to beat us at the moment. Zoe and Skon have been on fire recen—'

Sonja yanked down her face mask. 'Wait, Zoe's competing?'

'Yeh, of course, why wouldn't she be?'

Sonja thought a moment, then put her face mask back on. She shrugged. 'I don't know. I just think kids need time to process things, that's all.'

Dad and Sonja shared a glance, and then Dad cleared his throat.

'Let's get started.'

Sonja draped a heavy, cream-coloured apron over me while Dad swung the tube head of the wall-mounted X-ray machine over to my left cheek.

They stepped behind a small white wall with a see-through plastic shield from nipple-height up.

Beep

They re-joined me from behind their protection.

'I like how the X-ray is dangerous enough for you to shield yourselves, but you're quite happy to put it right next to my face. No wonder people out here are getting cancer,' I joked, but I really felt the 'punch' of my own punchline. No-one even cracked a smile.

They shared a glance and got on with business.

When I was younger, Dad would always threaten to withhold anaesthetic, but his threats were as empty as the bottles in Tully's Mum's recycling bin every morning.

I had my mouth wide open, and Dad jabbed me in the back of my jaw with a needle so big it looked like one of Fabian Malik's javelins. It made Dad look like the sort of crazy doctor who keeps well-manicured tulips in his front yard, and well-sedated subjects in his basement.

Dad poked me right in the part that tastes sour when you're about to throw up. Both sides. Seconds later, he got to work, and I pictured a miniature council worker jackhammering my back molars while three others sat around on my tongue and smoked cigarettes. They all had tattoos.

'Ugh!' I jerked.

Pain. Just below the left ear. It felt sour, like chewable vitamins.

'Is it hurting?' Dad asked.

'It doesn't hurt, it just …' I tried to find another word for 'hurt'.

'We didn't have sensitivity last time?' Sonja muffled.

'Well, we have it now,' I sniped.

Dad reloaded the huge needle and pumped another giant wad of anaesthetic into my jaw, while Sonja stuck a sucky tube deeper into my throat, wiping my chin.

'Does it tingle, or feel fat?' he asked.

'Does what tingle or feel fat?' I asked, before realising he was tapping my lip with his fore and middle fingers.

'Oh.' I gave him a thumbs-up.

Dad started drilling, but I groaned again, only this time it wasn't from the pain. Dad's dental van was starting to feel like Mum's hospital room. Too white. Too clean. Too … medical.

He sighed, putting his tools down. 'Mike, I have to see other people.'

'Mike, are you OK, dear?' Sonja asked, patting my face. She moved behind me, then lifted my head up and cradled it in her hands. 'Take as long as you want.'

'Please, Mike, you should be numb by now,' Dad said.

'He's hurting, Marvin,' Sonja whispered; caringly. Patting me, again.

Sonja wasn't just talking about my teeth, and it really pissed me off. My veins felt like they were running through solar heating panels on a hot tin roof in summer.

I pushed Dad off me and jumped out of the chair, suddenly the whole room just felt too 'close'; my ears noticing the dry air-conditioning pumping loudly into the van.

'Why are you being so nice all of a sudden?' I turned to Dad. 'Did you tell her about Mum?'

'Sit down, Mike,' Dad tried to calm me.

'Why are you telling strangers about Mum?'

'Mike, Sonja isn't a stranger.'

'Mike, darling, you're dribbling —' Sonja tried to interject.

'It's none of her friggin' business!' I yelled, pointing at Sonja.

'Here, Mike. Let me just clean you up.' She reached out and started sucking at the dribble patches on my school shirt with her little suction device.

'Why was the seat warm?' I asked Dad. I asked them both.

'Mike, you're dribbling everywhere, making a mess,' Dad muttered.

'Of course I'm dribbling everywhere! I can't feel my face. You really pumped me full of that stuff. Are you trying to kill me?' A bead of liquid presented under my chin, then slowly trailed down my neck.

The top half of my face was hot, and I was getting short in the chest. Everything in between had gone AWOL.

'Don't tell anyone at this school about Mum, OK? I see how you're all treating Zoe and she hates it. I hate it. I just want things to be normal here.'

'Mike, please sit down. We need to do the fissure sealing,' Dad said gently.

Instead, I ran out, down the short steps at the van's front door, past Moses Matakefu, who was waiting to be mouth-mutilated by my dad next.

'Mike, that story about the lifesaver, you mind if I read it? I wanna know what happens at the end!'

Without a word, I rifled through my bag and shoved the pages into Moses' hands.

'Cheers, cuz! I'll give it back soon, promise.'

I shrugged, and walked out into the school yard. I didn't have time for small talk.

I couldn't risk being spotted by someone. My lips were too numb. I was drooling like a rabid dog. If Skon saw me like this, he'd have a field day. Probably call me 'the Human Sprinkler' or some lame shit that would stick with me until graduation day.

I needed to hide.

I needed to go 'Under the Bridge'.

•

The Bridge was actually a concrete stairwell that led to the very bottom floor of the school's science block. More like a basement, the Bridge was dark, and damp. Renowned more as a place to be avoided, than one to be seen. It smelled like a pedestrian tunnel, of sweat and urine.

Named 'the Bridge' thanks to Gabe McCormack.

Gabe had excused himself during class to go to the bathroom, but all the cubicles had been full, and desperate to expel the sexual wantings of his teenage urges, he'd quickly run downstairs, to the very bottom of the building, and hid under the steps of the science block to do you know what.

Under 'the Bridge', because – with his bright ginger hair – he referred to his penis as a Red Hot Chilli Pepper.

I kneeled down in the dank darkness and prayed I wouldn't feel moisture where I sat.

I sat in that darkness with my thoughts, thinking about Sonja patting my damn face. I didn't need sympathy. I needed a cure for cancer. I needed the tears itching at the corners of my eyes to go away. I needed to be home with Mum and away from Dad.

I sat down there in the darkness, with my mind racing, when all of a sudden:

I heard a giggle.

At first I thought maybe I was imagining it, but no. This giggle was real, coming from the darkness opposite me, in the corner of the basement, right under the concrete steps.

I wasn't alone.

Suddenly, my pulse was in my ears like I'd dived head first into my own heart.

Someone was with me, watching, waiting, warning.

'Boo!'

I screamed, and reeled back, bashing the back of my head against the cold concrete wall behind me.

Zoe had appeared opposite me. Smiling.

Actual, real, object of my affections, Zoe Ingham. Inches away from my face right now, really laughing.

I honestly thought I'd died.

'Jesus, I thought you were a ghost,' I whispered, trying to make sense of the fact that moments ago I'd been yelling at Dad and now here I was – hiding with Zoe Ingham, under the Bridge.

'Wow. Haven't heard that one before,' she said, rolling her eyes.

'No, I mean, I thought I was alone –' I tried to cover up what I was saying.

Zoe giggled, 'Don't worry. I don't often make a point of scaring the shit out of people.'

'Why are you here?' I asked.

'Why are we all here?' she joked in a hippy voice, then shrugged, 'I have to hide from the sun sometimes. Just one of the perks of having skin like mine. You don't exactly have an excuse though.'

I looked at my brown arms that almost disappeared in the darkness of the Bridge.

'I'm hiding,' I mumbled. 'I just feel a bit numb.'

Zoe's eyes lit up just the tiniest bit.

'Me too,' she said. 'That's really why I'm here. To hide. I'm sick of people feeling sorry for me.'

I didn't really know what to say, mainly because I did feel sorry for her. The story seemed to be everywhere. Even that morning on the radio I'd heard a news story about six other ferry terminals in the city that didn't have adequate safety measures.

'You know what happened, right? With my sister?' she asked.

I nodded. 'Yeh, I heard. That really sucks.' That's all I could say, really.

'Thank you,' she said.

'For what?'

'For not saying "sorry".' She looked away in thought for a second.

Then – suddenly – a spark.

I don't mean a metaphorical one. I mean, a real-life, actual spark.

Zoe had a cigarette lighter in her left hand that she'd cranked the flint on, before holding the flame to the cigarette she held in her right hand.

She offered the smoke to me.

'Do you know how?' she asked.

I nodded, reaching out to take the durry by its crunchy white body, just above the yellow filter, trying to hide my doubt with blind confidence. Zoe raised one eyebrow, unconvinced.

'Remind me?' I said, an embarrassed smile forming between my flushing cheeks.

Zoe smiled back. 'You have to suck in the smoke, and then take a breath in afterwards. You'll feel it kick you in the throat,' she said, pointing to where boys have an Adam's apple. It made me wonder whether Apple from Apple and Eve had an Adam's apple in his throat. Apple Adam's Adam's apple.

I found my lips, put the cigarette in my mouth and took a big puff, breathing in, waiting for that 'kick'. At least, that's what I tried to do, but I suddenly felt a sharp burning on my chest. I was terrified. I'd heard cigarettes were bad for your health, but I didn't think they'd give you a heart attack straight away!

I went to grab the cigarette out from between my lips, but it wasn't there.

My lips were so numb.

I looked down and realised the cigarette had tumbled out of my mouth and was now burning a hole through my shirt. I wasn't having a heart attack, but I had reason for one. How the hell would I explain this to Dad?

I squealed, swatting the ciggie off my chest, suddenly choking and coughing on the smoke that I'd managed to scavenge before it took a high dive from my mouth.

'Shhhhh!' Zoe laughed, slapping at my chest.

Touching my chest.

She was touching my chest.

I'd consider setting myself on fire like a self-immolating monk if it meant more slapping from Zoe.

'You'll ruin my secret spot,' she whispered.

'I think Gabe already ruined it,' I laughed.

'The Red Hot Chilli Pepper. What a sicko,' she said, finally satisfied that I wasn't going to go up in flames. 'He showed us how big it was on a ruler in Maths the other day. Twelve centimetres.'

'Is that all?' I snorted. But then it struck me, was twelve centimetres a lot?

I'd seen Gabe in the lockers after PE before. Despite his tiny frame, his 'thing' looked healthy, surrounded by substantial tufts of thick red pubic hair, while I always changed under a towel because I was still what Skon liked to call a 'skinbag'.

Zoe sparked her lighter and scanned for the remains of her cig. She spotted it. 'Oh man, it's all broken,' she said.

'I'm really sorry,' I whispered through gritted teeth, blowing down the neck of my shirt across my nipples.

'Plenty more where that came from.' She shrugged and put the lighter back in her pocket. 'Mum started smoking again. She leaves these all over the house. It's about the only thing she gets out of bed for. Meanwhile, Dad's the opposite. When he's not working, he's running. Running everywhere. He has these terrible blisters that leave specks of blood all through the house. It's like he's pretending it didn't happen,' Zoe said.

'I've only seen my dad run when we're putting up posters for his nightclub and he's seen a police car,' I said.

Zoe smiled. 'I keep looking at the phone, expecting it to ring, expecting to answer it and hear Georgia on the other end of the line, telling me that she just ran away. That she needed to fake her own death, for some reason. And I'd tell her that it wouldn't matter. That nobody is mad with her because we all just miss her so much. Is that crazy?'

I shook my head.

'Well, it feels crazy.' Zoe sighed. 'So, that's my life story, Mike Amon. Tell me something about you.'

I love you.

That's what I wanted to say.

Let's run away together. Live in a big house in the country, miles from anyone. Somewhere with a pool that we could float in all day, and where we could eat cherries and drink frozen cokes and play Sega.

'My mum's got cancer,' I said, the words unexpectedly spilling out of my mouth.

Zoe's eyes widened, she stared at me, for a second, maybe it was a lifetime.

I was sure she was about to say something, when we heard footsteps coming down the stairs, and voices echoing around the cold concrete.

One belonged to Tyson Brickford, the other to Calvin Barnes.

'OK, so that's it there,' Tyson said.

'Fuck, is that all?' Calvin said.

'Mate, that's ten dollars' worth, but that's all you need.'

'So how do I do it?'

'Here, I'll show you.' There was the spilling of liquid on the cement, and then the crackling of an aluminium can. 'So, you put the weed on that bit there, and then you light it, and you suck through the part where you usually drink from.'

'Fuck, that's hectic,' Calvin said.

'Haha, yeh man, you'll be knocked out. Make sure you've got something to eat. Chips or something, and don't mix it with alcohol, man, or else you'll be falling everywhere. Cooked.'

'I'll end up like that girl in the Swamp,' Calvin laughed.

Tyson scoffed. 'No, dude, my dad works on the Council. He reckons she was pushed.'

I looked back at Zoe, hoping she hadn't overheard. Her eyes were narrow, her mouth a straight line, as though she was visualising the most brutal forms of torture.

'No way, who pushed her?' Calvin said.

I felt rage bubble up from my guts and in my chest. I wanted to stand up, to walk out.

I had to say something.

I propped myself up on my knees, ready to stand up –

'No, don't!' Zoe put her arm out to block me. She held her finger up to her mouth. *Shhhh!* She pointed above our heads.

Clopping.

'Who's down here?' a stern, intimidating voice echoed around the walls.

It was Ms Harris.

Zoe quickly flicked her cigarette out from under the steps, like it was a cat's eye marble, and it slid, bobbled and rolled along the ground before coming to a stop right in between the feet of Calvin and Tyson.

'What the fuck?!' Calvin yelled.

We watched as Ms Harris' black block heels appeared before the boys, right over the smoking gun.

'Right, which one of you boys has been smoking?' Ms Harris asked.

'Neither of us. It just came out from under the stairs!' Tyson whined.

'Sure it did. In which one of my classes have I taught you that stairs have lungs?'

Silence.

'Exactly. Stairs don't have lungs; therefore they can't smoke, therefore, you're both coming with me,' Ms Harris growled.

It was music to my ears, listening to all sets of feet scurry right back up the stairs and out of sight.

I would've felt guilty in any other situation, but not after what had happened.

Not next to Zoe.

'Zoe,' I said, surprising myself. 'Would you like to –'

Right then and there, the bell rang. End of lunch.

'Would I like to what?'

I paused. 'Nothing,' I said. 'Would you like to head to class now? That's what I was going to ask.'

She smiled as we came out from under the stairs and into the light. When I looked down, I noticed that Zoe's skirt had somehow tucked itself into the left cheek of her underpants. They were bright red, as red as my face was feeling just from spotting them.

I quickly turned my head away, like I'd been punched by a heavyweight.

'I'm not looking!' I said, holding my hand over my eyes.

She looked down and giggled, a little bit embarrassed, but cool, and corrected herself. When I took my hand away from my eyes, she was smiling and staring at my chest. I looked down and realised my nipple was poking perfectly out from the cigarette-burnt hole in my school shirt. It was so perfectly positioned it looked like some sort of kinky costume.

'Jesus. How was I going to explain this to any of the teachers?'

Zoe took a badge she was wearing and carefully pinned it on my shirt.

The badge was small, just bigger than a nipple, and was traffic-light green. It said GO FOR IT in chunky, white, impact type.

'Give it back to me another time,' she said, with a light shrug.

'Another time,' I repeated, letting the sentiment sink in.

A date.

We parted ways out in the light, at the top of the steps.

'Mike,' Zoe called out.

I turned back.

'About your mum,' she said, looking me right in the eyes.

'That really sucks.'

She wasn't wrong.

•

Ms Harris' science class was usually one I had the most fun in. Who doesn't love mucking around with a Bunsen burner? We'd be in rows in the lab, two to a desk, surrounded by brightly coloured posters of planets and the periodic table. But today I wasn't thinking about science.

I couldn't stop thinking about Zoe, and I was suddenly filled with this weird, tight, hot feeling. A feeling like I wasn't quite able to do what I wanted to do.

It was the same frustration I felt when I used to stand in the newsagency, looking over the shoulders of the men who browsed the nudie mags that sat right next to the gaming ones. I'd catch glimpses of nipples, and pubic hair, and I'd have to tuck my thing up into the waistband of my shorts, and I'd just feel so damn frustrated. Like, what next?

I just couldn't get rid of my erection, and I was having moments where I thought I'd pass out; like there was too much blood downstairs and not in my actual brain.

'Everything OK, Mike?' Ms Harris asked. 'You haven't tried to disrupt me all class, I'm wondering whether you are alive.'

I looked up, startled.

'I'm talking about crabs and you haven't once mentioned anything about pubic hair,' she said.

'That's because Skinbag doesn't have any!' Skon yelled.

'Congratulations, Mr Helpmann. I'll be seeing you after class for that remark.' She wrote his name on the bottom left corner of the whiteboard.

'I went to the dentist, Miss,' I said. 'I don't feel great.'

'Do you want to go to the nurse?' she asked.

'Nah, no, it's fine. I think I might just put my head down, if that's OK?'

I thought she might force me to go, but she was interrupted by a knock on the classroom door. It was Mr Bortey. Ms Harris met him just outside the room, whispered a bit and then came back in.

'Calvin and Tyrone, Mr Bortey would like to see you outside.'

Calvin and Tyrone looked at each other like they'd been summoned to the gallows.

They both walked outside to Mr Bortey, who ushered them around the corner.

Zoe and I looked at each other across the room.

'Anyway, as I was saying, a "keystone" is the central piece at the crown of an arch,' Ms Harris said, walking back to her desk. 'The top rock. It holds all the other pieces into place.'

A small set of blocks built into an arch sat on her desk. The top piece had a crab picture on it.

'Crabs are a keystone animal. They play a crucial role in the way their ecosystems function. Take away the crab, and the ecosystem changes dramatically, or …' she plucked the top block from the arch. Both sides crumbled inwards, clanking onto the tabletop. 'Or even cease to exist.'

To be honest, that sounded like my mum. I felt like she held my ecosystem together.

'Depending on the species, crabs live in fresh, salty, or brackish water. Does anyone know what "brackish" water is?'

'Is it what Chinese people call '"blackish" water?' Skon yelled out. The class laughed.

Ms Harris put a small "x2" next to Skon's name on the whiteboard.

'Brackish water is the type of water you'd find around the Brindlewood River. A mixture of sea water and the fresh water coming down from the mountain. Has anyone seen any crabs in the river here?'

I lifted my head to tell my life story. I'd grown up with those crabs, catching them in the Swamp, Dad leaving them in the laundry tub for days on end until they ended up on our plate. I was basically a crustacean Mowgli.

'This is not up for discussion!' The scream boomed out in the classroom corridor, bouncing in the through the glass windows.

The whole class sat up.

Poor Calvin and Tyrone were getting an absolute hounding.

'Does anybody know what the Latin word for "crab" is?' Ms Harris asked, ignoring the scolding happening outside.

'You will not be representing the school in any way, shape or form!'

Finally, Calvin and Tyrone slunk back into the room, heads down, eyes to the floor, shells of their former cocky selves.

The whole class pretended they hadn't overheard.

Zoe and I looked at each other again, our mouths open in shock. We'd done this. And I'd moved up the reserves for the relay team two spots in one foul swoop!

Two gone. Fifth in line to the throne ...

'It is believed that the Greek physician, Hippocrates, was the first to use the word in a medical sense when he noticed a mass of cells, and the swollen blood vessels around it, that reached in every direction. It reminded him of a crab. And when Hercules kicked a crab so high into the sky, it got stuck, hence the constellation we all know it as today. Does anyone know the word?' I heard Ms Harris ask.

The class collectively shrugged. It was hard to concentrate when we'd just heard Calvin and Tyrone cop it from Mr Bortey so spectacularly.

'It's "cancer",' Ms Harris said.

And it was like I'd been pinched.

'The word "cancer" is actually the Latin word for "crab",' Ms Harris said.

Then the bell rang.

•

When I got home, I found Dad in my room with a measuring tape so old and yellowed it could well have been used to size-up Tutankhamun's tomb. He was stretching it out along the wall underneath the window that looked out over Tully's backyard.

'What's going on?' I asked, dumping my bag on the floor.

'I'm just ... you might need a bigger bed. This one is too small,' he said, pointing to the little spring single that sat only centimetres above the carpet. It was almost like a cot, or the type of bed I imagined a drug addict would sleep in.

'My one at Mum's is a queen,' I said, hoping he'd take the hint and not just buy me a double. He was prone to being stingy like that.

'Yes, I'm seeing if it would fit here.' He looked away, almost guiltily. 'Whether something *like* it would fit here,' he corrected.

Dad finished the measuring with a furrowed brow, and then placed the tape measure on my small study desk in the corner and walked out. 'I'll go put on your chicken nuggets.'

I closed the door and looked around my room, with my TV and my Sega Saturn, and my small set of drawers that held all the clothes I ever needed for staying at Dad's, and I imagined the room with a nice big bed in it.

I looked down at my study desk and saw the measuring tape Dad had left there, lying like a lifeless, flat tapeworm.

Twelve centimetres, Zoe had said, about Gabe's penis.

Was twelve centimetres a lot?

I picked up the tape and measured out twelve centimetres between my thumbs. It didn't look like much.

I couldn't stop thinking about how I'd seen Zoe's undies. Bright red. Something about being that close to her; feeling her breath against my face. Seeing her with that cigarette. Seeing her pale, white leg, and the slight fold of her left buttock as it met the top of her thigh with those fine, white hairs.

I just kept thinking about that fold of Zoe's bum as it met the top of her thigh.

So white —

The seam of her bright red underpants that sat just above that line. I desperately wanted to see what was under them.

I wanted to touch the skin there, and between her thighs. To put my hand on the part of her undies that draped ever so slightly down from there. To put my finger inside, and ... I didn't really know what after that. Were you supposed to move it once it was in there?

I could feel myself getting hard, and I looked at the tape measure I was holding in my hand.

Twelve centimetres. Is that all? Haha.

I was sure I was bigger than that.

I lowered my shorts and undies down around my thighs, and looked at my hard, veiny stiffy, poking diagonally up and away from me, bopping ever so slightly up and down with the rhythm of my heartbeat. Then I put the start of the tape measure at its base, right where it met the rest of my body, and I slowly guided the tape measure up and along to the tip.

With each centimetre revealed as I ran the tape up, I could feel my heart beat with nerves. I was running out of penis to measure! By what I considered to be the halfway mark, the tape unfolded to reveal only the number five, and by the time I reached the start of the head, there was only an eight.

I couldn't believe it. I reached the very end of my manhood and felt my heart sink. I almost wanted to cry. How would Zoe ever like me when my stupid little chode was dwarfed by Gabe's coke bottle?

Just when I thought things couldn't get worse, god managed to have an ace up her sleeve.

A quick rap of dad's knuckles on the door.

And then the sound of the door opening.

I scrambled to pull up my shorts and cover my ass, but I still had to zip up my fly and tuck my boner away.

'Don't!' It was more like a primal moan than a request. A guttural heave that sounded of secrets and shame.

I had my back to the door as Dad burst in, holding a polystyrene tray with freezer frost all over it.

'Mike, we only have five chicken nuggets. Do you want more chips instead –' Dad stopped, dead in his tracks.

He looked down at me as I turned around.

I looked down too.

I'd tucked my boner into my waistband, but I'd managed to tuck it *outside* of my shirt. So, there it was, my little mushroom poking out the top of my pants. On top of that, I'd gotten the tape measure all tangled up too, and it was sticking out from the waistband of my pants and dangling down to the floor. It looked like I had two penises. One stubby, hard, brown one, and one flat, floppy, white one with numbers on it.

The worst part was, Dad didn't even leave.

'Oh, I'm sorry,' he said, turning away.

'Dad, get out!' I screamed.

'Is five nuggets enough?' he asked again, his back now to me.

'Yes, it's enough!'

'OK, I'll let you know when it's ready,' he said as he closed the door.

I ripped the stupid tape measure out of my pants and tucked everything back in, flopping myself down onto my stupid little bed, and stared at the ceiling.

I hated my life and I hated living with Dad. I thought living here was going to be all video games and chocolate milk, but it was actually just interruptions and nothing good in the fridge.

That stupid little bed. Dad's dumb African music. His annoying accent and not knowing when to leave me alone.

I couldn't wait to move back to Mum's place.

With the air-conditioning, and that sweet view over Brindlewood.

The sooner she got better, the better.

•

The gymnasium's spinning shadows were calling me, sucking me into their hypnotic whirl. It'd be hard to stay awake this assembly.

I'd spent a whole sleepless night feeling super bummed about the size of my thing, wondering how much it would hinder my chances with Zoe, and trying to work out what I could do to make it grow bigger. I wondered if there were any books in the library on the subject, but then I realised there was no chance in hell I'd have a book like that on my rental history.

This is why we needed to get the internet.

We sat baking in the gymnasium. A sea of school diaries were flapping like fans in the hands of their cross-legged keepers.

A row of teachers sat, facing us, on plastic chairs at the front of the room, next to the lectern. Zoe was sitting with them. Every time she looked to her lap, I'd stare at her in wonder, wishing, hoping. Every time she looked up at us, I'd go back to the hypno-whirl.

'What's going on with your Mum?' Tully asked.

I immediately snapped out of my daze as my heart dropped into my pelvis.

'What do you mean?' I asked.

'I saw your bedroom light on last night. How come you aren't staying with her at the moment?'

'Oh,' I thought about telling her, but looked back up at Zoe. A teacher patted her on the back and gave her a patronising smile, and she smiled back and I wondered how many fake smiles I really had in me.

'She's getting the carpets cleaned. My bed's currently sitting in our unit's garage as we speak!'

'Well maybe offer me a lift to school tomorrow. I'm sick of needing to get to school before the breakfast rush.'

Skon poked her in the small of her back. 'Shhhh, Chunks!'

'Fuck off!' She slapped at him with her diary in retaliation.

Ms Harris squatted down to their level. 'Congratulations, you two.' That's all she had to say, writing their names down on a small notepad.

Mr Bortey droned away up front. 'These vaccinations are part of a national initiative and are *not* compulsory; however, we highly recommend that every student participate. If you choose to participate, you will be allocated a time tomorrow, and be required to attend the procedure *instead* of your regular scheduled class.'

Everyone started cheering.

'Alright, alright, calm down,' Mr Bortey said.

Next to me, Jon Qi was the only person not excited. 'Needles are the sharpest things in the world,' he whispered, a bead of sweat suddenly born on his brow.

'Now, with just over two weeks until the Dobson Dash, I'd like to welcome our Year Eight athletics captain, Zoe Ingham, to the stage, to announce the charity that every Brindlewood High Harrier will be raising money for on the big day.'

The crowd clapped robotically.

Zoe stood up, straightened her skirt, and gathered a set of palm cards just slightly bigger than her hands from her pristine school blazer.

She stood at the lectern, her red hair glowing under her navy-banded, straw school boater.

'Launching four years ago, the Brea—' She was faint.

Mr Bortey jumped up and adjusted the bendy lectern mics to her level.

'Thank you,' she whispered, then smiled out at the crowd, and continued. 'The Breast Cancer Foundation's aim is simple: to stop deaths from breast cancer. They fund large-scale, world class research in their aim to stop this deadly disease in its tracks. That is why I have chosen the Breast Cancer Foundation to be our charity this year for the Dobson Dash.'

I sat in awe, my mouth hanging open as though I was sitting in Dad's dentist's chair, while kids clapped and cheered around me.

'A very noble cause, Ms Ingham,' Mr Bortey said, adjusting the mics back to his height.

Zoe collected her palm cards and, as she sat back down, she spotted me in the crowd.

And she smiled.

CHAPTER TEN

TUESDAY, 24TH MARCH 1998

I was surrounded by boobs.

Plastic.

Jellyfish.

A small room with a clinical sanitation that put Brindy Shopping Centre to shame, I was down a wing of Mum's hospital floor that I hadn't seen before, and I'd found myself in a little walk-in wardrobe-sized storeroom, standing in the doorway. There were waist-high cupboards, and two stainless steel shelves that wrapped around the whole room, stacked end to end with all the materials you'd need to make a breast.

There were nipples in buckets. Boobies in bins. Posters on the wall listing different types of 'areola'.

Dad poked his head into the room. 'Mike, come back out to the waiting room, they're going to call our name soon.'

'What's an areola?' I asked Dad.

He looked around and realised where we were. A room full of boobs. He cleared his throat. 'Oh, um, it's the dark, outer ring of the nipple.'

'I thought it was a dipping sauce.'

Dad stepped inside the room to take a squiz himself. Father and son, surrounded by jelly.

'You were four years old when you stopped breastfeeding,' Dad said.

I almost dived into the rubbish bin, I was so embarrassed. I looked around to make sure that nobody was within earshot, and then I regathered myself.

'I thought I invented those memories,' I said.

'We thought it was time to stop because you were tall enough to serve yourself.'

I looked around as the heat in my cheeks subsided.

'Who are we meeting with?' I asked.

'Just a doctor,' Dad said.

'Is it the doctor who's looking after Mum?' I asked.

'Um … sort of,' Dad said, avoiding eye contact.

'Mike.' A stranger at the door. He had a thick mop of black hair, a beard the same colour, and the shoulders of his dark-blue shirt were covered in dandruff, the way a chocolate cake looks with a dusting of sugar. He had big red welts that crept out from his hairline, down towards his bushy eyebrows. Welts like spreading stains when Tully's Mum spills a bottle of pinot on the carpet.

'Ready for our appointment?' he smiled.

'Where are we?' I asked, poking a boob with my finger.

The doctor held his hands up as though he were the guide at an art gallery. 'The treatment of breast cancer often requires the removal of breast tissue, and sometimes the whole, or even both, breasts. As you can imagine, the removal of one's breasts can be quite a traumatic experience. Part of what we call "the surgical journey" involves finding a replacement implant that the patient feels comfortable with to match their age, shape, and wants, moving forward. This room gives them those options.'

'Are you a plastic surgeon?' I asked.

The doctor smiled. 'I'm a psychologist, Mike. Part of my job is helping patients *and their families* confront the mental barriers they might have about such a transformation.'

We'll do whatever it takes …

No, we won't.

I looked up at Dad who wouldn't meet my eye. 'You think I need to see a psychologist?'

The doctor looked at Dad, then back at me. He cleared his throat.

'Let's head on through to my office, hey?'

He guided me out, and down the hall.

Dad stayed behind with the boobies.

•

His name was Dr Jarnipf. Pronounced 'Yah-nif'.

His office had no windows, but one wall was glass, and it looked out into the waiting area of Mum's hospital floor, where a receptionist and male nurse flirted behind the welcome desk. Off to the side, an old man sat staring wistfully into memories of his youth, and a bald lady in a white gown made a call on the public phone while she played with the tube that ran from her hand cannula to her IV stand.

Jarnipf closed the blinds to that wall.

We sat opposite each other on two cushioned chairs in the middle of the room. Behind him was a dark wooden desk with a computer monitor, pens, a stack of papers, scattered books, and a framed glamour shot of Dr Jarnipf and his wife, straddling a motorcycle.

I couldn't tell if it was a joke or not.

Jarnipf, with his short-sleeved, dark blue button-up, and white undershirt, looked like someone who mistook his bullying at school for companionship.

His wife, with her puffy-sleeved pink dress, boxy chestnut bob and blunt fringe, looked like someone who considered marijuana as deadly as heroin.

I absolutely could not take my eyes off it.

'The most important thing to understand from here, Mike, is that there is no right or wrong way to behave. It's absolutely crucial to explore all your emotions,' Jarnipf said. Child psychologist. Adult fuckwit.

He'd been yapping away for about twenty minutes, asking me about school, and my hobbies, and all that, but pretending he was my best friend or something, and then suddenly started talking to me like I was still eating mushed apples and pumpkin for meal time.

'Now, I know this may sound like a silly question, but I need to ask any child under the age of thirteen this question: Do you understand what "death" is?'

'Never heard of it,' I said. 'Is it some kind of dipping sauce?'

Jarnipf smiled. 'It's just a question, Mike. I honestly mean no offense.'

My knuckles whitened as they gripped the armrests of my chair. 'Yes,' I said, quietly.

'OK. So, in your Mum's case, we have to look at all the possible scenarios here, Mike. Even the worst ones, including death. Have you thought about the consequences of your mother dying much?' It was the first time anyone had actually even mentioned the word, to be honest. It made me even more mad with Dad. Did he know more than he was telling me?

'Yes,' I said.

Jarnipf nodded. 'Good. That's important. Is there anything you want to talk about?' he asked.

Of course there were things I wanted to talk about. My mum was in a room just down the hall. Just down the hall! I was failing at athletic greatness, losing to that smug freak Skon and ever since I'd measured my penis, I'd been so bummed out. My dad thought I was going crazy, and now I needed to worry about whether my mum would actually survive.

'Mike?' Jarnipf waved his hand in front of me.

'Is my mum going to die?' I asked, snapping out of my dorm-room of distress.

Jarnipf took a big breath and ran his hand through his beard. 'I'm not entirely sure of her exact situation, Mike. So, I'm sorry, I won't be able to answer –'

'Do you *think* my mum is going to die?' I asked, sterner this time. Testing him.

Jarnipf took another big breath. 'There is always a chance that your mother will make a full recovery, Mike. We try to remain hopeful with every situation,' he said, nervously clicking his pen, 'but really – I'm not her doctor. There are so many outcomes that we might arrive at through this journey, and the main thing you need to prepare yourself for, is to be strong. Where your mum is at, there's no easy way out. You will need to become a bigger person, no matter what.'

He kept clicking his stupid pen. One of those four-colour ones.

*click*click*click*click*
*black*blue*red*green*
Who uses green ...?

What a fucking weakling. Couldn't even look me in the eye and tell me the truth. I wanted to spit on him. *Just TELL me the truth!*

'So, I'm not sure when we'll be catching up again, but your dad will probably join us next time, if that's OK?' Jarnipf asked.

*black*blue*red*green*

'Whatever,' I shrugged, already knowing full well that I would be wagging the next catch-up. No chance I wanted to ever hang out with this fucking loser ever again. Either tell me the truth, or fuck off.

*click*click*click*

'Is there anything else?' he asked.

I thought about it for another moment.

'There's no "wrong" way to behave, right?' I asked, double-checking his own mantra.

'That's right,' he said, ever so seriously.

I thought for a second, and then I calmly reached across, took the pen out of his hand and walked over to the glamour shot of him and his wife on his desk. I used the red pen to add a tiny rash to the hairline of Motorcycle Jarnipf.

'That's better,' I said, then dropped the pen on the desk.

I waltzed past Jarnipf to leave his office, but as I opened the door, my heart dropped.

It was the voice I heard first. A boy's voice. A familiar one.

'I don't need some fucking shrink telling me what to think,' was all I heard it saying before I realised where it was coming from.

And then I saw him, and he *almost* saw me.

It was Skon. His usual baseball cap with the white sweat stains doing laps of the brim. He was flanked by a woman I assumed was his mother. She had dyed blonde curly hair, and was wearing a white power suit, lots of make-up, and earrings so long and weighty they almost gave her a shoulder massage.

'Don't you try anything in there, Skonny. I swear,' she said, softly. She didn't even look at him, just stared straight ahead, chewing gum, lost in thought.

I quickly slammed the door closed, and spun back around to face Dr Jarnipf, who was wiping the red marking off the plastic pane of his picture frame.

He stared at me a second.

'Mike, is everything OK?' he asked. A few specks of scalp had made their way to his facial hair and you could see each fleck desperately holding onto his moustache with each gust of breath from his nose.

'Umm,' I had to think. 'I'm sorry about your photo.'

'This condition that I have, I don't like it much. It's something that I battle with every day. Even the choice to wear this shirt I didn't make lightly. I do it to prove to myself that I won't let it hold me back. I'm not going to lie, Mike – I don't appreciate what you've done to my picture.' He held up the photo. 'I felt good that day. My psoriasis had eased. You think it looks bad, but you have no idea how painful it is. I thought I'd do something fun.' He paused for a moment. 'She died a year after this photo. Non-Hodgkin lymphoma.'

'I'm sorry,' I said.

'It's fine, Mike. I've seen much worse,' Jarnipf shrugged. 'But please understand, you're going through something very hard right now, and stealing happiness is a fool's errand. You need to grow your own. I can help you plant that seed. OK?'

I nodded. 'Could you please walk me back to my mum's room?' I asked, like I was a lost six-year-old at Brindy Shops.

Dr Jarnipf's face softened.

'Of course I can.' He put his arm on my shoulder. I felt my body shiver so fiercely that I worried it might've made a sound like a wobble board. Dr Jarnipf opened the door, and, as we stepped outside, I buried my face into his chest, wrapped my arms around his waist, and pretended to cry. This guy was the worst, but I'd rather pretend he was helping me than let Skon see my weakness.

From a peek out the corner of my eye, I could see Skon was too busy playing his Gameboy to look up.

We walked around the corner together, towards Mum's room, just as Dad was walking down the hallway towards us.

'Is everything OK?' Dad asked.

Jarnipf guided me into his arms.

'He's a little rattled. It was a very successful session,' he said softly, before disappearing back around the corner to his office.

I stepped back from Dad and got my oily eyes on. Stupid Jarnipf.

'Mike, what's going on?' Dad's eyes narrowed.

'Nothing,' I said.

Dad grabbed me by my arms, and squatted down to talk to me. The problem was that I was almost taller than Dad these days, but I guess parents always feel bigger than their kids; so when Dad crouched down, he talked to my belly button at first, until eventually I crouched down too, so we were at the same height.

Father and son, crouching in the middle of the hospital hallway like a couple of scrawny brown sumo wrestlers.

'Did he do something to you?' Dad asked, looking over my shoulder, and then his own.

'No,' I said. 'I just don't like him.'

Dad nodded. He looked over his shoulder again and whispered. 'I don't like some of these people either, Mike. I don't trust them. If anyone ever does something to you, I will chop their throat. You understand?'

Lol. What a silly old man.

Dad was almost smaller than me. I could probably chop *his* throat!

But there was a look in his eyes that made me feel something for him, which was a bit rare for me and Daddy Marv.

I had to look away quickly. Think about other things.

Because if I thought about silly old Dad for any longer, I'd get a little bit upset about the whole situation we'd been chucked in together.

I think he meant it.

I really think he meant it.

And when we got home, I sat in my bedroom and played *Street Fighter* in the dark, with the curtains closed, so that Tully didn't know I was home.

And I wondered if this was how it was going to be from now on.

•

WEDNESDAY, 25TH MARCH 1998

The following afternoon, half of our grade was sitting in plastic chairs along the ground floor hallway of the main senior-school building – the old, three-storey building at the tallest point of the senior campus. The building made of red bricks, with yellowing, white trim, arches, and a shiny, glass elevator tacked onto the outside to remind you of yesteryear's indifference to wheelchair accessibility. The building with the school shield above the main doorway, visible to traffic on City Road, that reminded you in Latin that *knowledge is the gateway to life*, while you sat in your car feeling more like *peak hour is the gateway to depression*. The building that doesn't quite fit with the rest. The building that exists in old sepia photos behind moustached white men wearing top hats and petticoats, back when kids caught the horse to school and the tuckshop served boiled mutton with a quarter-pound of damper or some shit.

The building otherwise known as A Block.

Tully and I sat side-by-side, outside the nurse's office. Jon Qi, the long jumper, was sitting right at the nurse's door, next to us, his face red, his eyes wide, sweat on his brow, his right foot tapping so vigorously it looked like he was a drummer in a thrash band. He was next in the queue, then Tully, then me; all waiting to be cured of something we hadn't caught yet.

'Do vaccines even work?' Tully asked, picking at a flake of custard paint that was peeling from the cracking concrete wall behind us.

'My dad grew up in Ghana. He wasn't vaccinated and he's fine,' I said.

'Really?' Jon Qi asked. 'Do you think we can just drink it? Instead of, you know …' he mimed a needle in his arm.

'What are we even getting vaccinated for?' Tully kept picking.

'Measles, mumps and rubella,' Jon Qi said.

Tap. Tap. Tap. Tap. Tap.

'I don't know what any of those diseases are.'

'I think that means they work then,' I said.

Tully gave one last pick and a huge shard of paint dropped off the wall and crumpled on the maroon tiles.

Silence.

Tully looked around. No teachers in sight.

Tap. Tap. Tap. Tap. Tap.

An A3 poster hung on the corkboard opposite us, its header reading: COVER YOUR MOUTH WHEN YOU SNEEZE! WATCH FOR SYMPTOMS OF COMMON COLDS AND FLU! It had a cartoon boy with a bright red nose, and tissues overflowing from his pockets.

'I swear I've got some symptoms,' Tully said, peering at the poster.

One of the arrows pointed to the cartoon boy's ears and it read MIDDLE EAR INFECTIONS/LOSS OF BALANCE.

'What do ears have to do with balance?' Tully asked.

'My parents' six-stack CD player at home has a dial for balance,' Jon Qi said, proudly.

Next to it was a poster titled: COMMON SIDE EFFECTS OF DRUGS. It had a diagram of the human body with hair like a Ken doll, with arrows pointing to different body parts and organs, linking side effects with various drugs. Of all the drugs listed, alcohol made the most appearances, yet it and tobacco were the only legal ones on the list. Weird.

The only drug that affected your genitals was steroids. According to the poster, steroids caused shrinking of the testicles, but also increased hair growth. I guess you win some and lose some.

Next to the poster about drugs was a poster titled: CONTRACEPTION. It was split into quarters: MALE CONDOM, FEMALE CONDOM, THE PILL, and OTHER METHODS.

'If I get that job, I might ask Mum if I can go on the pill,' Tully said.

'The pill?' I shifted in my chair, making sure no gossips were in ear shot. 'Do you really need it for, you know, fingers?' I asked.

'You dummy, the pill isn't just about sex. If I go on "Diane", it'll clear up my fugly skin, regulate my period so I don't have to carry a stupid jumper in my bag all the time, and best of all, it'll make my boobs bigger. It's a wonder drug.'

'Drugs are bad, m'kay,' I said, doing a Mr Mackey impression from *South Park*.

'Here's some advice,' Tully said. 'No impressions. Girls do *not* think they're cool.'

'Anything else?' I asked.

She shook her head. 'First one's for free. Any more and I'll have to start charging.'

'Dude, I'm as broke as you.'

'That's a shame, because I had a very interesting chat with a certain someone that I think you might be interested in.'

The nurse's door opened and she poked her head out. 'Jon Qi?'

Poor Jon looked like a ghost.

'Good luck, Jonny Qi!' Tully yelled, as he disappeared into the nurse's office.

As Jon stepped in, Zoe stepped out, her left sleeve rolled up, a small, circular band-aid on her bicep, her dark blue sports skirt exposing pale bright legs that I'd spent the last few days guiltily dreaming about.

'Hey chica, can I please have your stems for a day?' Tully said.

Zoe smiled. 'You don't own enough sunscreen for these things.'

'Too late. They're already red hot. See you at training, girlfriend,' Tully said.

'See you there,' Zoe replied, then looked at me. I glanced straight to the floor. 'Bye, Mike,' she said, before walking down the hall.

I let out a huge sigh, welcoming my ability to breathe again.

Tully bashed me on the arm. 'Second tip: How about you actually talk next time the love of your life is near you, ya weirdo! That's two for the price of none. You owe me.'

'Who does Zoe like?' I asked, watching her match-red ponytail disappear out the front door of the building. 'Please, just tell me. I'll owe you forever. Promise.'

'Promises don't work at checkouts, Mike. I need the cold, hard stuff.'

'Tully, I don't have any money. I don't have any girlfriend. I have nothing,' I said. 'You're fine. You have Danny.'

Tully rolled her eyes. 'You're probably too young to understand this—'

'I'm only three months younger than y—' I said.

'You're probably too *immature* to understand this, but men look at us, OK? The teachers. Men on the street. Dads at the track. They look at us. Girls, I mean. The girls with boobs get the most looks. That's a scientific fact. So, unless you can magically grow me a big set of boobs like those bitches at Mt Saint Margaret's, I need to know that Danny's being faithful, I need a job, and I need the pill.'

'No!' The scream came from inside the nurse's office. 'I can't do it!'

The door flung open and poor ghost-faced Jon bolted out of the room and down the hallway so fast you had to wonder if there was a long jump pit at the end.

He was gone.

The nurse poked her head out of her office. 'Tully Maxwell?'

I looked hopelessly at Tully, with her frizzy hair and her chunky trunks, her cheeks flush with red sparks and reaching capillaries. She jumped out of her seat and rolled her sleeve up. 'Shame we couldn't do business, sir.'

She went to step inside. I sat up.

'I can get you boobs,' I said, the words jumping out of me. I lowered my voice to a whisper. 'Fake boobs.'

Tully raised an eyebrow. 'Mike, you wouldn't know where to get a haircut, let alone fake boobs.'

'I know a place, it has fake boobs, and fake nipples. Everything you need.'

'Alright, MacGyver. You get me boobs and I'll tell you who Zoe likes.'

'I'd have to steal them,' I said, checking again for stickybeaks.

'And?' Tully asked.

'What if I get caught?'

'Whaaat if I get caaauuuughttt?' she mocked. 'This is why you're single, Mike. Take it or leave it.' She turned to walk into the nurse's office.

'Deal!' I yelled, quickly.

She turned back and reached out with her pinky up. We locked little fingers. Deal.

She checked again for eavesdroppers then leaned in. 'It's no-one,' she whispered.

My heart dropped. 'Who's No-Juan?' I asked. 'Do they sit at the Wog bench?'

'I mean "nobody", you idiot,' Tully said, whacking me on the arm. 'She said she doesn't like anybody.'

'Did you ask if there was anyone who she *didn't* like?' I asked.

'What? No, we don't talk about people she doesn't like,' Tully said.

'OK – so there's nobody that she likes, and there's nobody that she doesn't like, so that means there's nobody that she doesn't *not* like. So, she could still like me one day?' I asked.

'You're lucky you're not Jon Qi, buddy, cos I'm about to get straight to the point,' Tully said. 'Zoe is going through something that you will literally *never* understand. All she cares about at the moment is the Dash. She wants to win. I think it has something to do with her sister. So, maybe quit worrying about who you like and who likes who and blah blah blah. You're a great athlete when you're not falling over yourself, Mike. We could use someone like you.'

The nurse poked her head out again. 'Come on, Tully, hurry up.'

'Coming, Miss!' Tully said, following her into the room, before turning quickly back to me. 'Size 12C, Mike,' she said. 'I want them on my desk by Monday.'

She closed the door.

CHAPTER ELEVEN

FRIDAY, 27TH MARCH 1998

The signs around the Brindy Shops bus interchange read: BILL POSTERS WILL BE PROSECUTED.

I could really relate to this Bill Posters guy.

I'd nominated myself for membership to a club that offered five-finger discounts; I'd committed the thievery of two handfuls of silicone. On top of that, now I was an accessory to crimes relating to nightclub promotion.

This was not my style. I wasn't a criminal, I was a triple-jumper.

Dad and I were parked, roadside, at 11pm, and barely a rat stirred around the bus station.

During the day, a never-ending stream of buses screeched through here, their brakes squeaking as drivers found their marks, their engines churning as they exited the station left to the suburbs, or right to the city. Things were always moving here, people coming and going, checking their watches, tapping their feet to the tunes of their discmans.

At night, though, the place was dead.

Except a man and his dog, sitting conked-out and cooked at one of the bus stop benches, obviously settling in for the night because there were no buses this late. His dog asleep on the cold concrete platform floor next to him, tied by a leash to a metal timetable stand, its wagging tail casually slapping against a shoebox-sized steel ashtray as it dreamed in blue and grey.

I was sitting in the passenger seat next to Dad; a one-litre tub of runny glue sitting between my legs, an old paint brush jutting out the top like you know what.

'I'm so bored. Can't we just get some videos out, eat fish and chips, and do what normal people do on a Friday night?' I asked. 'Ever since Mum went to hospital, all I've done is put up posters and eat nuggets. I mean, have you ever thought about exploring your astrology through a cheap dice game?'

'Look, we can go crabbing tomorrow if you want to spice things up, but we need to put these posters out tonight, Mike. I have a radio interview in the morning. The posters need to be up and ready when people hear that interview. This is how you self-promote,' Dad was explaining. 'If you run your own business, you need to be good at promoting it.'

'When do we see Mum next?' I asked.

'Tomorrow. Now, Mike, please listen to me. The targets are on our backs, so don't do anything. If we get caught, we'll be in a lot of trouble.'

'How long until she gets better?' I asked.

'Mike, this is serious,' Dad said under his breath, nervously cocking his head in all directions like a turkey. 'If you see any headlights coming, you hide, OK?'

'How long until she gets better?' I asked again.

'We attack the electricity box across the road, then go for the light poles.'

'Dad, you wouldn't let me do skirmish during the holidays because you said you were against war-like activities. Why are you pretending this is covert ops?'

'On three.' Dad put his hand on the car door. 'One, two, thr—'

I went to open my door, but I bumped the tub between my thighs and the glue spilled out from my lap and into the footwell of the passenger side of the car.

'Oh, shit!' I yelled. 'Oh, sorry for swearing.'

'My new car!' he yelled, diving head first into the footwell in front of me, trying to stop the glue from running into all the hard to reach places.

'*Second-hand* new car.'

'Save the glue, Mike! We need to promote!'

He was trying to scoop up the muck with his hands and fling it back into the tub.

We both had our heads down when the flash of headlights swiped across our windscreen. I peeked up over the dash to spot a police car cruising past, heading towards the bus stop, slowing, stopping.

Two officers jumped out and approached the man with the dog, their heavy belts jiggling around their hips. I always wondered whether I'd be able to grab a gun from their belt and hold them hostage with it before they could stop me.

I recognised one of the cops. The young one. Dukes. The one with the aquamarine eyes who'd got me in the park. He was standing back, eating a hamburger. The older one nudged the man with the dog. The man wasn't stirring.

All good. Nothing to see here.

It looked like the boys in blue were about to be on their way.

But the dog stirred. The dog stirred, stood up, and noticed it had visitors.

Did you order home delivery, good pooch? Twenty minutes to your door or it's free.

The dog took an innocent swipe at Dukes' burger, missing by miles, but making Dukes rock back out of reach, and step directly onto a big piece of poop that the dog had obviously dropped earlier in the night.

'Oh, you fucking bitch,' I heard Dukes scowl, checking the heel of his thick boots. Police boots. Deep grooves.

Dukes picked up a handful of cigarette butts from the ashtray that was propped against the cement pillars of the bus stop, opened his hamburger, and dumped the butts in between the two buns, right on top of the meat like I usually did with chips on a cheeseburger. A ciggie butt butty.

Dukes whistled, real lightly.

The dog sniffled along the concrete, until it was right in Dukes' lap, then it snooched the whole thing. Almost in one go. Butts and all.

Now, here's the thing: I hate dogs. I think they're gross. I think they're wet. I think they're needy. And they killed my cat. But I don't reckon they should be tricked into eating old ciggie butts.

'Dad, did you just see that?'

'Shhhhhh,' Dad had long forgotten the glue, peering through the gap in the steering wheel, just above the airbag section.

Father and son; peeking on police.

I put my hand to the door handle. 'We can't just watch her die ...'

'Don't, Mike ... Don't do anything,' he whispered.

I looked down at my hand. 'How long will Mum be in hospital?'

'Mike, please.' His voice strained, desperate.

I started pulling the handle. 'How long?'

'Mike, I'm begging you. Don't. There's nothing we can do.'

'Are you talking about Mum or the dog?'

The door popped open, and I put my foot out into the gutter.

'I don't know!' He sounded so desperate that I froze. He took a breath. 'I don't know how long. All I know is, when you walk down the hallway, you've seen the other rooms. Three, four people in each. Your mum has her own room. That's so you can visit, any time. How do you think she's paying for that?'

I put my foot back inside the car, and closed the door, quietly.

'I can't afford to get in trouble right now, Mike. I need to put these posters out. I need people at this show.'

Dad looked tired. For the first time ever, I noticed grey hairs in his beard. Like he'd dipped his chin in salt.

The sound of screeching tyres broke our silence, as the police drove away.

The dog started sneezing. The man started to stir.

Dad and I sat upright, silent, breathing.

'Let's just go,' Dad sighed, as he started the car. 'It's late. Your mother starts treatment tomorrow.'

We didn't talk the whole way home.

There's nothing we can do.

•

SATURDAY, 28TH MARCH 1998

My hands were peeling.

Not skin, but glue. It looked like I had some kind of gross skin disorder.

It was the next morning, and Dad and I were sitting on a red couch in the waiting room of the local radio station, surrounded by posters of concerts gone by on old wood-panelled walls.

I sat next to Dad, peeling flicklets of dried glue off my hands just by rubbing my fingers together, watching them flutter to the floor; sometimes dropping vertically, and other times tumble-drying off to the sides, left and right, bouncing off invisible walls, switching direction before landing on the typical multicoloured carpet that usually adorned RSL restaurants to distract you from dropped beer and food stains.

'Just what we need. More mess.' The words came from a lady, sitting at a desk near me. She didn't look well. Her pale eyes weighed down by dark, sagging bags. Her head obviously bald under a floral bandana. 'As if the recent budget cuts didn't leave enough mess around this place.' She was older. Fifty, maybe? She dressed like a woman who'd buy clothes for the whole family. 'But of course, let's build a brand-new ferry terminal while *we* all sit in squalor.'

'I'm sorry,' I mumbled. I hated getting in trouble from older ladies. Guys I could handle. Guys I could fight. But getting in trouble from women really hit me for some reason. Women spoke in emotions, and that was a language I still couldn't speak.

I got down on my knees and picked up the small flakes, cupping them in my hand. Glue confetti at a wedding for a couple that won't stick together.

The lady's stern glare softened. She reached into a small cupboard near her desk and pulled out a dustpan and brush. She came over and knelt down next to me.

'I'm sorry,' she said, as she started to wipe up my flakes of glue. 'I'm not feeling well.'

She swept the final few glue crumbs up.

'I'm Dot,' she said.

'Mike.'

'Would you like to use the computer?' Dot asked, pointing to her desk. 'It's got the internet.'

'Is that a trick question?'

She slid the keyboard towards me.

Oh sweet mother of god, the internet. The world at my glue-crusted fingertips. I had so many questions, but none that I wanted Dot to see me asking.

'Nothing that's made you curious of late?' Dot asked, peering over my shoulder.

There was one thing.

Twelve centimetres …

Dot turned to Dad, who was muttering to himself, practicing his pitch.

'I'll take you inside the studio now, Mr Amon.'

Dot led Dad into the radio booth and sat him down at the bulky wooden desk, which wrapped around the host of the program, Sian Fox. Dot fiddled with Dad's mic so that it was at mouth-level, and then chatted to Sian whose big, curly, blonde hairdo and cherry-painted lips deserved more eyes than the world of radio could offer. Sian adjusted her microphone and forced a bright red, ear-to-ear smile at Dad that told me she'd woken up the same time the rest of Brindlewood was falling asleep.

I looked at the computer screen in front of me, and clicked that small text box that sat midway up the snow-peaked Altavista mountain logo. The world at my fingertips. And I typed:

How to make your penis bigger?

Pills.

So many pills.

So many hyperlink results with so many capital letters. So many exclamation marks. So many X's and L's and percentage signs.

I scrolled all the way down to a link that looked more like a website than an advertisement, checked around me for peeping eyes, then clicked.

It was a forum dedicated to a technique called 'jelqing'. The idea was to stretch your penis every chance you could get, and it would essentially elongate every little fibre in it. Then, there would be more room in each cell to fill up with blood when you got a stiffy.

Through the big monitors that were sitting near Dot's desk, we could hear the radio show that Dad was now being interviewd for, live on-air.

'A health professional during the day, and a party animal by night! He's the man behind one of Brindlewood's most cultural night events, and something I used to pencil into the calendar every Saturday night; the owner of "Afro Good Times", please welcome Marvin Amon to ABC Local Breakfast!' the host chirped.

'Yes. Hello?' Dad said nervously, jutting his head back and forth, trying to find the right distance from the mic.

'Now, you're from Ghana, which is in West Africa, yes?'

'That's correct.'

'Amazing. What a brilliantly rich culture.'

'Thank you. I can't take credit for all of it,' Dad said.

The radio host laughed, too much. Dad wasn't *that* funny.

'Amazing, amazing,' she said, again with too much gusto. 'The whole region is not without its share of turmoil, though. How do you feel about the political standings in Somalia at the moment?'

A look of worry flashed across poor Dad's face.

'Oh, I'm not sure. It's seven countries away from where I was born.'

'Mmmm, but what's going on there really is horrific, isn't it?' Sian Fox said, earnestly.

'Yes,' Dad was stuttering now. Trying to find a way out. There was no way out though. Poor Dad was now speaking on behalf of one billion people. *All* of Africa.

Happy with the direction of the show, I saw Dot discreetly exit the studio and make her way back towards me.

Jesus Christ! I couldn't let her see what I was looking at. There were diagrams and everything for god's sake!

She was smiling as she approached, and my heart started thumping in my chest.

I clicked the cursor into the address box and typed the first thing that came to mind: how to cure cancer?

As the hour-glass curser started doing somersaults, and the bandana-wearing Dot arrived back to the desk, my heart sank. She handed me a small orange juicebox but then spotted the screen and her smile dropped.

'Why are you looking that up?' she asked, like I'd missed a staff meeting about etiquette.

'Oh, it's not because of you ...' I mumbled. It was true.

Dot thought, then nodded. 'Then why?' She asked.

I didn't have an answer. I didn't want to tell anyone about Mum.

'Surely, we should be calling on the president of countries like the Democratic Republic of Congo to release the stronghold of resources and the funds that arise from it?' Sian asked, with a furrowed brow.

'Oh, umm ... I don't think I have his number,' Dad joked.

Sian Fox wasn't laughing. 'I mean, ultimately, it's about responsible governing and administration. A priority to serve the people. Take for example the current calls for our council here to finally take responsibility and revamp the boardwalk and jetty area down at Jenkins Reserve so that it can extend the larger catamaran services from the City and turn the Swamp into a thriving hub for the community. Can you think of any reason why they shouldn't do that?'

Dad swallowed. 'Well, umm, I guess some locals might think it a shame to see the end of fishing and crabbing in the area ...'

Sian Fox's mouth dropped open. She turned up Dad's mic discreetly as she leaned forward. 'Dr Amon, are you suggesting that catching fish is more important than saving lives?'

I didn't know where to look.

I could barely watch poor Dad.

I could barely watch poor Dot. She was seated next to me, absent-mindedly picking at her fingernails while she watched the interview unfold.

Dot in her bandana.

'Does it hurt?' I asked.

'Does what hurt?' She looked around the room curiously, touching the back ties of her head scarf with her fingers.

'I'm sorry,' I said. And I really was, because I was thinking about my mum.

'No, no, it's fine, pet. Not many people have asked me that.'

Dot took a moment to gather her thoughts. 'Did you know, in the middle ages, sometimes if you were sick, or acting "abnormally", they would drill holes in your head, to let out evil spirits.'

'I'd act abnormal if people drilled holes in my head,' I said.

'Well, that was their medicine at the time. You could spend all your money on the best doctor in town and they'd drill a hole in your head.' She laughed, and lightly touched her head to reconfigure her bandanna. Her laughing had made it slip away slightly, but also – it seemed – maybe she was checking for head holes.

'Back in the day, the scariest thing in the world was scurvy,' she continued. 'It killed so many people for thousands of years. If you were a sailor, or an explorer, it was always a terrifying possibility with no explanation of ailment.'

Dot took a sip of water.

'And you know all it was that cured it? Oranges. Lemons. Limes.' She shrugged, almost smiling.

The saliva in my glands was suddenly mirroring that tart reminder of the chewables Mum forced me to take every week. I always wanted Flintstone vitamins but Mum reckoned they weren't good for you.

Make up your mind. Are vitamins good for you or not?

'Vitamin C,' I said, dreamily.

'Exactly!' Dot said, cheerily. 'That's all it was. Vitamin C. Centuries upon centuries of people dying, and all they needed was a margarita.' She rocked back and really laughed.

'A pizza?' I asked, confused.

Dot chuckled. 'What I'm trying to say is – right now they're drilling holes in my head, because they genuinely think that's the best cure.'

'But maybe you just need an orange?' I finished.

She smiled. 'Well, aren't you switched on. Your mother's very lucky.'

I nodded, not really sure what to say. Truth is – my mum and this lady were both as lucky as each other.

'All I'm saying is – one day, we'll probably look back and realise the cure for cancer was as simple as an orange,' she said.

I held out my juicebox, and Dot laughed again.

'Maybe it's not an orange, though?' she continued. 'Maybe the cure is something we don't even know exists yet. There's something out there, simple as an orange, that could save us all. Mark my words.'

I believed her. These days, oranges are right in front of our eyes, all day every day. It's amazing we just take them for granted.

I thought about everything else that we take for granted every day. I thought about 'happiness', and all the nights I saw Mum crying on the phone talking to Linda. The stack of envelopes on the kitchen bench. I thought about the day we inspected her apartment and I had begged and begged for her to move there because I loved it so much, and she'd said it was too expensive, but then a week later we were moving in and you couldn't wipe the smile off my face or the troubled look off hers. I thought about the night when I burst into her room to tell her who shot Mr Burns and she'd just been sitting on the edge of her bed, staring at the wall.

'What's wrong?' I'd asked.

'My contract at work is going to be up soon,' she'd said.

'What are you going to do?' I'd asked.

And she'd just kept staring at the wall. 'I don't know, chook,' she'd said. She didn't look away once.

'It was Maggie who shot Mr Burns,' I'd said. Then I ran back down the hall and triple jumped into the lounge room to watch more TV.

I wondered how happy she really ever was. I thought of all the times I must have irritated her with my questions or my jokes. I would have to make a better effort when she was home to show her how much she meant to me.

Maybe 'happiness' was going to cure my mum. She couldn't be happy, lying in a bed with all those damn tubes. I'd have to capture the happiness. Take it to her.

We heard the nearby studio door open and Dad emerged, sweating like he'd just run a marathon. He somehow looked like the sickest person in the room.

'Jesus Christ, I died in there,' he said.

Me and Dot looked at each other and smiled.

I knew what I needed to do.

Make the team. Get the girl. Become an adult.

Achieve my dreams. Bring Mum home, cancer-free.

All the oranges in the world.

•

We'd come out to the Swamp after Dad's radio interview and he'd kept muttering to himself about how 'certain people' didn't understand that humans had been fishing and crabbing since the dawn of time and that it was a way for family to connect and bond, especially through hard times. Mind you, I could definitely think of more exciting ways to bond. Watch paint dry, maybe?

I looked around at Dad's equipment splayed out across the dirt where we were crouched, about ten metres from the base of the Jetty. Crab pots. Knives. Buckets. Bait.

'I used to feel sorry for crabs, but they're actually quite angry creatures,' I said. 'I mean, you can't shake a crab's hand. They're always like, "Oh look at me, I'm shit at paper, scissors, rock".'

Dad wasn't listening. 'Mike, hold this,' he demanded, holding out a piece of string, and I winced, turning my face out to the side as I grabbed it; the piece of string all slimy in my grip.

'Your mother starts her treatment today,' Dad said, his eyes superglued to his hands.

It was so gross. He was tying a BBQ chicken carcass to the centre of his fourth and final crab pot. He was really getting his hands properly up the poor chook's rear end with a piece of shiny green twine, attaching it the metal cage that he planned to leave on the muddy river banks. He looked like a surgeon performing plastic surgery. The circular trap – his rusty, cage breast; the carcass bait his new nipple.

'She might be feeling quite sick, so we can only visit her for a short time.'

I could smell fish heads rotting in the autumn sun.

'Crabbing really is a glamorous sport, isn't it?' I said, whiffing in the delicious chook-carcass/mullethead combo. 'They should make a new deodorant in its honour. Lynx Crab.'

Dad finally looked up, sweat on his brow.

'She will be uncomfortable, OK?' Dad said, motioning for some old red-handled scissors.

I opened the scissors to snip, but froze. A metal cage breast. I looked to the blue sky instead. So many sprites, flashing in every direction. I could feel my heart punching me. Was I fainting?

'You know what makes me uncomfortable?' I handed the scissors to Dad. He could finish his 'work'.

'Lynx Crab makes me uncomfortable.'

'Mike, look at me,' Dad said, grabbing me by the shoulders and really looking me right in the eye. I noticed lots of freckles on the whites of them. 'I need to know you're hearing what I'm saying.'

Eyes to the ground, I nodded. 'Yeh. Treatment. I heard you.'

He nodded. 'OK, well … she might not be herself.' He cleared his throat. 'I'll be back soon.'

'What am I supposed to do?' I asked.

'There's some glue still left in the car. Put some posters up on the jetty pillars, but keep a lookout for thieves!' Dad yelled, carrying four baited pots away as he ducked into the mangroves that lined the riverbanks.

Keep a lookout for thieves.

Anyone desperate enough to steal a handful of stinking mullet heads, some discarded twine ends, and some kindergarten scissors.

Keep a lookout for thieves.

I walked to the end of the Jetty and stared at my reflection in the water.

Found one. Mission accomplished. I got butterflies just thinking about stealing those boobs for Tully.

Your mother starts her treatment today.

Suddenly those butterflies turned to stones, I felt sick to my stomach. I don't know why, but I ached any time I thought about Mum and her treatment.

Are they going to cut off your breasts?

We'll do whatever it takes.

No, we won't.

I stood at the end of the Jetty as Dad struggled through the mangroves, two traps under each armpit, stopping every now and then to reclaim a mud-swallowed sneaker; weaving through the wild like a crab himself.

I thought about Dot, with her bandana and sagging eyes, who probably feared for her own breasts daily.

I stood at the end of the Jetty on this autumn afternoon and thought about Dot, working in those stupid studios, eight hours a day.

I stood at the end of the Jetty and thought about Mum.

Your mother starts her treatment today.

That's when I noticed them.

At the end of the Jetty. My worst nightmare.

Jellyfish. Hundreds of jellyfish. Thousands.

Gently pulsing. Their blue blubber illuminating the murky brown waters.

I'd never seen that many in the river before. Ever.

I still had the scissors in my hand. The scissors that had been my favourite all through primary school, that I'd used to cut perfect squares of origami paper with, that I'd then fold into flapping cranes and flipping frogs. Mum even kept some of those paper animals on the dressing table in her room. But those same scissors were the scissors that Dad was now using to snip stinky fish strings.

I didn't know what 'treatment' meant, exactly. What to expect. But I had my own treatment plan in place. I needed to make Mum happy. *Happiness is oranges.*

I started cutting. Cutting my hair. In crude, ill-thought jags, I hacked at it sporadically, sometimes chopping through the air, sometimes getting so close that the blades would scrape my scalp.

If Mum was losing her hair today, I'd lose mine too.

Dot and those damn studios.

In fifteen years, those same studios would be forced to close down because of what's called a 'cancer cluster'. Between 1994 and 2006, sixteen women who worked there got breast cancer, and twelve more had developed breast abnormalities. They were getting cancer at six times the state average. Ten of them had worked at the very desk I'd been sitting at the whole time Dad had been talking on the radio. Talking to the lady with the bandana. Talking to Dot.

That's what I was looking at now, standing at the end of the Jetty. As the 'slink' of scissors sliced around my head, and I watched pinches of black, curly locks bounce off my shoulders, then off the Jetty, and into the water. A swarm of jellyfish daintily bopped away down there, no care in the world about the pain and suffering they could cause.

A cancer cluster.

The craziest thing is Mum and I lived just two doors up from those studios.

Before she got the cancer.

Right on the very same street.

Only two doors up from Dot and the others.

Crazy, huh?

•

'What have you done?' Mum blurted. A look of genuine horror across her face.

She reached out and grabbed at my scrappy 'do.

My stomach dropped, because she looked genuinely upset, I thought she'd know I was doing it in solidarity. Maybe it would make her laugh because I'd done such a crappy job of it – instead she looked devastated.

Also – she had all her hair!

We'd come to visit Mum while we waited for the tides to go up and down again, and hopefully gift us some crabs and found her playing cards with Linda. To be honest my hair wasn't the worst of it, we were still stinking of fish guts and mud – definitely out of place in this sparkly clean hospital room with all its white linens.

'I don't know what he was thinking. I was just putting crab pots out and he cut it all off,' Dad said, covering his own salty ass.

'I thought you started treatment today.' I didn't really want to speak too loudly because I felt on the verge of tears, and I was scared my voice might crack. It'd really made me sad when her eyes didn't light up at what I'd done. I thought she'd be happy with it. I could tell her all about Dot and why I wanted her to feel like she wasn't alone.

'She did start treatment today,' Gretchen said, as she entered the room carrying a small tray. 'Radiation therapy. You did very well, didn't you, Anne?' Gretchen arranged Mum's sheets and placed the tray in front of her, then pressed a button next to her bed.

'I don't understand why you cut your beautiful hair?' Mum said, as her bedding inclined into more of a seating position, her face contorting, like she was getting miniature electric shocks in her neck.

She reached up and touched my badge. The one that said GO FOR IT. I'd worn it since Zoe had given it to me that day we'd talked under the Bridge. Mum touched it, and I looked down, forgetting that I'd put it on, and I felt butterflies swarm in my stomach like they do on a rollercoaster, and then suddenly get sucked out of me. I felt my body hollowing.

Because I wanted to tell Mum about Zoe.

I suddenly had that feeling again. That feeling where I could feel my heartbeat in my ears, and I realised I needed to step away from the whole situation. Nothing was going how it should.

'I swear, I turned my back for a moment, and he'd cut it all off,' Dad said.

'It's just disappointing, Marvin,' Mum said, trailing off.

She looked terrible. She could barely open her left eye.

I walked back over to the window. The trusty window, where I didn't need to see anyone's questioning looks, could avoid eye contact. Looking out over the city, somewhere I could escape – get out of the cold white box of this hospital room.

'You know, it's his birthday soon,' I heard Dad whisper to Linda.

'Oh god, as if there're not enough things to worry about,' Linda whispered back. 'How old is he this time?'

In the reflection of the window, I saw them turn towards me.

I gritted my teeth, leaning my forehead against the window, watching the glass haze – then clear up – as I channelled imaginary fire through my nose.

God it made me mad. Saturday night. I wanted to be at Tully's watching TV, or playing *Athlete Kings* on my Sega Saturn.

I started rubbing my fingertips over my scalp, filling my head with a scratching sound; watching shavings of hair flutter onto the floor. I kept rubbing, watching them fall, and before I knew it I was really scrubbing my scalp, with both hands, just watching hair filings tumble to the tiles, doing everything I could not to hear Dad and Linda's punishing conversation about me becoming a teenager.

I probably would have scratched my scalp off if it wasn't for a cool, calm hand landing on my forearm.

'Well, don't you look even more handsome with a sharp hairdo like that,' she said.

Gretchen was the embodiment of when lips touch ice-cubes in a cup of room temperature tap water. I looked up at her beautiful, soft smile and I felt myself fall in love with her. Not a sexual love. A real love. A love that brings families together at Christmas, even when they know it will end in fighting.

Her face lit up with colour and the sky filled up with sound.
We looked out the window to the world.

Popping. Bursts.

Fireworks.

Shooting up from the showgrounds, their golden tails wiggling through the black before bursting into rainbows of crackly colour. Green. Gold. Red.

'They must be testing for next weekend,' she said, her face changing colour with each explosion. 'Are you excited for the show?'

We looked out over the blueprint of The Brindy Show. The Ferris wheel looking almost complete, the food carts proudly spruiking hot chips and Dagwood Dogs under Hollywood lighting, but with nothing yet in the bain-maries.

I didn't answer. I wasn't even interested in the show this year.

Dad walked up, 'Low tides, Mike. We need to collect the pots. I'll meet you in the waiting area.'

When I turned around to leave there was a twenty-dollar note on the table. From Linda.

·

And then I was running.

Towards the end of the Jetty. Away from the man, and his gun. It was now I realised that this was the same guy from the bus shelter. The night I spilled glue everywhere. The night I saw the cops feeding a dog cigarette butts.

'Is your dog OK?' I'd whispered.

'What do you know about that?' he'd croaked, stepping forward.

I wanted to tell him about Constable Dukes, and the ciggie butt sandwich, what I'd seen, but I didn't think I had time.

So I started running, sprinting down the wooden catwalk towards my greatest fear, my ridiculous new haircut offering little resistance to the wind, and as I leapt off the edge of that jetty, into the jumble of jellies, I couldn't help but wonder if it was all connected. If it was all happening for a reason.

I thought about Dot at the radio station, her big drooping eyes, gently pulling the skin off her skull. They were drilling holes in her head, and Mum's. I thought about the box of bullets, and the ciggie-butt sandwich the policeman fed to the dog. I thought about poor Georgia Ingham getting swallowed by the underbelly of that ferry, her tiny hands feeding the crabs we were catching.

I thought about all that as I leapt off the edge of that jetty, heading towards the cluster of jellyfish.

My legs hit the water first, and the sharp pains shot through my stomach.

The stings had started.

The cancer cluster.

CHAPTER TWELVE

When I resurfaced, I was looking down the barrel of a gun.

'Don't shoot!' I screamed, spluttering muddy salt water from my lips.

'Stop screaming,' the man said, with his thick gravelly voice.

'It was the police,' I said. 'The police did it. Please don't shoot me.'

'For frig's sake,' he grumbled. 'It's not a bloody gun. It's a walking stick.'

Suddenly, under the sharp moonlight, it became completely clear.

'You need to get out of there, fast.'

I was scrambling, treading water, but my head kept going under because my legs weren't working properly. 'I've been got,' I said. 'I can't move.'

'Jesus Christ, grab on.'

I grabbed the thick, wooden base of his walking stick, and doggie paddled desperately as he guided me around the end of the Jetty, and to a small ladder bolted to its right edge.

'You saw them get my dog, did you?' he asked. 'Saw that with your face eyes?'

'They're my only eyes,' I said, panting.

He shook his head. 'The mind's got eyes too, kid. After all, you thought I had a gun.'

I looked again at the end of the walking stick I was holding. 'I didn't notice you with it before, that's why.'

'So you made something up, like how babies dream in the womb.' He motioned behind him, towards The Goat Track. 'That hill's not kind to the ankles of old men. Not when you're dragging your best friend along too.' He looked out to the water. 'What'd your face eyes see?'

I climbed up onto the Jetty and unfolded on its uneven, rough wooden planks, panting. Gusts of bitter night wind sweeping across my soaked skin.

'The cop fed him cigarette butts.' I was panting. Shivering. 'I wanted to do something. I should've, but I didn't –' I couldn't finish. I clutched my guts and groaned in pain.

'Where? Where'd you get got?' The man asked, squatting down close to me. He smelled sour like wet bus seats, emphysema on his breath. I saw his face, properly, for the first time. Hazel eyes. Freckles under the dust. Lips dryer than pork crackling.

'I heard a splash. Mike, where is my torch?' Dad grumbled, wading back through the marsh towards us. A swamp thing covered in sweat and mud, clutching his catch-sack and pots. He spotted us. 'What the hell is going on?'

'He took a fall,' the man said. 'He's been got by something.'

Dad ran over and squatted next to me.

'Mike, are you OK?'

'Everywhere,' I squirmed. 'The Irukandji. They're in my pants!'

'Irukandji?' The man asked confused. 'No Irukandji this far south.'

I was writhing around, clutching at the crotch of my shorts.

'Where does it hurt?' Dad asked, quickly kneeling down next to me.

'My waist. My pants. I think they bit me on …' I trailed off.

'No Irukandji, but there's definitely bullsharks in that drink that'll take off your ankle.' The man pointed out to the water. 'That's why I was telling you not to jump. You seen that poor girl. Bodies don't just float six kilometres downstream.'

'Step back,' Dad said to the man, who obliged. 'Where does it hurt?' Dad asked again, kneeling over me as I thrashed around on the dirt.

'My – my –' I'd never really said the words in front of Dad before. 'My dick!' I finally blurted.

'Dick is Richard's nickname,' the man muttered. *Why was he even still here? Go away!*

'He's right,' Dad said. 'You mean your "penis"?'

'Stop being a Richard!' I wailed.

Dad thought for a second. 'I'm sorry I have to do this.'

'No! Don't piss. It doesn't do anything. Ask my teachers.'

Dad stopped. 'Why would I do that?' He rubbed his hands together like a weightlifter dusting his palms, then calmly reached for my scrotum.

'What are you doing?' I screamed, the words coming out in weird elongated, differently pitched groans. I couldn't control my waist or stomach from jerking around. Another gust of wind. I was drying out. Sandpaper skin of silt and salt.

'Shhhh,' he said. He cupped my balls in his right hand, and with his left hand he pinched my thigh.

'You're a freak! Assault!' I yelled.

'Get in the car,' he said, standing up, concern suddenly awash over his face.

'I can't get in the car. I can't move. It hurts!' I screamed, on my back, looking behind me to the car, the world upside down, the Jetty on the roof, the sky on the floor, the car in the dirt carpark, dimly lit by a single orange parklight, looking a million miles away.

'I'll help,' the man said.

They both picked me up off the ground and carried me towards our car.

'Jesus, Mike, you need to do some more exercise,' he groaned.

'You need to learn to cook something other than chicken nuggets!' I replied, feeling flicks of the Reserve's dry scrub as they carried me down the path towards the dirt carpark.

This upside-down world where dirt was the ceiling. The car getting closer. I was in a tunnel. Just the car. Sparkles filling the darkness around.

'Am I dying?' I asked.

'No, you're not. Not at all,' Dad said, really puffing now.

'Then why are we running?' The man asked, hand-me-down smoke dousing me with each of his gravelled huffs.

'I don't want to alarm you, Mike. But I think you've twisted your testicle. If we don't get you to the hospital soon, you could lose it.' Dad could barely get his words out too.

'I'm alarmed, Dad!' I screamed.

The car door opening, my body tossed across the back seat with a grunt.

I stared at the roof of the car as footsteps ran from the back-left passenger to the driver's side.

I didn't want to lose a testicle. I'd only just started getting to know them.

We'll do whatever it takes.

No we won't.

'Time is of the essence,' Dad said, furiously turning on the car, and backing out of the imaginary car space that was allocated in the dirt carpark of the Reserve. The man waved to us with his walking stick as we reversed away. 'If you don't untwist your testicle soon, you might lose it.'

'Can't I just untwist it?' I asked.

'Go for it,' he said.

I pulled down my shorts, and ever so gently touched my ball sack, and it was like I'd clamped my scrot in Mum's red-hot hair straightener. Whatever jellyfish stings I might have copped were completely forgotten as my scrotum sent electric shocks to every part of my body.

'Arrrgh!'

'No luck?' Dad's smug smile was audible through his question.

I lay back down and stared at the street lights reflecting in different polygonal shapes off the roof of our car. I guessed by the car's turns where we were, doing everything I could to distract myself from the pain.

'Am I a Nazi?' I asked.

'What?' Dad asked. 'What on earth were you looking at on the internet today??'

'Because of Linda,' I said. 'My granddad. He was a Nazi, wasn't he?'

Dad turned around to check on me, flicking his eyes back and forth between me and the road.

'Yes.' He corrected the steering wheel just in time to stop our Corolla from bashing into a road guard. 'No. It's more difficult than that, Mike,' Dad said. 'A lot of Germans were Nazis back then. That doesn't mean they all killed Jewish people. It just means they wanted to keep living their normal lives.'

'Is that why Linda hates Mum? Because she married you?'

'What?' Dad really spun around at me on that one. 'Mike, Linda doesn't hate your mum. She's just not good with kids.'

'But Mum's so old,' I said.

'Yeh, but your own kids never grow up.'

I thought about that for a second. It felt like the sperm in my scrot had been replaced with fire ants.

'Why did you and Mum break up?' I asked.

I saw Dad's shadow shrug on the roof of the car, and I started to smile to myself. For once, I was getting some answers.

Then I started to scream.

'ARRRRRGH!' I jerked my left hand up from where it had fallen onto the floor of the car.

'Mike, stop moving. I promise, we will save your testicle,' Dad yelled behind him.

'No, there's something alive back here!'

'Oh, it's probably just a crab,' Dad said. His voice suddenly more matter-of-fact.

'*Just* a crab?' I asked. 'You mean there's a crab back here?'

'Of course,' he said, hesitant to turn his head to look back, trying desperately not to hit the wooden blockades that lined the dirt road through the Brindlewood Reserve. 'You were whingeing so much, I didn't have time to tie them up.'

'*Them?!*' I asked, my body instinctively rolling away from the car floor so that I almost kneed myself in the chin, sending further pain from my ball sack up into my stomach. 'ARRRRGH!' I shrieked again.

'Oh come on, they're more scared of you than you are of them,' Dad muttered.

'Are they, Dad? Did they tell you that before you offered them a lift?'

We screamed out of Brindy Reserve and onto the main road that led from the highway to the hospital. As the car sped around the corner, I heard the clinking of empty bottles.

'Have you been drinking?' I asked Dad, my stomach churning with pain.

He pulled over.

'What are you doing?!'

Dad turned around and looked at me. 'Yes, I've been drinking, Mike. I thought we were just trying to catch some crabs. I thought we could walk home and we could come pick everything up tomorrow morning. But you ended up in the river with your testicle halfway to your ribcage, tangled up like a pretzel. The doctors may have to chop it out. It's not my testicle, so I don't care. But if you're worried about my drinking, by all means, let's pull over to the side, and we can wait for a taxi as the cranky crabs nip at your ankle. What do you say?'

I hated him so much in that moment.

'My granddad was a Nazi, my uncle is schizophrenic, my dad gives free rides to mud crabs. The men in our family are cursed. Maybe I shouldn't have children.'

Dad cast his eyes to me through the rear-view mirror.

'Trust me, Mike. If we don't get to the hospital soon, you might not even have that choice.'

And then his pedal hit the metal.

CHAPTER THIRTEEN

We screeched into the driveway at the Royal Brindlewood Hospital emergency entrance, and I couldn't help but feel a pang of sadness. I'd been here before. The same driveway we'd screeched down the night Mum had come to hospital.

It was only ten days ago.

This time I was in the back, and Dad jumped out of the car, his footsteps disappearing to where the light was shining through the back-seat window.

'Dad?' I asked.

Just the scratching of crabs, somewhere in the footwells.

I heard sirens. Maybe I was dying. Maybe I was blocking the way for people who were dying to not be dying, while I died.

'Dad?' I felt hot in the chest.

More scratching. I thought about Mum. She came here ten days ago and hadn't left. Would I still be here in ten days?

The car door flew open. The cool night air sucker-punched my still-damp head, which was dangling, wrong-way-up, over the edge of the back seat. Dad was upside down, with a wheelchair. Behind him, the pearly gates of testicle rescue.

'Sorry I took so long. I was trying to find a good cushion.'

Marv grabbed me by my shoulders and manoeuvred me into the wheelchair, my hands cradling – but not touching – my scrote, protecting them from any sudden jiggles.

'Can I have one of your posters?' I asked.

'Of course. For your bedroom wall?'

'No, I'm freezing!' I shivered, and Dad wrapped a poster around my shoulders.

We burst into the emergency ward, Dad's muddy runners leaving a slick trail of brown through the pristine tiled foyer, my 'Afro Good Times' cape flapping in the air-con, my eyes crushed under the crude, fluorescent lights, the hairs in my nose catching a sanitary waft. The clientele look sadder on a Saturday night. Someone always has something 'stuck'.

We rolled straight to the desk. 'We think he has a twisted testicle.'

'No problem, darl.' The young, loose-locked receptionist grabbed a form, barely looking up from her computer. 'Well, not a problem for me, anyway. We need ID and a Medicare card.'

Dad reached into his tattered leather shoulder bag and suddenly yelped, snatching his hand back.

'I can't give them to you right now.' He lowered his fingers to below the counter.

'We need your details, sir.'

'Just give her your cards, Dad!'

'One moment, sorry,' Dad smiled. He turned back to me, and leaned in. 'There's a crab in my bag, Mike. It almost pinched me.'

'Tip it out,' I whispered. 'I need to save my nut!'

'Mike, I didn't tell you the whole truth before. The thing is, I caught four crabs. Only three were ...' he looked guiltily over his shoulder. "'Of size". One was too young, Mike. I didn't have time to throw it back.'

'You've kidnapped a crab?'

'Shh! Mike, please, you can't mention this to anyone. There's already too many eyes on us fisherman right now. They might take away my equipment.'

'They might take away my testicle!'

His eyes narrowed while he weighed up what was more important. It seemed to be a closer battle than I'd hoped.

He reached into the bag and winced. When he pulled his hand out, there was a crab attached, dangling adventurously from his index finger like a cliff hanger. Dad jumped back, shrieking, flailing his hand wildly, until the crab flew up into the air, a muddy pinwheel. The oxygen in the room was sucked away by the collective gasp of every onlooking punter awaiting their treatment.

The crab cartwheeled spectacularly through the air, twisting and flipping every which way, before landing square in front of me, perfectly on its back four legs, with better technique than Nadia Comaneci. It reared up, held its two big pincers up in the air and then smashed them together.

It literally clapped its hand in front of me, as if to say, 'bring it on, motherfucker', and let out what must've been an almighty roar in crab-talk, but sounded more like the air escaping a hole in a BMX tyre.

The receptionist jumped out of her chair, backing up to the shelves of folders and paperwork behind her. 'Sir, we have a no-animal policy. Get it out of here!'

Dad was clutching at his finger as it dripped blood all over the floor, and I sat in my wheelchair holding my crotch.

Two idiots vs one baby crab.

The crab smashed its claws together and then took two steps towards me, and I freaked.

We had the attention of the whole waiting room, and I'm not proud of what I did.

I still feel bad. I really do.

I kicked it.

I kicked the crab.

My adrenaline kicked in, and I kicked out; standing up from the wheelchair, taking two steps forward and booting the crap out of that little baby Sebastian, its claws exploding off, the rest of its body sliding along the glossy floor of the hospital, right out the emergency doors.

GOOOOOAAAAALLLLLLL!

'Don't worry!' Dad had his hands up, one dripping with blood, trying to settle the audience of confused onlookers, all nursing their own strange ailments, as he chased the crab out the door of the hospital. 'It's just a crab. An adult crab. They grow their claws back!'

On his way past, he leaned in. 'Thank you, Mike.' Then he was out.

'Are you aware you've got a claw on your footwear, sir?' The receptionist was straightening out her blouse, re-taking her seat.

I looked down, and sure enough, there was a big ol' crab claw clenched firmly on the rubber strap of my right thong.

I couldn't take it off, though. I couldn't even make it back to the wheelchair. I just collapsed on the floor, clutching my stomach in pain.

Are you aware you've got a claw on your footwear?

No, I wasn't aware.

I was not aware I was wearing a crab.

•

The doctor stood over me as I lay stretched out on a gurney in a side room just down the hall from the main emergency area. The blue curtains had been drawn and Dad sat on a stretcher of his own, next to me, a nurse holding what looked like a giant metal toothbrush, scrubbing furiously at the large gash in Dad's index finger. My 'Afro Good Times' cape had been replaced with a white towel, that I'd wrapped right around my arms and shoulders, and I was looking up at the man in charge of saving my nut.

The doctor was in his late thirties, tall, with black hair, and the kind of jaw-heavy face and soft green eyes that Ally McBeal would soon describe as 'dreamy'. The type of doctor who you felt pursued medicine, not because he had passion for the job, but because he'd looked like a doctor since he was fourteen years old. I could imagine him discussing career changes with his wife over a half-drunk bottle of red, at their dimly lit dining table after the kids had gone to sleep, uttering phrases like, 'We'd have to move outside of the catchment zone,' and 'Yes, but there's just no money in that.'

His name was Jones, Dr Jones. 'Yes. Like the song,' he said, before I could even ask. He reached for my waist. 'We may be able to fix it manually. I'm just going to try and take off your shor—'

'No!' My hands snapped straight to my waistband.

'Mike, follow procedure.' Dad's face was all scrunched up. The nurse was really scouring his wound, like she was cleaning mould from the corner of her shower before having her in-laws stay the weekend. Dad stuck his non-crab-snipped left hand out Doc Jones' way. 'Dr Amon. Senior Dentist for the south-west Brindlewood region.'

Doc smiled, politely, then came back to me. 'Mike, I understand you might be feeling self-conscious, but we're going to need to examine the whole area properly, so it would be ideal if you let us do our jobs as best we can, OK?'

'It's just …' I was really clutching on.

'Oh, come on, Mike, this is a medical emergency!' Dad put his non-crab-snipped hand over his eyes. 'I won't look.'

'Your father is right, Mike. We really want to help you. I'll turn around, and you can cover yourself with a sheet, but I need to examine the area.'

I slid my legs under the bedsheet I was lying on, and tried to take my shorts down, but felt an immediate stabbing pain in my stomach. 'Argh, I can't do it!'

'Nurse, get some scissors.' He pointed to a cabinet behind him. 'I hope these aren't your favourite shorts.'

The nurse retrieved the scissors, and the doctor started snipping up the legs of my favourite black stubbies. Each snip sending shivers up my spine, the same way snips near the ear send shivers down it.

'I have to explain.' I cried out. His snips getting closer.

'Mike, puberty happens to everyone at different times of their life. You don't need to feel embarrassed about anything.' Snip. Snip. Snip.

'He's a late developer. He breastfed until he was four,' Dad said.

'Dad!'

Doc kept going. 'That's perfectly healthy too.' Snip. Snip.

'Oh.' He stopped.

'Oh? What's oh?' Dad straightened.

The doctor was staring strangely at my groin. 'Oh, it's nothing.' He turned to the nurse who was now bandaging Dad's finger. 'Nurse, we are going to need …' He looked closer at my crotch, and I wanted the heavens to open up and rain Irukandji upon this very room. Impending doom sounded like a walk in the park compared to this.

'I don't know how that got there,' I croaked pitifully, looking down at my crotch.

It was hair. Not pubic hair. Head hair. My head hair, clumsily pasted to where real pubes should be.

'We're going to need adhesive glue solvent?'

I gave the world's smallest nod.

Dad sat forward to look. 'Is that why there were curls in my glue bucket?'

'It must've fallen off down there when I cut my hair today.' I was turning in a performance that could probably have earned me a Razzy.

'It's fine.' Doc patted me on the arm; the smile he was trying to hide behind his face mask betrayed by the crinkle at the corner of his eyes.

'Hopefully we can do this without surgery,' he said.

And then he reached for my bits.

And everything went black.

•

When I awoke, I was being wheeled down a corridor of bright lights by a nurse who was humming the theme song to *The Nanny*.

'What happened?' I was lying down, hair net on, scrubs draped over me, up to my neck.

'Miiiister Shefffiieeeeld,' she screeched, 'you're going into surrrrrgery.' She caught herself, mid-Fran Fine impression, cleared her throat, and dropped the accent. 'Sorry, darl. Was in the moment. We need to put you under, my dear. Untwist that testicle of yours.'

We stopped at the doors of an elevator and the nurse pushed the button. I had no idea what area of the hospital we were in but it was dead quiet, except for the nurse, who'd gone back to humming the theme song. She smiled down at me. 'How you feeling?'

'I feel like I've napped out of control. Like a truck has hit me.'

Pounding, in my groin, like Dad had my bits in his mortar and pestle. Pounding like a bass drum. A techno remix to the nurse's hums.

Oonce. Oonce. Oonce. Oonce.

The floor numbers of the lift descended: 4. 3. 3. It stopped on 3. Stopping on 3, but the beat never stops.

Oonce. Oonce. Oonce. Oonce.

A triangle now. *Ding!* The lift had arrived. Doors opened.

Vocals now added to the mix. A scream.

Not a European pop princess, singing sultry hooks about the summertime.

A voice I knew.

'No!' Another scream. 'It's not fair. I fucking hate him!'

Sound of a body collapsing onto the elevator floor.

'I know, baby. I know.' A mother's voice. 'Get up, Skonny, please.'

Skonny?

'There's nothing we can do. He's gone.'

Two bodies coming out from the elevator now, past us. Faces I'd seen in this hospital once before, outside Dr Jarnipf's office. Skon and his mum.

'I know, baby. I know.' His mum was almost carrying him now, a shoulder under one of his armpits with her hands around his waist, as he sobbed. The type of ugly-crying you do when your gut wants out via your mouth. When you question where your next breath will come from.

My heartbeat matched the pounding in my lap. As we crossed paths at the door of the elevator, my head turned away from them both under my hair net.

The nurse wheeled me into the lift and we waited in silence as the doors closed.

Then we were alone.

'One of the hardest parts of this job,' the nurse said. 'Watching young people like that lose someone. Young people don't deserve suffering. It should be saved for after puberty. That's when we learn how to inflict it on others.'

For a second I'd forgotten about Mum, about Zoe, about my nut, but it all rushed back to me now as I thought about Skon's visible pain.

'I really feel for that poor young boy,' the nurse said.

The lift dinged.

'First floooooor!' she screeched, as she wheeled me out. She wanted to be Ms Fine.

But nothing was fine.

Bring the beat back.

Oonce. Oonce. Oonce. Oonce. Oonce.

•

The operating theatre didn't look as fancy as the surgery rooms on the TV shows. It was less *ER*, and more glorified examination room with some screens and machines. I wouldn't be tuning into this program any time soon.

A young Asian man in full scrubs had his back to me, standing at a metal trolley with gadgets attached. Everyone was wearing face masks, including Doc Jones, who re-entered and calmly picked up the clipboard below my trolley.

'Well, it's definitely testicular torsion,' he said. 'How's the pain?'

Oonce. Oonce. Oonce. The extended remix. The organs all around my abdomen were joining in. A choir of agony singing staccato through my stomach. Nurse Fine put a canula into the top of my left hand, and I barely felt the needle pierce the skin. The choir wasn't going to let a little solo artist drown it out.

'Right now, I wouldn't care if you cut my balls off like you're snipping through the twisted skin between Woolworths snags,' I said.

The doctor laughed. 'Sounds like an eight. Let's get you untorsed.' He walked around to my right side and placed a hand on my bicep.

A nurse placed a face mask on me. 'Here, play Darth Vader for a bit. It's just oxygen.'

The air was smooth, clean, cool on my nose and mouth.

Doc looked over me, a silhouette. 'The anaesthetist is going to inject you with what I like to call a "test serum". It's not the anaesthetic, it's just a primer to get your body prepared, so I'm going to get you to count down from ten, and when you get to zero, we'll inject you with the real deal, OK?'

The Asian man walked over to my left side, where the canula was. He squeezed something in.

'So, this isn't the anaesthetic?' I asked.

'Nope,' Doc smiled under his face mask. 'Now start counting.'

'OK.' I took a big breath. 'Ten.'

And then I was out. Completely out.

Motherfucker.

•

I dreamed I was walking through the Reserve. It was sunny and it was right at the Swamp, near the Jetty. There was a dog walking a man. I repeat, a dog walking a man. It was the Dancing Dog. The dog I'd been when I danced out at assembly to the news of Georgia's death. The Brindy Harrier. The Brindy Harrier was walking a man on a leash. The man was Dukes. The man was sniffing around the end of the Jetty, barely dressed, only in black underwear briefs. He had smooth, swimmer's legs, smooth like his bald head, a triangle of wispy, brown hair on his chest, the only speck on his whole body. He had a leash around his neck and a muzzle around his mouth and was sniffing down at the mud. Sniffing around for –

Cancer.

Crabs.

The man-dog sniffed. The Dancing Dog leaned down and pressed Dukes' nose into the mud.

And held it there.

And held it there.

And held it there.

Dukes' arms and legs were wobbling, kicking out everywhere, convulsing.

You killed my cat, you fucking mutt.

Dogs can smell cancer.

What did Tully's dog smell in Gypsy?

Irukandji.

Before it –
Put it out of its misery.
– mauled her to death.

Dukes' convulsions started to slow. He fell over on his side. Face and tips brown. Just like my cat.

•

When I woke up, the truck had hit me again, and this time it had reversed for good measure.

I was back in the curtained-off area down from emergency. Dad was sitting on the same hospital stretcher next to me, a heavy bandage over his index finger, reading a black-and-white leaflet, printed on a piece of computer paper folded in thirds. The front page read RECOVERING FROM ORCHIOPEXY.

It had two cartoon testicles that had twisted around each other; one was smiling, the other had a little bandage around its testicular head and was frowning. They reminded me of Apple and Eve. But I guess these two were both boys?

'What does it say?' I mumbled. I weighed a thousand kilos. Heavier than the conscience of a cheating spouse. The bass drum was back, but dampened. Muffled. My pain receptors were waiting in the cue outside the club now.

'You need to rest a lot, and get lots of fluid,' Dad said, scanning the leaflet. 'No heavy lifting, no baths or spa baths, no running, no –' He trailed off.

'No what?' I was feeling so cold.

He cleared his throat, and calmly committed to the words on the page: 'No masturbation.' He folded up the leaflet.

'No, the one before that.'

'No running,' he repeated.

'But the Brindy Schools Cup is in two weeks!' A knot forming in my stomach. I needed to run. To jump. For Mum. For Zoe.

'Not for you it's not.' Dad stood up. 'Stay here, I'm just going back to the car. I need to make sure the crabs haven't killed each other.'

I waited for him to leave before I lifted my gown to survey the damage.

There were small white butterfly bandages sitting over a stitched-up incision down the side of my scrotum that looked like it had been leaking a little.

How the hell was I going to hop, step and jump?

I felt tender from guts to gooch, and it all looked so swollen. Big.

Bigger.

I guess every cloud has a silver lining.

·

SUNDAY, 29TH MARCH 1998

The morning sun leaked through the closed blinds. Mum's room wasn't as cold when the sun hit those walls. The halls outside were quiet. Quieter. Not as many footsteps. Not as many whispers. A *Woman's Day* magazine sat on the small table, a pen keeping the pages open. Linda hadn't finished the crossword.

Next to the crossword was a bunch of flowers I hadn't seen before. A note attached read *'Thoughts and prayers for a speedy recovery!! From Iris and the team at Woolvin Park.'*

Dad was at the gates of The Show, promoting 'Afro Good Times'. Gretchen was away. Another nurse, who I hadn't met before, had popped in to fiddle with dials, and to leave a small container of hydration jelly next to Mum's bed.

'You need anything, you just yell out, OK?' She'd said on her way out. She didn't bother telling me her name.

Mum was hooked up to machines, and the bags under her eyes looked big enough for airlines to charge excess. I was sitting opposite her in Linda's chair, icepack in my lap, in proper hysterics as I told her the whole story. About the crabs, and my testicle.

'Anyway, I'm guessing the stitches are made from Dad's promises to start going to the gym because they'll apparently disappear in two weeks.'

I laughed heartily, pretty chuffed with that one. Serving up some oranges for breakfast.

'Stop fucking lying,' Mum rasped.

My heart almost stopped. I looked around, knowing full well that we were alone, but double-checking the nurse hadn't walked back in.

'I'm not lying.' I slapped the icepacks in my lap. 'Ask Dad when he gets back.'

'Who?' Her eyes rolled, closed slowly, re-opened, she drooped her head to her right and spluttered a mouthful of sticky, thick saliva onto the collar of her hospital gown. I wish I had Sonja's little sucky thing.

'Dad. My dad.' I could hear a high-pitched ringing in my head, like tinnitus.

Her eyes were gliding, never rolling, but never focusing.

She couldn't seem to move the left side of her face. She took jagged little gasps in through the right side of her mouth, exposing her teeth like a snarling wolf.

'And where's your mother?' She was looking right at me, her eyes glassy, barely open.

I almost laughed. 'She's right here.'

'Where?' Eyes gliding side-to-side. Invisible tennis.

'It's you.' This wasn't funny anymore. 'You're my mother.'

'No, I'm not.' Staring. Snarling. Spitting.

'Mum, it's me, Chook.' Sparkles were closing in from the outsides of my eyes. I could feel the panic rising in my chest.

'Who?'

'Mike,' I said.

She dribbled onto her gown again. 'I don't fucking care who you are.'

I felt like I was standing in the whitewash of Friendly Beaches, as the water raced across the crests of my feet, rushing back to join the ocean, sucking sand past my ankles, with a force that made it difficult to stand.

How could a mother forget her own child? It's the thing that stops them feeding us to the wolves. The reason we aren't left to bake in the back seat.

How could I know who I was, if Mum didn't know who I was?

'I don't care who *you* are,' I whispered, holding everything in.

There wasn't anything to hold. My insides felt hollow.

I didn't want to be a stranger to her.

I thought about the joy I felt each night, when an ad break would come on the TV, and I'd run down that stupidly long hallway of our apartment, underneath the revolting, mini chandelier, and burst into her room to update her on my day – what had happened at school, games I'd played, things I'd seen, jokes I'd heard.

I just wanted to talk.

To let her know that I loved her.

That she was the best person in the whole world.

That I needed for her to be with me, watching, making sure the oranges I plant grow properly, so that we'd know they would cure something; loneliness. Sadness. Scurvy of the heart. So that when we're buried in the dirt, and our peel rots, and our flesh is eaten, and our juice runs down the neck of Mother Earth, the oranges we hold can grow into more trees with more oranges, dropping fruit for our children until they can reach for themselves.

I didn't want to cry. You can kill trees with salt water. But the tears dripped down my face, as I choked on the sounds that I didn't want to escape. All I wanted was my mum. Happiness is an orange that plays 'Stars and Dice'.

She was coughing now, loudly. A whooping, dry cough that sounded like she was clearing her lungs of secrets from Woodstock '69.

'Here.' I stood up and walked to her bedside, my hands shaking as I reached for the little container of clear hydration jelly next to her. 'Have some water,' I said, peeling off the lid. I put it to her lips and squeezed a gloopy chunk of it. 'That should help,' I said.

She got through a mouthful of the water-jelly and then turned her head away.

'I don't need any fucking help!' Her arms pushing at me, weakly, her voice echoing around the empty room. The container flew from my hands as Mum struck me and it splattered out onto the floor. A jellyfish, swimming in the tears of a stranger.

'Yeh. You don't need help,' I whispered as I felt tears start to break through. Soon the jellyfish would really be floating.

I hobbled over to her window and opened the blinds.

Rides. Kids. Laughter. A sea of oranges amongst carnies and cow shit.

Dad was at the front gates, a handful of flyers, catching people headed in and out while they waited to cross the road at the traffic lights. A nuclear, Akubra-sporting, RM Williams-wearing family, who looked fresh from the Tablelands, completely ignored him, and for just a second I saw a hurt boy too. He looked up towards the window, trying to spot me, and when I put my hand up, he waved back. He pretended to hit me, and I dodged it and smiled.

He still knew who I was.

The eerie silence of pre-visiting hours for those who weren't in private rooms was suddenly broken by the sound of choking behind me. It was coming from inside the room.

It was Mum, convulsing in her bed.

The hydration now gurgling up from her throat, bubbling out of her mouth.

Her chest lurched upwards as if being shocked by invisible defibrillators, and her eyes were clearly moving underneath her closed eyelids.

Mum was –

Dying.

– choking.

My heart started racing as I rushed over to her bedside, my finger aimed for the bright red button that read 'HELP' just above her bedhead, but I slowed as I got closer to her.

I don't need any fucking help.

I took my finger off the button.

Beeping. Numbers flashing on her IV stand.

Her face was as red as the HELP button, the vein on her forehead – which you only saw when she was mad – popping out like a TV cable running from her brain to her brow. I put my finger out again, pausing on the button, waiting.

Waiting for what?

I closed my eyes.

I was starting to get tired.

So tired.

Tired of finding a park outside every afternoon.

Tired of keeping my eyes to the ground as I walked through the halls. One, two, three, four, five, six.

Tired of thinking every phone call would be the one.

It had only been ten days, but it was all I could remember. Loops in the car. The smell of disinfectant. The soundtrack of whispers. And now she didn't even know who I was!

My hand on the button.

'What the hell is going on?'

And then I pushed. I pushed the big, red HELP button, so hard I thought my finger could have poked right through the wall and itched the head of whoever lay next door. A small siren rang out somewhere down the hall, and I heard footsteps suddenly scatter towards us in the room.

I opened my eyes and turned around to see Linda in the doorway, wearing one of her blue flowing dresses, with her big draping jewellery hanging off her neck and arms, holding a gigantic coffee, with her handbag perched over one wrist.

'Jesus fucking Christ, Anne.' Linda flung her coffee onto the ground and raced over, she wrapped a section of Mum's hospital gown around her index finger and started scooping stuff out of her mouth.

'I tried to get help!' I said, pressing the button again, just to be sure.

Two nurses ran into Mum's room and pushed me out of the way. Linda stepped back, and a third nurse wheeled in a small machine.

'Let's get some saliva control going please!' A nurse with black hair yelled.

A young, blonde nurse took a small tube from a cupboard, which she connected to Mum's bedside stand, and started sucking goop from deep in her throat just like Sonja, while the black-haired nurse placed oxygen straws up her nose, in between rounds of pumping air into her mouth with a face mask and hand pump.

The third, older nurse ran out of the room and returned with an injection, which she fed into the permanent intravenous spout that stuck out from Mum's wrist.

I couldn't watch after that, I turned away and stared blankly at the floor.

'Let's get her into 2B-11.'

I heard the sound of unplugging of cables and unlocking of wheels.

'She should be fine,' the young blonde nurse said, not Gretchen. Nobody was Gretchen. 'We're just taking her next door to be monitored more closely.'

I nodded.

Linda was still in the room, I could feel it. Her eyes, watching me.

'I was just about to press it.' I could feel droplets from my melting icepack trail down my shorts and drop onto the floor. That poor jellyfish wouldn't know what it was swimming in, what with tears, and coffee, and condensation.

'I'm sure you were, dear.'

I felt the icepack in my lap taking over my soul.

Footsteps walking up the hallway now. Dad walked into the room, sweating. 'I tell you what, it's hot out there –' His mouth dropped open, still holding a handful of flyers. 'What happened?'

I could feel Linda staring. 'They've just moved her to a different room for monitoring.'

'Jesus Christ,' he said. 'Mike, are you OK?'

'A bit rattled, aren't you, love?' Linda said.

I nodded. My face a salty mess. Looking out the window at the sea of oranges.

Dad ran out to see the doctors, and Linda just kept staring.

'I twisted my testicle.'

'Well, that's funny, isn't it?' she said. 'I suppose you'll get some days off school? Might be just what you need.'

'Yeh. Maybe.'

But no school meant no Zoe. And no running meant no Dash.

And, right now, they were the only oranges I had.

CHAPTER FOURTEEN

MONDAY, 30TH MARCH 1998

I spent the first day of recovery in the dental van.

It was like being under house arrest. I begged Dad to let me stay at home, but the doctors told us that I needed to be under constant supervision in case I got some kind of infection. I also had to lie down at regular intervals, and I had to avoid weightlifting, which I imagined I'd be quite successful at, considering I'd spent my entire life avoiding it. They'd stitched my ball back into place, and the stitches were going to dissolve by themselves over the next two weeks somehow.

Technology really is amazing. There are some things oranges can't fix.

It really sucked having to go to school, while technically being home sick from school. I kept peeking out the blinds for any predators. A sackwack was basically a handshake hello in Skon's book. If he saw me hobbling gingerly around the dental van and found out it was because I'd twisted my testicle, it'd be like spilling blood in a shark tank. He'd absolutely tear me a new one. He'd call me 'No-nuts Mike' or 'Sick Dick Mick'.

But then, I wondered if he'd even be at school after what I'd seen in the hospital.

'Dad, my icepack is warm!' I was kicking back on the dental chair.

'Mike, I am at work.' He was staring at a patient file, glasses on, in full work mode.

I hated Dad when he was in work mode, his face pursed like a cat's tush.

'Pop it in the freezer here, Mike,' Sonja said, pointing to the little bar fridge underneath a bench at the back of the van. 'Don't know what you'll do in the meantime, though. That poor little fridge couldn't chill out a surfer, so it might take a while to actually freeze anything.'

I waited until the stillness of class time before I dared venture outside. The nurse's office – through the handball court, past the assembly hall, over the overpass, under the science block, up the set of steps where you went Under the Bridge, across the courtyard, and into A Block – felt a million miles away with my bits being held together by the medical equivalent of fairy floss.

I decided to hit up the tuckshop next door instead.

Jon Qi, the long jumper, was sitting on the white plastic 'waiting chairs' next to the van door when I stepped out.

I did a double take. 'Jeez, Jon,' I readjusted my downstairs. 'I'm surprised you're within twenty feet of this place.'

Jon smiled, and then sneezed. 'Big needles in there, right?' He pointed up to the van. 'Your dad's gonna get me.' He laughed.

I joined in. 'You could always get it done without anaesthetic?'

Jon shook his head. 'My mum took me to see someone. This lady, she asked me if I liked fitness, I said yes, so she said, "we're going to climb a ladder", and I said "sure", but it wasn't a real ladder. She made me this thing called a fear ladder.'

'Every ladder is a fear ladder if you're scared of heights,' I said.

Jon laughed. 'It's about taking each step at a time, and before you know it, you can see the whole world. But my fear is called aichmophobia. Sharp things. So my first step was just thinking about a needle, and breathing. So, I did that. And guess what?'

'Your brain didn't get pricked?'

'Yes! Nothing happened. So then I sharpened all the pencils in our house. Sharp enough that they could turn paper into stencils, and I put my finger on the tip of them. And guess what?'

'You still got your fingers?'

'I've still got my fingers!' Jon Qi waved them in front of my face. 'So that's all I've been doing. Touching sharp things – the tips of pens, knives, skewers. I'm excited to see your father, Mike. I'm at the top of the ladder.'

Dad swung open the door. 'Jon Qi?'

Jon flung his hand up. 'That's me. I want to see the world, Dr Amon!'

Dad looked confused as Jon bound past him into the van. 'I can't show you the world, Jon, but I can show you how to floss.'

When I arrived at the tuckshop, the army of troops was arming the fort.

Tully's mum was standing in the middle of two parallel stainless steel benches, screaming demands at exhausted mums.

'Rita!' she screamed at a short, Indian lady with glasses whose hair frizzled out from her ponytail. 'Let's double the cheese-and-tomato toasties today, we'd run out by 1:25pm last Friday. That can't happen again. We've got vegetarians on this campus!'

I was almost too scared to approach.

Tully's mum took one look at me and her face dropped. She checked her watch. 'Shit a brick, Mike. You scared the living daylights out of me. I thought the rush was starting.' The colour was back in her face. 'Why aren't you in class?'

I pointed to my crotch. 'Stray cricket ball. With pace. Luckily it nicked the inside edge of my bat, which took some of the heat off, but it still got me fair in the nads.'

'Too much information, Mike,' she said, disappearing, then returning with a bag of frozen peas. She lumped them on the counter.

'Thank you.' They went straight below the belt.

'Tell me, what do you know about this Danny fellow, Mike?'

A lady behind her ran past with a tray of steaming hot sausage rolls, on a mission.

'We're out of sesame seeds,' Sausage Roll Lady said.

'Then they're gonna have to go out nude,' Tully's mum said, like she was leaving a man behind.

'Danny? Danny's fine. Rich family. We weren't friends,' I shrugged. 'I know she likes him.'

'That's what scares me.' She dabbed her brow with a tea towel. 'Look after her, will ya?'

I nodded. Me look after Tully? I'd have better luck looking after a wild bear.

There was a loud noise in the background, a tray went down. Rita screamed like she'd been hit.

Tully's mum kept facing me but closed her eyes. 'Those better not have been the fucking samosas!'

I had to hobble away, before me and my peas were smoke.

As I walked back towards the van, Jon Qi was walking in my direction, but it wasn't the jovial fearless Jon I'd laughed with minutes before. This Jon had seen a ghost. His bloodshot eyes wide, catatonic, staring – the type of stare that turns your hair grey overnight.

'Jeez, Jon, that was quick.'

He barely looked at me as he walked past.

I reached out to touch his arm. 'Hey, Jon, are you OK –'

'Don't touch me!' He slapped my hands away.

I froze, hands up. 'I didn't mean to alarm you.'

The man was broken. 'I'm sorry, Mike, you can't touch me.' His eyes started welling up. 'Your dad, he goes to check my teeth, but then recoils. He said I have spots in my mouth, red spots. They're called Koplik spots. I ask him what that means, and he tells me, I … I … I have measles.' He burst into tears. 'I climbed the ladder too late, Mike. I'm on top of the world, but someone turned the lights off.'

I went to hug him, but then totally remembered that was not a good idea. I took a step back instead.

'It's OK, Jon. It's not like you've got cancer or anything,' I said.

'I guess,' he sniffed. 'But it means no school for at least fourteen days. I'm going to miss the Dash.'

And just like that, I'd gone from seventh fastest boy in the grade to third in line to the throne.

•

WEDNESDAY, 1ST APRIL 1998

Two days later, and Mum had officially been in hospital for thirteen days.

That's an unlucky number.

It was 6:30am when I burst into Dad's bedroom. It was strewn with clothes, *Ebony* magazines and nasal sprays, and the boxy, 34cm TV opposite his bed was clearly still on from the night before because *Aerobics Oz Style* was on, and there was no way Dad had set the alarm for that one. Dad was lying in a pair of underpants that had so many holes I wondered whether they were made with slices of Swiss cheese, and the mere sight of me awake at this hour was enough cause for him to spring out of bed.

'Mike!' He grabbed a blue pinstriped cotton work shirt from the floor and covered himself. 'What? What's wrong?'

'It's leaking.' I pointed to my groin. 'It's all infected, and oozing. We need to go to hospital.'

'Jesus!' Dad was scrambling.

He took the shirt he was covering himself with and buttoned it on, but he mismatched the buttons with the holes, so it looked slightly diagonal on him. He fell back onto the bed, yanking his dark olive work slacks on, and it wasn't until he was putting on a pair of his favourite fishing socks, that he realised I was laughing.

I rocked back and bellowed, slapping my thigh, pointing at the old man on the bed, dressed all sloppy like a scarecrow.

Tears down my face. The good kind.

'April fool!' I said, as I closed the door and waltzed back to my room. I planned on squeezing another thirty minutes sleep in.

We didn't speak much on the drive to school and I spent another day in dental van purgatory.

Tully dropped by at lunch time and we took turns riding the dental chair up and down while Dad and Sonja went and got sandwiches from the tuckshop. Tully was behind the controls, I was on the chair.

'I got the job,' she said.

I was reclining. 'You're a paperboy?'

'A paper-bosslady, to be precise. My first delivery is next week. First paycheck the week after, but Mum is going to spot me so I can go visit Danny down the coast this Sunday.'

Now, the whole chair was moving towards the floor. 'Maybe you could invite Zoe and we could all go down together? I'm sure she'd appreciate getting out of this stuffy city.'

'It's funny you should say that.'

The chair stopped. I was lying horizontal, all the way down at Tully's waist. She lifted a knee and pressed it directly onto my chest, pinning me flat against the blue vinyl. 'You promised me boobs if I put in a good word, Mike.' She whipped Sonja's sucky saliva vacuum out of its holder and held it to my neck like a switchblade. 'Well, the words I've been putting in are mighty good.'

'Cut it out, Tully, I'm fragile!' I was actually struggling to breathe. Those tree trunks had some force. No wonder Tully could move down a running track.

'Words are like avocados. Good ones can turn bad very quickly.'

A stare off. Then footsteps. Just outside the van.

'12C. Don't you forget it.' Tully quickly whipped her knee up, and the chair returned to its regular inclined position just as Dad and Sonja opened the door and stepped back in.

I was rubbing my chest, regaining my breath.

'Daddy Marv!' Tully smiled. 'I heard Mike stopped your heart this morning!'

Tully's favourite party trick. Pretending she was sweet.

•

There were more cards on the table in Mum's room.

'Gee, it's very nice that people are thinking of you, Anne, but I'm losing space here,' Linda said, her head cocked at right angle, half her crossword hanging over the edge of the table so that the downs looked like acrosses and vice versa. There were more flowers on the table too now. And balloons.

'How was schooooool?' Mum dribbled.

'It was good,' I said, looking out my trusty window at the Showgrounds, hospital ice in my crotch. I always kept my head down walking down the hall to Mum's room, but lately I'd been keeping my head down even when I was in it.

Mum was partial to a cold sore or two during the winter, but usually only one or two. Right now, mid-autumn, I was struggling to find any inch of her lip that wasn't pussy and blistered. Her eyes never sat in the same place at once, that's if they were even open, and she had a permanent wet patch on her light blue gown that often trailed from her tongue that sat limply at her lips.

'I wrote a really funny story about a lifesaver who can only save lives by farting into people's mouths,' I said. Just trying to pick those oranges.

'Ha!' Linda honked.

'That's just silly,' Mum slurred, spitting onto her gown. 'You need to take school seriously.'

I let out a long, tired breath that splashed across the window like a ghost who hasn't worn a seatbelt in a car crash.

'Well, I actually got an A for it, so what would you know?'

A silence that stank of lies. Then the pages of a magazine closing behind me. Linda cleared her throat. 'I could really do with a coffee,' she said. 'Four sugars, Michael. Would you mind?'

I just nodded.

I was tired. *You should take school seriously.* I was always doing the right thing and this is how god rewarded me: a dying mum who was being mean. Cheers, mate. Time to pick a few oranges of my own.

And so it was that I found myself – once again – surrounded by boobs. The bright storeroom where I first met Jarnipf. The stainless steel shelves. The chicken fillets with aiolis.

12C. 12C. 12C.

I never understood bra sizes. They always reminded me of a number plate.

What size are you? I'm 383PCP, the Sunshine State.

A poster on the wall read: 'DIY Breast Implant Sizer'. It had pictures of stockings filled with white rice and discussed the importance of not relying on cup size due to bra manufacturer's inconsistency, the natural shape and lie of the desired breast, and whether you wanted silicone or saline.

On the shelves, I kept looking for anything that resembled the number 12 or the letter C, but all the labels were measured in cubic centimetres and grams. Under a collection of silicone fillets that all looked like jellyfish without the tentacles, the label read: '425cc, 396gms'.

I was sweating. Pretty soon Dad would be walking the halls asking where I was. Worst case scenario, he'd work out what I was doing. Best case scenario, I'd look like a pervert getting hot over some rubber boobs.

There's no good time to start your career as a criminal, except when there are no witnesses, so I quickly grabbed two jellyfish, and put one in each of my front pockets. I looked down and it was like I had a bum on my front; two large mounds poking up from my thighs. I took them out and put one in my back pocket. The other I was still working out a plan for when I heard a heavy stride approaching.

Black dress shoes on a shiny hospital floor.

With no other option, I stuffed the second boob right down my pants, and had to muffle a groan as it pressed up against my stitching. I backed up against the wall beside the room's door, hoping whoever was approaching would stroll straight past.

So, I stood in wait. The footsteps approached, then slowed as they got to the door.

A hand reached in, around the edge of the door, a silver watch hanging loosely around its hairy wrist, feeling with its fingertips like Thing in *The Addams Family*.

My heart was pounding as Thing touched along the wall, then onto my shoulder, then up onto my nose and face.

A head popped around the corner. Someone I'd been hoping to avoid every time we came back to visit Mum.

'Mike!' Dr Jarnipf laughed. 'I was just turning off the light in here. You really gave me a fright.' He checked his clipboard. 'We're not due to meet, are we?'

I shook my head, but didn't say anything.

Dr Jarnipf clocked the sweat on my brow, my rapid breath. His eyes narrowed. 'What are you doing here?'

'Nothing,' I whispered.

Jarnipf looked at me, his eyes tracking down until they rested on my lap. 'What have you got there?'

'I'm not stealing,' I said.

'I didn't say that you were, Mike. Now, I'm not going to be mad, but be honest with me – why have you got a breast in your pants?'

If I'm honest with him, we'll probably need to have another meeting. Some boring crap about how I wouldn't steal a car, so why should I steal a boob.

'I wanted to see what it would be like to be "bigger", like you said the other day.'

Dr Jarnipf's eyes widened. 'Gosh, Mike, I didn't mean "bigger" like that!' He cleared his throat and looked behind him for anyone else, and stepped into the room with me.

'Mike, listen to me, what you're going through is a very common issue that men of *all* ages face, not just kids.' He closed the door, so it was just us, the bright lights, the boobs. 'I know with the invention of the internet, you're probably seeing images of men or women, or even 3D dragons, that are setting very unrealistic standards that might make you feel inadequate.'

I made a mental note to never look at Jarnipf's search history.

He continued. 'Trust me, Mike, those feelings might resurface all the way through your life, even when you have a stable job, and a beautiful, caring partner. The fact is – we all feel insufficient sometimes. You're only very young, and you may not have hit puberty yet, so there's no need to feel worried about things like that. There's plenty of time to grow.'

I nodded, then turned on my biggest, most pathetic, sad face. 'I just feel like girls won't like me if I don't compare to those guys.' Oh man, I really wanted to get out of this room now.

Jarnipf smiled. 'Have you ever seen a statue of Hercules?'

'I'm guessing it's made of marble and he's draping something over his shoulder?'

'His penis is tiny,' Jarnipf said, beaming. Too happy. 'They all were. All the Greek heroes. In ancient Greece, a large penis was the badge of an animal. A pathetic beast who couldn't control his urges. The exact opposite of those who built the civilised world.'

It sounded a bit racist, to be honest. I'd heard plenty about black people and their things, and now it seemed like Jarnipf was implying the ancient Greeks were making up for a few insufficiencies.

'Think about an old English painting from the Renaissance,' Jarnipf said.

I thought about one.

'What do the women look like?'

'I guess they were a bit bigger? Chubbier?'

'Because curvy was beautiful back then. I mean, it still is as far as I'm concerned but back then it was the height of class and wealth and aristocracy. Now, some people consider it a sign of overindulgence and laziness. Discrimination is born by man, Mike, not god. All you can do is be yourself. Take pride in everything you do, and just be a good person. I guarantee, that'll make you more attractive than any stupid penis pump ever could, OK?'

My ears pricked up. 'What's a penis pump?'

Jarnipf laughed. 'Picture a vacuum, but for your penis.' He waved away the thought. 'I've said too much. It's a very silly product that offers minimal gain and can actually be quite harmful.' He patted me on the shoulder and guided me out of the room. 'Just know that girls will like you if you be the best version of yourself.'

That was something a person with a small penis would say. I wondered how well worn the pump under Jarnipf's bed was.

As he walked me back to Mum's room, I was glad he was next to me, not behind me, otherwise he would've seen the other fake boob I'd stuffed in my back pocket, making it look like I was doing half a Jennifer Lopez impersonation.

That and the fact he'd forgotten about the one down the front of my pants meant I had what Tully needed, and I dreamed about taking things to the next step with Zoe.

I also started wondering where I would get a penis pump from.

Minimal oranges are better than no oranges.

CHAPTER FIFTEEN

THURSDAY, 2ND APRIL 1998

The journey to Tully's house from Dad's was through a straight garden path, no more than three metres in length, that somehow presented its trekkers with more obstacles than a tough mudder. Lined by thick, overgrown weeds, trees, and shrubbery, the path was a spider's haunt of earthly delights, often crisscrossed with webs that hosted the long stick-like black and yellow legs and beige bulb of a golden orb, or the white zigzags of a St Andrew's Cross. At night, your best effort was to run through with both arms wrapped around your head, and then flail your body around like crazy just to be doubly sure nothing had dropped on you.

Once through the spider patch, you had to jump over the fallen, knee-high chain-link fence, being sure not to slice your shins on any of the split, rusted stray barbs, the combined tips of each wire-end probably holding ninety-seven per cent of the world's total tetanus bacteria.

After the gate, you had a one-metre drop off a wooden retaining wall, onto a rocky, uneven dirt patch that ate sprained ankles for breakfast. If you managed to stay on your feet, congrats. If you took a tumble, it was into a choppy backyard of dry grass and bindies, which you'd be picking off your clothes and out of your forearms for the entirety of your visit.

It was tough stuff, made even tougher with a groin full of stitches and a handful of boobs.

'Dad's putting up posters, and he reckons I'm a liability cos I can't run, so he's making me stay here.' I was standing at the back sliding door of Tully's downstairs rumpus room. 'Just in case something happens.' I motioned towards my nuts.

'In case your nuts start playing Twister again?' Tully laughed.

I held out two clear jellyfish boobs that wobbled under the fluoro lights of Tully's downstairs area. Tully grabbed them, held them close for inspection, and gave them a good jiggle. 'You done good, kid.'

She let me in.

The downstairs 'rumpus room' of Tully's house was one half of the original two-car garage that was underneath her aged, peeling-white-paint, Queenslander home. They only needed room for one car these days. The concrete floor was now covered in second hand carpet, it had a low ceiling and concrete pillars spaced evenly down one side that held the middle of the house up.

I sat down gingerly on her sunken, tan, fake-leather three-seater, covered in cracks and holes that exposed a white cotton filling.

'I'm glad you're here. Mum won't let me use the phone, but she'll let you. She hates looking like a bitch in front of my friends.' She opened a glass window behind the couch and yelled up towards the window above. 'MUM! Mike needs to use the phone! His nuts hurt and he needs medical advice!'

'Jesus, alright!' An old plastic Telstra handset crashed down from the top of the stairs outside, the top end firmly catching the long grass before springing back up on its coiled grey cable like a bungee-jumper. The body of the phone slowly followed, lowered down by its cord, like a little pulley system. Tully grabbed the whole lot, and pulled it inside.

'How long is the cord on your phone?'

'Long enough to do this.' She dragged the phone right across the rumpus and into her bedroom at the back corner of the garage, and we lay down atop the star-and-moon doona covering her single bed.

Tully's room was always cleaner than I thought it would be. Although tonight there was a plate next to the bed with crumbs that looked toast-related, plus a few discarded two-minute noodle packets laying discarded next to their empty silver flavour sachets, no bowl in sight. There was a dusty lava lamp, more igneous than molten, unplugged atop her bedside milk crate, along with *Girlfriend* and *Dolly* magazines splayed across the floor, the perforated pages of the sealed sections showing the hasty shreds of eager eyes.

She had posters of Jonathon Taylor Thomas, and Devon Sawa from the *Casper* movie, and a CD rack fit for fifty, but which only held four albums – three of which were different volumes of *100% Hits* compilations, and the fourth was a Christmas CD that proudly boasted 'Uncle Toby's' cereal branding.

The hallmark of the room was Tully's pinboard. A big cork board covered in 4x6 photos of all of Tully's primary school memories. I spotted myself a bunch of times on that board, and I couldn't help but swell with pride knowing I had a friend who felt me worthy of pinboard placement.

Tully threw the two jellyfish onto her bedside milk crate, and dialled.

We waited.

Heart suddenly in my throat.

I went to press the hang-up button, but Tully slapped my hand away.

A voice on the other end.

My heart now almost in my mouth.

Zoe.

Tully was off. Going on about some girl known only as 'Boobs' who apparently was trying to steal Danny from her. She was really slagging off this girl. I wondered what the hell this had to do with me.

I leaned in to try and hear Zoe's voice.

Tully shuffled across so that our skin wasn't touching. 'Watch it, bozo,' she mouthed.

'Sorry,' I mouthed back. 'It's just … get on with it.'

Tully rolled her eyes.

I took the boob implants off her bedside milk crate and put them back in my pocket.

Tully shot me a deathy. 'Hey, babe. Enough about Danny. Can I ask you something? Well, it's just I'm always talking about Danny, but who do you like?'

Silence.

I leaned away. I couldn't take it. If she said me, I'd die of happiness. If she didn't, I guess I'd only just started high school. It wasn't too late to move interstate, start school under a cool pseudonym like 'Victor Reed'. It might be my only option.

Tully rolled her eyes. 'You know what I mean, babe.'

I shifted around on the bed trying to find a good position for my legs, and stitches, on Tully's wafer thin mattress.

Tully shrugged. *I've done my bit.*

The fake boobs were going back into my pocket again.

Tully shot another deathy.

'Yeh, but imagine I have a gun to your head, and I'm forcing you to like someone. Who do you like?' Tully stared me right in the eye and pretended to cut her throat. *You're dead.*

Silence.

'It doesn't matter where I got the gun from! Let's imagine I got it from the Reserve.' Tully looked a little more serious.

Then there was a pause.

Tully's eyes lit up. She pulled me over, to really huddle in. I leaned down so my ear was next to the phone. I could *just* hear a murmur down the end of the line.

'If I absolutely *had* to like someone,' the murmur said, 'you know who it would be.'

I started biting my nails. There was nothing much to bite, but I started really chomping, peeling cuticles away from my right thumb with vigour. I was lying on Tully's bed praying for the right answer the way a farmer must lie in bed when they hear the rumblings of a storm. The rains were coming. The fruit could grow.

Oranges. Happiness.

With my left hand, I was pinching my leg to distract from the thumping of my heart, which was so loud that I didn't hear the footsteps coming down the outside stairs next to the rumpus room, or the sliding door open, or the footsteps walking across the carpet towards Tully's room.

'If you were holding a gun to my head, and I *had* to like someone – and I'm embarrassed to say this – it'd have to be that silly, skinny, dorky, awkward, not funny, guy.'

I paused on the edge of my sanity.

'Mike!'

I heard my name, and I should've been thrilled, over the moon, bowled over by a big bouncing orange.

But the voice that said my name was not Zoe's. The owner of that voice said my name with an accent.

The owner of that voice said *moskwito* and *mari-jew-ana* and *cuncer*.

Dad and Tully's mum were standing at Tully's bedroom door. Dad had glue smeared across his old shirt and jeans, and his forehead was beading like a hotdog hawker at the ballpark.

'Mike, we need to go!'

'What was that?' Zoe's words trickled out through the handset, and I almost tried to catch them, to stuff them back into the phone. Return to sender! There's been a mix-up.

Tully freaked. 'Sorry, babe. Mum's busting my tits. Gotta go!' She slammed the handset down.

I quickly jumped up and started shoving Dad out of Tully's room. 'Why did you have to come in here and do that? You ruined everything!'

I pushed him outside and closed the sliding door behind us. Just me and him under the bug-covered fluorescent light.

'Mike.' Dad lowered his voice. 'I'm sorry, I didn't tell Tully's mother anything, but I needed to get you. This is important.' Dad was not playing around.

'You couldn't wait just a few minutes?'

Dad shook his head. 'The hospital just called. They don't think she'll make it through the night.'

How could this be happening? Everything was on track. I'm getting closer to racing in the Dash. I'm so close to getting Zoe to like me. The oranges are within my reach!

I could only stare at Dad. He nodded. *It's real this time.*

So we ran home, up the retaining wall, over the fence, through the path, spiders and all, and when we got to the car it smelled like glue. And as we drove to the hospital in silence, I couldn't help but wonder: Were the oranges I'd planted already rotting?

•

The lights in Mum's room were dim, and there wasn't anywhere to sit because Linda and Uncle Greg were sitting in the only two chairs. Dad was looking for answers as usual. I stood at the window. The whole room felt extra cold tonight.

We had never visited so late.

I'd braced for more dribble, more yelling. But Mum was asleep when we arrived, her chest moving peacefully up and down. It was the most 'at peace' she'd looked in fourteen days, and I wondered – for the first time ever – whether maybe she'd be happier in the ground next to some of my oranges, and then I wondered which sort of hydraulic press I'd need to squash the guilt that I felt as a result.

Linda was back on her crossword, dry riverbeds of mascara down her cheeks, Greg next to her, a huge man, with shaggy brown mutton chops and glassy black eyes; the bottom rim of his gut sitting out over the waistband of his beige shorts, old thongs on callused feet, trademark stains on his blue polo shirt. No matter what Greg wore, it always looked like he'd just been eating.

'How are you, Greg?' I asked.

'Obese,' he laughed. He wasn't lying.

'He's lucky he's not locked up, Mike. That's how he is,' Linda said.

Greg shrugged sheepishly. 'They got me at a petrol station, Mike.'

'And what were you doing at the petrol station, Greg?' Linda asked.

'I was filling up my car,' Greg said.

'Stop bloody lying,' Linda muttered, shaking her head. 'The police arrested you because you threatened to blow up the service station.'

'Why did you want to blow up the petrol station?' I asked Greg.

'I know too much, Mike. And they know it.'

Linda put her pen down. 'Oh, for god's sake, Greg, stop fucking lying! You wanted to blow it up because you thought I was inside it.'

'I wasn't feeling very well,' Greg laughed. 'But I'm good now.'

'Back on your medication now, aren't you?' Linda said, patting him on the leg.

Greg nodded, putting his arm around her. 'Love you, Mum.'

Linda smiled, crunching up her mascara trails.

Gretchen came through the door, sporting eyes held open by invisible toothpicks. 'I'm sorry about the false alarm,' she said. 'Things were looking bad, but around an hour ago, all her vitals picked up, and she's the best she's been in days.'

An hour ago? I thought. *That's when I was on the phone to Zoe. Maybe Mum was listening?*

'Don't you dare be sorry, young thing,' Linda said, reaching for cigarettes. 'You want some fresh air, Gregory?'

Greg groaned to his feet. 'You know that stuff kills ya, right? But OK.'

He chuckled as they left.

I stood at the window again, looking out at the shut roller doors of The Brindy Show's sideshow alley. Two silhouettes stood smoking out the front of a stand that had pictures of cowboys painted on it, their cigarette cherries taking turns to flare in the darkness like fireflies dancing.

Gretchen walked over. 'Everything OK, little cutie?' She scrubbed my hair and gave me a light hug.

'You ever feel like you screwed things up so bad that the person you love will never forgive you?' I said.

Gretchen looked at me quizzically.

'I just eavesdropped on a phone call with the girl of my dreams.'

'Oh no, she found out?'

I nodded. 'I just wanted to know if she liked me. Now I'm pretty sure she never will.'

Mum stirred behind us and we both turned to watch. She settled. We turned back to the window.

'What do you think causes it?' I asked Gretchen. 'Cancer, I mean.'

Gretchen sighed. 'Nobody knows.'

I thought about those nights at Mum's apartment, Mum on the phone to Linda, yelling, screaming, crying. All the diets she used to go on. The fights with Dad after nights at Afro Good Times. The times she asked me to clean up my room or do my homework. Everything seemed like her life had been so full of unnecessary conflict.

'I think it's stress,' I said. 'A lack of happiness. I think if you unplug the lava lamp for too long, the lava turns hard like rocks.'

You could hear a faint whizzing sound from down the hall, gradually ramping up towards us.

'About this girl, Mike, if she's the girl of your dreams, you need to wake up,' Gretchen said. 'Say sorry. She might just forgive you.'

The whizzing got louder.

Kenny.

He screeched around the corner in his chair, his stupid ship in a bottle, rocking in his lap as he ground to a halt inside the door.

'I'm not too late, am I?' He said, eyes red, breath rushed, wearing full-body cotton navy pyjamas. 'Janet had left for the night. I had to call her back to get me out of bed. There were no maxi taxis. I had to wait. I thought about going to the train station, but some of the gutters. I can't do it. This fucking city.'

Kenny rolled right up next to Mum's bed. With a lifting, twisting action, he lurched his right hand off the joystick of his chair, and flopped it on the section of bed next to Mum's hand. Then he leaned forward, sliding his hand along the sheets until it touched Mum's. He clutched her finger.

'I thought I missed you, Anne,' he said. 'But I'm here now.' Then his face contorted, tears arrived, and he let out a guttural wail that bounced out the room and down the walls of the hallway like a squash ball.

CHAPTER SIXTEEN

FRIDAY, 3RD APRIL 1998

Mum's steadfast grasp on life was testament that even the tiniest green bud of hope on an otherwise withering plant is proof that the tree can still produce fruit.

I could make amends with Zoe, but like Gretchen said: I needed to wake up. I needed to apologise.

I'd been in testicle recovery for five days now, and I needed to get back into the swing of things – pun intended. I had things I needed to achieve. It was time to get my goals back on track.

With the Dobson Dash only a week out, training was at the showground for the first time, and even though I didn't plan to run or jump (or weight lift) just yet, I was going to stop in to the session, and hopefully bump into Zoe and make amends.

The Showgrounds were dead at 8am. Cleaners roamed the stadium, plastic bags in hand, using litter pickers to capture trash. After a week of woodchopper's comps and dirtbike stunt shows, the usually lush green grass in the middle was looking more and more like Tully's backyard.

I managed a medium-paced hobble through Golbourn Park, and by the time I arrived at the showgrounds oval, everyone was gathered in a circle, looking at something on the ground. I wriggled my way into the group to take a look.

It was a bird. Lying mangled on the bright blue running track.

Fabian Malik, the slicked-hair thrower, was poking the lifeless bird with his javelin. He looked like a young Tony Danza but with an even fuller, more drooping bottom lip, and a handful of tiny skin tags around his temples.

'Is it dead?' I asked.

'It's the blue track, bro. They think it's the ocean,' Fabian said, in his thick Lebanese accent, giving it a final poke; his stick-CPR proving futile.

'Imagine falling to your death like that,' Zoe said, a tinge of pain in her voice.

'Bro, that's Mike every time he jumps!' Skon said.

Some of the group laughed.

'Shut your crumpet hole, Skon, you gronk,' Tully said.

Skon really laughed too, and it suddenly hit me where I'd seen him last.

The hospital.

Skon was guffawing and slapping people on the back. A real show. He didn't look at me, though.

'Hey, is everything OK?' I asked, my words cutting through the laughter.

His smile faltered, and he blinked one too many times. 'What the hell do you mean by that?' He said it quiet, stepping up towards me.

'Nothing,' I whispered. Eyes were on us. 'I'm just asking how you are.'

'How the fuck are *you*, skinbag?' Really standing in my face now.

'I'm OK,' I said, quietly. 'Someone I know is really sick right now. So I'm trying not to be too cool about it.'

He was looking at my ghost, writing my obituary with the blood left on his knuckles. 'Good for you, Mike,' he whispered. 'Keep acting like a little bitch and you might end up in a stretcher next to them.'

I was on shaky legs, aorta clocking in overtime; if we had to fight, there was a really good chance I was going to end up with one or both of my already battered testicles stuffed into my mouth, the athletics team standing around us.

Then, a voice came down from the hill next to the stadium, slicing through the tension like a crab's pincer slices through Dad's mouse-clicking finger.

'Ayyyy! It's my team!' It was Coach Bortey, standing atop the small grassy hill that acted as a secondary bleacher next to the main showground stadium. 'It's the kids that I get to see more than every second weekend!' He looked a little winded from the walk up the hill.

'Jeepers, he looks happy,' Zoe said.

'He looks happy, but he doesn't look healthy,' I said.

'And fighting with Skon is healthy?' Zoe asked. 'Grow up, Mike.' She turned her back, and what little hope I had dropped out of me like groceries from the split in a shopping bag.

As Coach Bortey made his way into the circle, he spotted Skon first.

'Skon?! What are you doing here?'

The group looked at Coach, then at Skon, confused.

Skon's face went a pale pink. A rare chink in the armour.

'Why wouldn't he be here?' Zoe asked, stepping forward, eyebrows cocked, hands on both hips. 'He's our captain and he cares about the Dash, as opposed to *some* people.' She directed that at me.

Coach looked at Zoe, then at Skon, then at the group. 'Yes, of course.' He looked to the ground. 'Jesus. I've never been more jealous of a bird.'

'Everything OK, Coach?' I asked.

'No, Mike. No, it's not. We've just lost our discus star and second leg in the relay.'

'Moses Matakefu is gone?' Zoe asked, her Dobson Dash dreams collapsing in front of her eyes.

Coach Bortey nodded. 'Yep. The kid who insists on saying pacifically instead of specifically, has somehow received an academic scholarship to Sunshine River College, lo-and-behold only weeks before the rugby season starts. What a surprise.'

Coach hung his head and let out a big sigh, then he shook it all off and pretended everything was fine. 'A lap around the showbag pavillion, kids! They can steal our athletes, but they won't steal our spirit!'

Zoe took off, over the hill Coach Bortey had just come from, and into the main showground towards the hospital. Most of the team followed, including Tully, but I couldn't run, Fabian was busy poking the bird, and Skon had turned his laser beams back on.

'What the fuck did you mean by that before?' Skon said, still staring at me.

'About what?' I said.

'About what you said before. About someone you know being really sick.' He stepped up to me again, this time without a crowd of onlookers to hold him back.

My hands went straight to my crotch, prepped for a swift left jab or possibly even a knee to undo all of Doc Jones' stitchery.

Fabian had been staring at the bird this whole time, captivated by its stillness, and of all the moments for Fabian to speak up, now was not the time.

'He said "a *flap* around the showbags"!' Fabian yelled as he kicked the dead bird at me, but poor Fabian wasn't the best aim when it came to kicks. He did javelin, after all.

Poor Fabian absolutely shanked this dead bird off his right foot, scooping it up, somehow, and flinging it to his left; up and directly into Skon's face, and when I say into Skon's face, I mean – Skon had feathers for breakfast.

They reckon that before a tsunami, the water on the beach basically disappears. That people often die because they can't believe how calm everything is. They just sit there, bemused by the serenity as the water is softly sucked away from their sun spot.

And then the wall of water hits.

Punishing and unrelenting, causing bone-crushing chaos, and loss of life.

That's what happened on the oval this morning.

The tide went out of Skon's eyes. Stillness. Calm.

Poor Fabian took a walk to see the sands.

'Bro,' Fabian chuckled. 'Bro, I'm so sorry.' He put his hands up in surrender.

'It's all good, mate,' Skon said. His eyes widened as he took a very calm breath. The dude literally had a feather on his cheek, how he wasn't bugging out was beyond me. He just wiped his mouth and sort of nodded, as if he was having a fake conversation in his mind. 'A lap around the showbags, hey?' He asked, patting Fabian on the back.

'Yeh,' Fabian said, obviously calming.

And it was right in the middle of Fabian's response, that Skon struck.

Like a snake.

He darted so quickly you'd think he was the Flash, swinging his body behind Fabian and wrapping his arm around Fabian's neck. He bent Fabian's arm behind his back, at an angle so severe you had to wonder if there were more than 360-degrees in a full circle. It was like Skon was making human origami.

Restrained, and with no hope of escape, Fabian started squealing, hoping to get Coach Bortey's attention, but Coach was intently watching the new discus hopefuls about 100m away.

Skon dragged Fabian right out into the middle of the oval onto the patch of hard grass where there was usually a cricket pitch in summer, and thrust him onto the ground.

Fabian was lying, busted up, on his back, spread-eagled.

Skon grabbed him by the ankles, and started spinning; dragging Fabian along his back. After a while, he was really cranking, spinning round and round like the blades of a helicopter; all the hard grass and dust from the old pitch kicking up from the dirt.

The whole ordeal only lasted thirty seconds, but thirty seconds is a lifetime when you're a human lawnmower.

All you could hear was Fabian, screaming, jerking his body like a fish on the hook, trying to keep his skin off the ground as best he could.

With one final thrust, Skon flung Fabian away. He scuttled across the wicket, and lay facedown on the grass, completely still. Then the blood started soaking into his shirt, the way red wine would seep into a paper towel when Dad accidentally spilled a bit on the kitchen table.

Skon had been spinning for too long. He laughed heartily, then took two steps forward, lost his balance and stumbled, falling onto his face.

'What the heck just happened?' A scream from the grassy hill. Zoe. Leading the team back down towards us.

Coach Bortey finally caught on to the action behind him.

The team gathered around Fabian, checking if he was OK. I joined them at the back. Avoiding their eyes.

'What's going on here?' Coach Bortey asked, weaselling his way into the circle. 'How did this happen?' Coach asked, looking around like he'd just spotted the definition of 'confused' in the Oxford Dictionary and had seen his own picture.

'Fabian tripped on a hurdle, sir,' Skon said, brushing grass and dirt from his shirt.

Coach Bortey looked around. 'Where? Where is the hurdle? You're all going to get in a lot of trouble unless I find out who did this.'

'Did you see anything?' Tully asked me.

Coach Bortey waited. The whole team waited.

Skon, the tough guy, stared at me, awaiting his fate, and I remembered the boy. The boy crying in the elevator. The way I was bound to cry one of these days or weeks or months, who knew.

'I didn't see anything.' My eyes to the ground. 'I've been feeling sick. I can't train and I won't be at school today either.' Then I looked up and locked eyes with Zoe. 'I'm sorry. I really am.'

Eyes back to the ground.

'You want to know what happened?' Skon stepped forward and slapped Coach Bortey on the bicep. 'You fell asleep on the job, sir. That's what happened.' He jogged back to the jumping pits, ran casually towards the 11m board and, like it was nothing, took the world's easiest hop, step, and jump, sailing what must've been an easy 12m into the pit. 'We going to start training or what?'

An hour later, back at junior campus, class was in and the school was still. I was stopping into the tuckshop to pick up some frozen peas, en route to the dental van to start my day of testicle house arrest, when Coach Bortey caught up with me.

'Mike,' he was puffing, standing right up next to me, on the outside of the metal queue barrier. He'd gotten changed and now donned more 'appropriate' teaching gear. 'Fabian's been to the nurse and is now going to the hospital. They're talking about grafts, Mike.'

'What sort of graphs? Bar graphs? Pie charts?'

Coach slammed his hand down on the hollow steel barrier and it let out a twangy bellow that chased away some nearby pigeons feasting on the crumbs of a discarded breakfast croissant. Time to get off. I'd gotten the gong.

'Grafts, Mike. Skin grafts. He won't be able to run next week. We'll be lucky if the school doesn't get sued. Now, I know you know what happened. I know Skon was there. I just want to say, if you know anything – more than you're saying – then you need to let me know. I have a duty of care to my team, to the students. We can't have someone like that on our team.'

'Wait a minute.' It started to click. 'If Fabian's out, and Moses has moved to another school, and Jon has measles, and Calvin and Tyrone are suspended, that means you're down to number seven. Does that mean ...' I felt light in the head now, and held on to the rail to make sure I didn't pass out. I started wriggling my toes in my tight black clarks. 'Does that mean, I'm running the Dash?'

'Mike, please, focus!' Coach lowered his voice. 'I don't know what Skon's told you – what he's told anyone – but he's been going through a difficult time. Teachers are very understanding, and I promise, exclusion from the Brindy Schools Cup is a very lenient outcome. What happened this morning, Mike? Whatever you tell me, Skon won't find out.'

I wanted to run in the Dash. I wanted to run with Zoe. I wanted to run for cancer, for Mum. We needed to win, and I knew, sure as hell, that winning wouldn't happen without Skon on our side.

'What did you see, Mike?' Coach's big brown eyes, begging and bloodshot, waiting for a crack to appear.

I thought about the US President, about Bill Clinton, and how people could lie on trial. The whole world watching, fibbing through their teeth. I had one man watching and I felt as see-through as the wind, my conscience as cooked as the porky pies I was serving.

'Coach –'

'You mean "Mr Bortey".' He re-tucked his shirt into his slacks.

I'd made my bed, it was time to sleep. 'I didn't see nothing,' I said.

Coach stared. A beat. 'Jesus, Mike. It's I didn't see *anything*!'

He turned towards his office before turning back. 'If I find out you're lying, you're off the team too. No jumping, no running. You're gone. Understand?'

I nodded. The lump in my throat the size of Apple and Eve, combined.

•

I was limping pretty gingerly as I made my way back to the dental van as the exertion from just being at training had irritated my injury. Stitches in groin, peas in hand, but the news of Fabian's exclusion had put an unexpected spring in my step. I could feel myself healing by the second. I promised myself I'd be running next Friday, even if it killed me.

As I stepped up the van's steps, guarded by the privacy of its door, I wore a big stupid grin and thanked the gods, or whoever it was that invented bullies, and cigarettes, and measles vaccines that didn't come in a tablet.

I was going to run.

Run the Dash.

Run for cancer.

Run for –

Zoe!

I slammed the door of the dental van closed as thoughts of my romantic relationship flooded my mind.

What had I almost walked into?

I cracked open the door and peeked through.

Dad was holding some X-rays up to the light, and Zoe's mum, Mrs Ingham, sat opposite the dental chair, fanning herself with gross before-and-after pamphlets promoting treatment of gingivitis. She looked like she hadn't eaten in days.

Before I could close the crack and make my escape, the door flew wide open.

Sonja, wearing a mouth mask and rubber gloves. 'Come on in, Mike. It's too stuffy out here.'

I thought the whole van might shake apart from the pounding in my chest, like a toddler in gum boots stomping on floorboards. That the air-conditioning unit might rattle off the wall, and Apple and Eve would come tumbling from their rooftop.

'Mike, you should be lying down,' Dad muttered under his mask, barely looking up from his X-rays.

I hobbled in and took a seat near the back corner. I'd planned on dumping the peas in the freezer before anyone could ask about them.

'What's with the peas, Mike?' Zoe asked.

Mission failed.

I tore the green and blue bag open, and started shoving peas into my mouth. 'I just like them,' I said. Rock-hard frozen peas, churning away in my mouth.

I smiled. Nothing to see here!

'You have peas in your teeth, dear,' Sonja said.

Nothing compared to the rocks in my head, I thought.

Dad put the X-rays down, picked up his silver inspection mirror, and went back to looking in Zoe's mouth.

'There's certainly no functional issue with the gap, Zoe, so altering it could be quite a costly procedure for no necessity.'

'What if I just put rubber bands around them, and gradually pull them closer?' Zoe asked.

'If rubber bands could fix teeth then the postman would have my job.' Dad took off his mask and flicked off the light above Zoe's head. They both sat up. Dad took off his rubber gloves and threw them in the chairside bin. 'It's a cascade effect. You can't just close the top two teeth. It will throw your entire alignment into chaos.'

'So how much are we talking here?' Zoe's mum asked.

Dad shrugged. 'You'll have to ask the orthodontist.'

'Dr Amon, please don't make us pay two-hundred dollars to a specialist who will tell us we can't afford it.' Mrs Ingham pulled out a small calculator from her black handbag. 'The claim against the council is sucking us dryer than that saliva vacuum.'

'Please, Mum. I hate my gap, you know that.'

Mrs Ingham nodded. 'I know, dear, and I hate the council. And I can tell you now which one I'd prefer to see go first.'

I watched it all from the dark back corner of the van, the open bag of frozen veg pressed hard against my crotch, slowly munching away at peas. They weren't as bad as I thought. They might even go well with nuggets.

'How much?' Mrs Ingham asked Dad. 'Just throw out a figure.'

Dad took a moment. 'Three thousand dollars?'

'Jesus.'

'That's just a guess. It could be more, it could be less.'

'It could be more?!'

'Please, Mum!' Zoe said.

'Zoe, it's unnecessary.'

'Please, Mum, I just want to be normal!'

'You are normal, dear. There's a boy back there eating frozen peas for Pete's sake, you're normal!'

'I hate the gap so much. I feel like a gumball machine just waiting for a twenty-cent piece.'

'Do you really need braces?' Mrs Ingham asked Zoe.

'No!'

The voice shot across the room. My voice.

I didn't mean to, but I'd joined the conversation.

Now everyone was staring, as I almost broke my teeth on a particularly-frozen frozen pea.

'I ...' I thought about lying. 'I ...'

I looked Zoe right in the eye. 'I really like the gap.' I leaned forward into the main area, near the door. 'It makes you different from everyone else. And that's a really good thing. I mean, unless the gap is forcing your wisdom teeth into your brain, or you keep swallowing flies –'

'Quit while you're ahead, Mike,' Sonja whispered under her mask.

Point taken. 'I just think your teeth are really cool.'

Dark skin or not, my face felt as red as a stop sign.

Mrs Ingham threw her calculator back in her bag. 'You hear that, Zoe? The young man thinks you're as cool as his peas.' She stood up and walked past me, out the door.

Dad shrugged. 'It's true, there's really nothing wrong with your teeth, Zoe.'

Zoe stared at me, her green eyes knowing all my secrets.

Sonja started resetting the equipment. Dad swivelled his chair around and started perusing his next patient's file.

But Zoe just sat there, I could feel her staring at me.

I wish I had the guts to look up from my peas, but I was too nervous. I just shovelled a few more into my mouth and munched away. That single admission of dental admiration had exhausted every ounce of energy I had. I think I was due for one of my lie downs.

Zoe stood up from her chair, and unclipped the white bib she had attached to her school shirt. She picked up her schoolbag, and turned to Dad and Sonja.

'Thank you so much, Mr Amon and Nurse Sonja.'

'Good luck at the Dash next Friday,' Sonja said.

Then Zoe walked towards the door, just past me. 'Apology accepted,' she said with a small smile, and I fell through the gap again.

•

Zoe had barely closed the door when Dad grabbed me by the arm, and guided me to the dental chair. I'd wanted to stand in that spot forever, capture Zoe's breath from the words she'd whispered, and hold it to my ear in an invisible sea shell, her crashing waves of strength and softness always in its whorl.

'We need to do the fissure sealing,' Dad said. 'If we let it get out of control, we'll have to do a root canal.' A glassy look into the distance. 'You don't want a root canal.' It was like he was remembering the screams of every child he'd taken a drill to.

I'd really gotten used to not doing much of a day, sitting in the air-con, listening to numbed-up kids gossip about everyone in their grade. It was a real blow that Dad actually wanted me to help do his job.

'No.' I had way more things to think about than have Dad poking around in my mouth. 'Can't I just come to another school, another day?'

'Another school, another excuse,' Dad said, as he opened the door to the van. 'Sonja and I are going to get a sandwich from the tuckshop before all the kids get the good ones. You sit down in the chair. We'll come back and get started on your work.'

I took up the dental chair, plonked my peas onto my lap, and stared at all the instruments set up next to the dental chair. My eyes fell on the little grey suction hose that Sonja was always using to slurp away people's spit. I picked it up. The hose had a long, white nozzle attached to its end, which I plucked out of its metal head.

I just wanted to have a look.

The actual piping was about a finger's width, just like a standard garden hose, but less likely to cop a snipping from neighbourhood delinquents.

I took the hose for a different reason.

I was high on life.

High on the Dash.

High on Zoe.

High on oranges.

The hose wasn't on, there was no suction, and I was all alone, and I was just playing around.

It's a very silly product that offers minimal gains …

That's why I did it.

I lowered the hose down to my groin, slid the peas to the side, and pulled down the waistband of my shorts. I looked at the hose and I looked at my thing, just to compare. The area around the base of my thing, still an eggplant purple.

I put the hose right to the tip of my thing, just to see.

Just to check.

It wasn't the part of the hose that goes into people's mouths. They had nozzles for that. I was just playing around.

And before I knew it, it was in.

Just the tip, stuffed into the opening of the hose, the way a magician stuffs a handkerchief into his clenched fist.

I wondered if there was some way I could maybe turn the vacuum on, even for just a second, so I could get just a little bit of blood stretching out the cells. I just wanted double digits.

That's when the door opened.

I whipped my hands away, fixed the peas back into my lap, and lay dead still, expecting the hose to slip off my bits and onto the floor, but all the fiddling had sent a dash of blood to the region, so I'd gotten quite 'plump' in the pipe. The hose didn't just slip off like I thought it would. Pair that with the waistband that had snapped back when I let go, holding the hose flush in place, and there was only one way to describe my situation.

I was stuck.

I was in a pickle.

My pickle was in a pickle.

Dad and Sonja jovially threw their sandwiches aside.

Dad whipped on his usual rubber disposable gloves, clicked on the overhead light, and picked up his trusty metal mouth-mirror.

He leaned over me. 'Mike, you're shaking.'

'It's the air-conditioning,' I wiggled my waist, trying to unplug myself.

Sonja looked at the dial on the old wood-panelled unit on the wall. She shrugged, 'Says twenty-four degrees.'

'That thing's been broken for years,' Dad shook his head, frustrated. 'Never work for the government, Mike. Nothing ever works because people just take the "you-know-what".'

I nodded. I had a hose on my bits that were literally about to take my you-know-what right off.

'Let's get started, hey?' Mouth-mirror in one hand, dental probe in the other. 'Open your mouth and say '"ahhh"'!'

I opened my mouth, and could see my teeth reflected in his yellow goggles again.

I tried to sit up. 'You know what? My teeth feel fine –'

Dad put his hand on my chest like Tully had done with her knee. 'Mike, stop playing around, the sooner we get this done, the sooner you can head to the back of the van,' he said. 'Suction please!'

'On its way,' Sonja said, pulling her mask on. She flicked a switch and I jolted. Full on jerked. My waist convulsing almost out of my chair as I felt a cool sucking on the end of my thing, a weird squeal coming from my lap like water draining out of a plug.

'You're worried about pain again?' Dad asked.

I nodded, as a bead of sweat appeared on my forehead, evacuating my body, escaping the train wreck of a human it used to call home. I hit my hands across my lap; trying to detach the hose.

'Sonja, get an extra 10mg of anaesthetic this time please,' Dad asked.

'10mg of anaesthetic, Dr Amon,' she said, and instead of reaching for where the suction hose normally was, she turned around to prepare a needle of anaesthetic.

'Your friend, Zoe, she seems very nice,' Dad said, waiting.

'Cool,' I said.

Sonja handed Dad the needle, and he injected me in the mouth with the anaesthetic.

'She said she is running in the Dash,' Dad said.

'I'm running in the Dash too,' I said.

'Oh!' From Dad and Sonja.

'Your mother will be very proud,' Dad said, tapping my lips on the left side with his fingers. 'How does that feel?'

'Good,' I whispered. I wanted the anaesthetic to take over my body.

'Let's get started,' Dad said. 'Can I get the 190mm evacuator please? Mike sure likes salivating.'

Sonja was there, ready. She reached for the suction cord that was second nature to her, but made an air-swing. Her hand grasped nothing.

She looked confused. 'Sorry, must've fallen on the ground.'

She followed the base of the cord from the machine, tracing her hands along the hose.

I imagined I was back in the surgery room. Covering on my face, Euro beat pounding in my lap.

Heart rate is climbing.

I was going to be sick.

Beep. Beep. Beep. Beep. Beep.

Gentle tugging on my thing now. Sonja's hands working their way up the hose, and into my lap.

Beepbeepbeepbeepbeepbeepbeepbeep–

Her mouth dropped. 'Oh my god,' she whispered.

'What?' Dad said, his voice muffled by his dental mask.

We're losing him!

Then Sonja squealed.

Then I squealed.

Then Dad squealed.

I'd never heard him squeal before.

Beeeeeeeeeeeeeeeeeeeeeeep.

•

Mum really couldn't stop laughing. This weird, lurching, dry belch that forced its way out of her chest. Her face was red and contorted, but she was definitely laughing.

'Can you believe it?!' Dad was furious. 'I've had to submit the request this afternoon, for a complete and thorough sanitisation of *all* the equipment in the van, because of what Mike did.' Dad was shaking his head.

'He's your son,' Mum said, laughing.

'He's *your* son!' Dad said. Now he was laughing too.

It was the first time I'd seen Mum seem happy since the first day we'd visited, she was really laughing.

'So, you're OK?' Mum was looking at me with the most 'Mum' in her eyes that I'd seen in days. There would often be times when I'd be playing 'Classic Catches' with a bouncy ball in Mum's apartment – bouncing it off the wall next to the TV and diving across the carpet, plucking it from the air before it hit the floor – and I'd look up to find Mum staring at me.

Whenever I asked what she was looking at when I caught her staring like that, she'd say, 'Nothing.' Then, she'd go back to 'Stars and Dice' or her *Woman's Day* magazine or whatever. That's the look Mum was giving me right now, again, for the first time in ages. She was Mum. 'You're so funny, Mike.'

'What's everybody laughing about?' Gretchen appeared at the door.

Mum and Dad shared a glance and then both burst out laughing again.

'Well, whatever you're on, save me some, please.' She tapped an area of bed next to Mum. 'Shower time.'

Arms held out, Gretchen waited for Mum's reach. Instead, Mum slowly rolled onto her side, put her legs out over the edge of the bed, then tilted up into an upright sitting position. She pushed Gretchen's arms away.

'I want to do it myself,' she groaned.

'Well, that's a shame, because I was hoping to work off the flab from my tuckshop arms, but I guess I can let you do it all by yourself,' Gretchen said, winking at me. 'I'm just going to stand right next to you with my arms up, though, just in case – but I'll definitely let you do all the work.'

Primal was the moan; one eye basically closed, Mum pushed herself onto her feet, overcompensated, and started falling forward. Gretchen quickly grabbed her, as Dad ran around too, and I dived onto her bed like Superman, clutching onto the back of her gown with my fist, ready to tug her backward, just in case.

But she didn't need it.

She was upright.

Gretchen's arms were more gym than tuckshop, as she flexed to keep Mum on her feet, and Mum started walking towards the bathroom.

Stepping. Shuffling. Wobbling.

Crying.

Each shaky snatch of breath filling her with determination to fight. Each sob providing a soundtrack to each step.

Each step closer and closer to the door, I imagined myself racing in the Dobson Dash. Each tiny, wobbly step met with imaginary crowds cheering, white noise louder than Tasmanian beaches, a tortoise racing a cancerous hare.

When she reached the door, her hand clasping the handle, I realised my cheeks were as wet as hers. I couldn't help it. I wanted to be strong for her, prove that I was growing up, but oranges are ninety per cent water.

She really was herself.

The treatment was working.

She was still herself, she still had me, she still had her breasts. She was still a mum.

She stopped at the door, leaning against its white frame, and smiled through her cracked, cold-sore-ridden lips. 'Mike, I forgot to ask. What's her name?'

'Gretchen,' I mouthed.

A laugh. 'No, I mean "Stars and Dice". It landed on "Love". What's her name?'

'Oh.' A salty trickle knocking at my mouth. 'Her name's Zoe. Zoe Ingham.'

Mum smiled. 'Is she smart?'

I nodded.

'Is she funny?' Mum asked.

I nodded again.

'Is she confident in herself?'

I really nodded.

Mum gave me that 'Classic Catches' look again, in pain, but so lovingly, that I felt like the only person in the whole world. She used one hand to gingerly point down at my crotch.

'Then, she doesn't care about that,' Mum said.

Gretchen started to giggle. 'It's true,' she mouthed from behind Mum, smiling.

Mum kept going. 'If she likes you, she likes you and there's no reason she wouldn't like you.'

'Muuuum!' I whined, the tears on my cheeks were about to start boiling.

Dad had been hanging back in the corner, watching. He stepped forward and patted me on the back, his eyes red too.

'Are you crying?' I said.

'Mike, if I'm crying it's because I'm thinking about how much trouble I'm going to get in from the region supervisor about requesting new suction hoses for the van, OK? Now, let's go.'

He put his arm around me and guided me towards the door of Mum's room.

As we were about to leave, I heard Mum yell out. 'Mike!'

She's fallen –

Mum hobbled to the door of the bathroom and poked her head out.

'I've lost eight kilos,' she said. 'This diet is wonderful.'

She smiled.

And I laughed and cried at the same time.

Dot's cure was working.

Oranges are happiness.

CHAPTER SEVENTEEN

'Mike! You have visitors.'

As always, Dad's timing was shocking.

I was in my room, curtain closed, two CPU characters duelling in *Street Fighter*, with the volume up, so Dad would think I was gaming on.

Truth is, I had the tape measure held out against my penis again. The swelling had almost completely gone, and I felt like my old self, *except* I'd grown. 9.9 centimetres. So close!

'Coming!'

I stashed the measuring tape, walked downstairs, and peeked out the glass pane next to the front door.

I dived to the floor, back against the door, my pulse running a Dobson Dash of its own.

Was I dreaming?

Or was Zoe Ingham really standing outside my house?

I checked through the bottom of the window, right at floor level, and fair enough, there were a pair of bright white Asics, stuffed with lean, white ankles that led to the hems of a pair of three-quarter length jeans.

I needed to open the door, I knew that.

I reached for the handle. *Should I?*

I went to turn it. *No, I shouldn't.*

I stopped. *No, I definitely should.*

I jumped to my feet and raced back upstairs to my room.

Dad came out of the kitchen. 'Mike, what are you doing? Talk to your friends!'

Talk to my friends? I rummaged through the small set of white drawers I had next to my dumb little trundle. *The Ninja Turtles* pyjama T-shirt that I got when I was eight would do all the talking for me!

My cool clothes were still at Mum's! And my fave purple Tassie polo was a bit worse for wear after the day I took a swim with the jellyfish, so I settled for a cherry-red, dark grey and black Manchester United jersey that I'd retired the previous year due to their second placing in the league.

I looked in my mirror, tried to control my badly snipped curls with a few palm pats, and then took a deep breath.

Should I? Shouldn't I?

I should.

I rummaged through the pile of dirty clothes in the corner of my room and found what I needed. I unpinned it from the school shirt it was on and stuck it to my chest.

I checked the mirror. There it was. GO FOR IT.

When I opened the door, Zoe was still there, her long, rich red hair sitting lazily across the shoulders of her black tee, like the tails of sirens on the coastal rocks of Santorini.

'Oh, damn, you win!' Zoe said.

Win what? I thought.

Tully sprung up from behind Dad's Corolla. 'Ha! Told ya.' She bounced around the car in her grey tracksuit pants and baggy white T-shirt, standing next to Zoe. 'I bet Redlocks here, two bucks, that you lived next door. She didn't believe me.' She put her hand out to Zoe. 'Carn, babe, pay up.'

Zoe reluctantly put two dollars in Tully's palm.

'That'll buy me and Danny a Frosty Fruit tomorrow.' Tully kissed her coin. 'What are you up to tonight, Mike? I've got a bit of a sore throat, and I don't want to be sick for Danny tomorrow, so we're going to get some movies from Blockbuster. Keen?'

'No!' I cried. 'Tonight is Dad's concert at Hotel Brindy. He's got this band called Serwaa and the Swingers playing. They're touring all the way from Ghana.' I lowered my voice. 'He's forcing me to help set up. Maybe you should report him for child slavery and I can meet you in the new release section?'

Tully made a farting sound with her mouth. 'You stink!'

Zoe smiled. 'Can we come?'

Tully looked at Zoe, shocked. I looked at Zoe, shocked. 'Really?' We both said at the same time.

'Jinx! Personal jinx! White rabbit!' Tully socked me in the arm.

Zoe laughed. 'I've never heard African music. Maybe it'll be my new jam.'

'No, Zo, I should be resting for my man.' Tully started rubbing her sinuses.

'Let me check.' I spun around as Dad arrived at the door, sliding his kente kufi hat onto his head, a brimless cap that stands up like a short cylinder. On his mainframe was a blue, black and white dashiki over black jeans.

I could barely breathe I was cringing so hard. Why did he have to wear his stupid African clothes in front of the most amazing girl in the world?

'Wow! Cool shirt, Dr Amon,' Zoe said.

Cool??

I looked at Dad again.

I guess it was different.

'Dad, can these guys come to Serwaa and the Swingers?' I asked.

He checked his watch. 'If you can be ready to leave in five minutes, then sure. I'll even give you half-price tickets.'

All three of us raised an eyebrow.

'OK, free tickets. But you have to help me set up the chairs. And let's get you some suitable outfits to get those Ghanaian good times flowing!'

Zoe looked at Tully, eagerly, waiting, and I sent a tiny prayer to whichever higher being was checking their inbox.

'Fine!' Tully submitted.

It was a date.

My first date.

I felt a tremble through every nerve in my body. This was the moment I'd been waiting for, and it was all turning up oranges. Even if Tully and Dad were going to be there. And we had to wear dumb African clothes.

•

Hotel Brindy knew the word 'revamp' like the back of its 'EST. 1894' sign. A two-storey heritage-listed beauty, built around the skeleton of an original Queenslander, it had a stunning balcony on its second floor, the band room floor, that wrapped around two sides of its mostly white, square frame.

It had always been a place to drink your sorrows, but even in my twelve short years, only six of which I could really remember,

I'd seen it change from family gastropub, to university chug-den, to its current incarnation: a casino away from the casino.

The bottom floor housed a small bar, a TAB for horse-betting, and a restaurant with all the basics, specialising in handheld snacks, to give punters some free fingers to poke the ocean of gaming machines that filled the rest of the room.

Upstairs was still haunted by the ghosts of vomits past, with splotchy, stained, well-trodden and worn maroon carpet that stopped five metres from a small black stage with basic can lighting and two stacked speakers on either side. The walls plastered with so many old posters you couldn't see the faded, peeling wall paint below. If ghosts did haunt this floor, they'd surely be lonely, as it was only open to the public when a gig was on, and Dad was quickly becoming one of the only brave souls left battling the electronic reverse-Rumpelstiltskins that were sucking in gold and spitting out hay downstairs.

The setting sun was casting orange blades through the balcony windows of the bar and band room when Dad, Tully, Zoe and I walked up the stairs and into the space. I'd swapped Manchester United for the streets of Accra with a kente cloth Ghanaian smock that I'd found buried deep in the cupboard – previously unworn. Tully and Zoe were wearing black T-shirts with the Ghanaian flag on the front, and the word GHANA in giant print.

Sonja, wearing a leopard print dress and tassel earrings that could have been snatched from Ms Harris' jewellery box, was already putting out chairs with her son, Pete.

'Mamma Mia,' Tully whispered, as she watched Pete – his athletic build, in his bright yellow Nautica polo, and baggy white jeans, enabling him to easily reach the top of even the highest stack, and fling chairs around like they were playing cards at a poker game. The guy barely broke a sweat, though his shiny cheeks and neck were still red; the calling card of Roaccutane treatment.

The bar manager, Solomon, wasn't too far behind us. A stocky Ghanaian man, Solomon looked like a brick, on a bigger brick, on top of two slightly skinnier, long bricks, all wrapped in a black Hotel Brindy polo and black jeans. He handed Dad a black money box. 'Nii Adjetey!' He pointed to my shirt. 'Finally, you look like an African!' He let out a huge hearty laugh and then gave me a long, enthusiastic handshake that ended with both of us clicking fingers.

'Who is Nii Adjetey?' Tully asked, looking at me confused.

I tried to ignore her. 'Solomon, this is Tully and Zoe.'

Solomon's jaw dropped. 'Ay! You don't tell people your real name?' He put his arm around me, spun me around to my friends, and patted me on the chest. 'Don't be fooled by this "Mike" business. This man is Adjetey."

'Whaaaaat?' Tully said.

'Yep. Pronounced like "a jetty", so feel free to pay me out every time we walk through the Reserve.' I rolled my eyes, awaiting the teasing.

But nothing came.

'Do I have a different name?' Zoe asked, genuinely excited.

'Are you the first-born girl in your family?' Solomon asked.

Zoe nodded.

'Me too!' Tully said.

'Then you are Adjeley,' Solomon replied.

'Pronounced like, "a jelly"' I said, burying my face in my hands. I knew exposing my friends to this was a bad idea.

'Coooool,' they both said, at the same time.

Coooool ...?

My jaw almost hit the floor.

The only 'cool' thing about this whole experience was the wafts of air-conditioning I was copping through my extremely baggy smock.

Dad called out from across the room. 'I'm really sorry, guys, but this is a licensed venue, so you won't be able to watch the concert from the crowd tonight.' He was counting the money for the till that would greet punters at the top of the stairs. 'You can sit backstage. You should be able to hear from there. Mike, you know the drill.'

I sure did.

We were greeted backstage by a collection of bottled liquors on a table, next to some clean glasses and a big stainless steel bowl of ice.

'That's the rider,' Pete said.

'What's it riding?' I asked.

Zoe cracked up, and I smiled, pretending I'd made the joke on purpose.

'It's the band's drinks, dummy,' Pete said.

'Yeh, dummy!' Tully said, edging closer to Pete.

We'd been sitting around chatting and drinking Pepsis for about twenty minutes, when Dad burst into the room. He was trailed by a big, beautiful black woman with huge tied-up braids, dressed in a flowing rich midnight blue dress, followed by three dark dudes, all dressed in black T-shirts and jeans.

Dad kept rubbing his palms on the back of his slacks and stumbling over words. 'OK, so this is the greenroom, here is your rider.' Dad pointed to the collection of bottles set up on the table, then he pointed to me. 'And this is your servant for the night.'

The lady who I assumed was the 'Serwaa' part of 'Serwaa and the Swingers', chuckled, in a beautiful deep voice that I didn't know if I was hearing or feeling or both. 'You can take the night off, little man,' she said. 'Everything looks as it should.' She patted Dad on the back, and looked at the rider. 'Except I thought we asked for vodka?'

The nod of her bandmates backed her up.

Dad double-checked the table. No vodka.

His eyes straight to me. 'Mike?'

'You dressed me in a gown, Dad!' I said, standing up and airing all my laundry in the gale of the cheap backstage pedestal fan. 'Trust me – I wish I had room to smuggle things.'

Dad narrowed his eyes, then looked at the rest of us. Zoe, Tully, me and Pet—

Sonja entered. 'What's going on? There's a line outside! It's looking like a sellout. I could use some help out there –'

Solomon entered backstage, and now Dad went for him. He was blaming his next of kin. If it wasn't his son, it was his best friend.

He started talking to Solomon in Ghanaian, flailing his arms about, pointing to the drinks buckets. Solomon pointed to us kids, and then to the band members and then to Serwaa.

Serwaa then started talking to her band members in Ghanaian and pointing to Dad and Solomon. Then her band members started pointing to me and Dad.

Serwaa was now screeching in the Ghanaian language that my Dad could somehow not understand, and was pointing at the frayed carpet in the greenroom floor, the single pedestal fan in the corner, the blown bulbs in the Hollywood make-up lighting window, and then at all us four kids hopelessly taking up a quarter of the room, until eventually Dad held his hands up in surrender.

'Look, let's not fight about this!' Dad yelped, bringing Serwaa to a holt. 'You guys go do your soundcheck and I will sort it out.'

Satisfied, Serwaa and her band grabbed their instruments and exited towards the stage.

'What was she saying?' I whispered to Dad.

He shrugged. 'I don't know, Mike. They're Ashantis. We are Ga's. Not everyone from Ghana speaks the same language, but body language is pretty universal, so I'm guessing if I don't buy some more vodka soon, we're not going to have a show.'

Defeated, he walked past us, and out of the room.

Once the adults had gone, Pete jumped out of his seat, grabbed a big bottle of Pepsi, four plastic cups, and limped past me towards the fire exit door. 'Carpark, now,' he whispered.

Tully, Zoe and I watched Pete crack the fire-exit door, check for clearance, then wave us through, holding his vodka-bottle shaped crotch, as he limped out the door and out of sight.

•

Pepsi and vodka. The mark of a rookie. Like ordering an 'expresso' or asking for your steak well done.

We'd found the perfect hiding spot, behind a concrete wall to the side of the neighbouring thrift shop, and had topped up our Pepsis with dribbles of vodka that turned a perfectly good cola into some sort of cleaning agent that kicked you in the glands with every sip. The hum of the concert had pulsed through the carpark for two sets of forty-five minutes, and during the break you could hear raucous chatting from punters who piled out onto Hotel Brindy's band room balcony and puffed durries until the top floor looked like it was wearing a cloud.

When the music finally stopped, Tully and Pete had disappeared around a corner to the back of the shop. Their giggles and gropes and the occasional cough, bouncing lightly off the concrete surrounds of our hiding spot, were joined by sporadic ear-catching clinks of an empty glass vodka bottle rolling across cement. Zoe and I sat on the ledge of the wall and watched cheerful punters stumble out the Hotel Brindy exits in each and every direction, the occasional group of three babbling blindly and without pause to their one poor – sometimes pregnant – friend, carrying a set of car keys.

Zoe and I watched all the cars go, until there were only a handful left. I kept stealing glances at her under the buzzing street lamps and moonlight.

'Can I ask you something?' Zoe turned to me, catching me mid-steal.

The answer is 'I do', I thought.

'How's your mum?' Zoe asked.

I stared at an old gum stain on the ground, thinking about all the lies I could tell. Maybe it was the vodka, or maybe it was Zoe, but before I knew it I was completely spilling my guts.

'She's been in hospital for the past sixteen days, and I keep thinking that she'll get better, but it's taking so long. I really miss her. I miss living with her. I just want things to go back to normal.'

'Normal is what you make of it,' she whispered. '"Normal" used to be Mum waking up to do a 5km run before coming home to make our school lunches. Now, "normal" is waking up in the middle of the night because she's wailing in her sleep.'

We stared at the near empty carpark for a moment, the street light casting circling shadows of bugs the size of birds. Another cough in the background from Tully. A loud laugh from one of the last punters on the balcony.

'Hold out your hand,' she said.

I held out my hand.

Zoe took a pen out of her purse and wrote on my leg. Her phone number.

'I want you to call me if you ever want to talk about stuff.'

Talk? I was flat-out just trying to breathe right now. 'I won't lose it,' I mumbled.

Zoe smiled. 'I know you won't, that's why I wrote it on your leg, dummy. I can't believe you've still got this stupid thing.' She giggled, plucking the GO FOR IT badge off my jersey. It tumbled off her fingers and down onto the uneven concrete of a car space clearly marked 'RESERVED', and I watched as it spun on its edge briefly, before finally landing on its pin side; print-side up.

There it was.

The message I needed, my whole life, whispering to me from the twinkling drip-pond of car air-con sweat.

Underneath the moonlight.

Go for it.

It was a calling.

Zoe gazed, her sparkling eyes making me question my sanity. 'Whoops,' she said.

How could I possibly deserve to live in a world where people so perfect existed?

She smiled, just the tiniest bit, and I realised there and then, that I was saying goodbye to childhood.

I had to commit. Be a man. I'd been talking such a big game. Now it was time to follow through.

I couldn't think about it too much.

I had to surprise myself.

I just had to go for it.

No hesitation.

So, I went in like the bold swimmer who doesn't dip his toe, leaps blindly in faith, into the pool, temperature unknown. I would kiss Zoe, at all cost.

And just as I leaned in –

She leaned in –

And our teeth collided.

Hard.

Zoe screamed, quickly grasping her mouth.

It took a second for the sting of the enamel wasp-bite to spread like bushfire up the front of my face, from my top front gums, right up through my nose to the spot between my eyebrows.

'What are you doing?' she said, through clasped fingers.

'Why were you leaning forward?' I asked, clutching at my front teeth too.

'I was just trying to pick up your badge.' She was clutching at her front teeth.

Oh my god, have I ruined the gap? My heart started beating, slightly delayed from the dull throb of my pulse that I could now feel under the bridge of my nose. 'I was trying to kiss you.'

'Oh no,' she said.

'I – I'm sorry,' I stuttered. 'I'm sorry I tried to.'

'No, I'm bleeding.' She held up her fore and index fingers, their tips wet with red as though she were about to apply war paint to the face of a warrior.

Then she uttered the one sentence that killed romance quicker than a swift slap squashes a mosquito.

'We need to see a dentist.'

•

It took my eyes a second to adjust under the bright lights of backstage, but I saw what I saw. Ain't no doubt.

Dad and Sonja, in the otherwise unromantic surrounds of a discarded band greenroom. Crushed beer cans strewn across the carpet. Empty bottles of wine upturned into buckets of ice. A discarded guitar string that curled curiously out of the bin like the love child of an earthworm and a slinky.

Dad and Sonja. Their eyes closed, heads touching at the brow, standing in each other's arms as a cheap white pedestal fan provided the soundtrack.

As soon as I walked around the corner they split apart.

'Mike, I was just about to come get you. We should go home soon.' Dad cleared his throat, eyes darting to the ground.

I stood there, hand over mouth. I was hurt, and shocked. 'You were kissing,' I said.

'Mike, it's not what it looks like,' Sonja protested. 'Truly.'

'Mike, let's just go,' Dad said.

'Do you know where Pete is?' Sonja's eyes couldn't meet mine for longer than a second.

I wondered if my mouth would work with my body this tense.

'I think Zoe's hurt her teeth,' I said.

Screw them both.

I know what I saw.

•

'There's no cracking or obvious chipping, so it should be fine, but there's always a chance that the nerve is now dead, so if you notice discolouration, then you need to come see me in the van immediately, OK?'

Zoe nodded, still unable to talk with Dad's hands poking around in her mouth.

I was sitting next to her, both sunken into the old, mismatched velvet sofas of the greenroom. Sonja was putting things back in order. Dad had the front of his dashiki up over his mouth, playing dentist.

'You said you hit it on a bottle mouth?' Dad asked. 'What were you drinking?'

Zoe looked across the greenroom to the rider. 'Ummm. Pepsi,' she said.

Dad nodded. 'Well, make sure you eat some cheese to neutralise the acids, but be honest – did you mix some vodka with that Pepsi?'

'Dad, let it go!' I grumbled next to them. 'We didn't take the stupid vodka.'

Dad whipped his dashiki down and sniffed in front of my mouth. 'Mike, your breath stinks too,' he said.

'Now you know how all your patients feel,' I said.

'Of *alcohol*,' he said.

'Mike.' Sonja was nearby, stacking up chairs. 'You shouldn't be drinking.'

'I shouldn't be drinking?' Hand to my chest, my drama queen coming out. 'Who do you think stole the vodka? Where's your precious little Pete?'

Dad turned to her. 'I knew it was him. I've argued with Solomon all night about that bloody bottle.'

'Jesus, Marvin, they're kids! Am I supposed to keep a chain on him?' Sonja said, slamming the chairs down on the pile with force.

'You're all worried because you've done a shit job of looking after us,' I said.

'Don't talk to us like that, Mike,' Sonja said. 'I understand you're going through a tough time, but there's no need to be so rude.'

'Rude? I'm just being honest! It's pretty obvious you're a bad parent.'

Sonja gasped.

'Mike!' Dad turned to Sonja. 'He doesn't mean it. He's drunk.'

'What you said is very cruel, Mike. I want you to know that.' She picked up her bag. 'I'm going to find Pete.' She walked out the fire-exit and into the carpark.

Dad was death-staring me. 'Get your things. We're going.'

'Why? Why should I get in the car?'

'You're pissed,' he grumbled.

'I'm not pissed!' I yelled. *Man, booze really loosens your tongue.* I started to feel really warm all over.

I reached over the arm of the couch to the small plastic bin with the guitar string curling out of it, and I vomited. It felt so hot, and spicy. Uncontrollable. Wet. When I thought I was done, my stomach had other ideas. Dad was shaking his head as I wiped my weeping, vomit eyes; Zoe, giggling through her tipsy ones.

'I'm just having fun,' I gasped. 'Meanwhile, Mum's ... Mum is where she is and you're kissing other people.'

Dad took a breath. 'Mike, your mother isn't –'

'JUST STOP!'

Zoe jumped in her seat. 'Umm. I might go check on Tully,' she whispered, hopping up off the couch.

'No, don't. Please,' I said, reaching out with an arm, trying to hold onto her hand.

She looked at Dad, thought for a moment, and then sat back down.

I looked up at Dad through wet, bloodshot eyes. 'She's getting better, Dad. You saw her get to the bathroom. After tonight she'll be even better. And soon we won't have to go to that stupid place. I'm sick of it, Dad. Sick of the laps. Sick of the beeps. Sick of the whispers. I'm tired. I'm really tired. Just let me have fun, for once,' I said, wiping the vomit from my mouth with my forearm.

Dad thought a moment. 'I'll let you know when I'm finished packing up.'

He walked through stage door and out into the empty venue. Everything had gone quiet. It was just me and Zoe now.

'I really like you, Zoe,' I said.

Simple as that.

That's all there was to say.

We stared at each other and I remembered the badge. Go for it.

So I slowly leaned over, butterflies ravaging my guts, I closed my eyes, and went for it.

'Mike,' Zoe said.

I stopped.

'Is it my breath?' I held my hand up to my mouth and took a whiff.

Zoe smiled, with that killer gap. 'You've got something on your chin. It's really gross.' She laughed as I mopped it up with my sleeve.

I sat back in the couch and closed my eyes. I could suddenly sleep for days.

Then, a finger on my finger. I opened my eyes and spotted our two pinkies – one brown, one white – touching slightly on the edge of the couch cushion.

Call 000, there are two fingers here about to start a fire.

I looked up at Zoe, our eyes locking.

The carpark door slammed open.

'Oh my god!' Tully stumbled in, her eyes went straight to the small table and chairs next to the rider. 'It's beautiful. So much lace.'

Tully wobbled over to the table and picked up a blue satin bra with a lace trim that was draped over the chair in front of the greenroom mirror.

Tully turned to us, and I quickly sat up straight and pulled my hand away from Zoe's. 'This room stiiiiinks of spew!' She threw the bra on over her baggy tee. 'What were you fighting with Daddy Marvino about?'

'He wanted to go see Mum,' I said.

'Why? What's your mum doing tonight?' Tully asked.

I could feel Zoe's eyes studying me, waiting. 'I think she had a toothache,' I said. Zoe's eyes went to the ground, but I kept mine on Tully. 'Where's Pete?'

'His Mum took him home after she busted us,' Tully said.

'Busted you doing what?' Zoe asked.

Tully slumped onto the couch, right between me and Zoe, and let out a big sigh. 'I think I need to break up with Danny tomorrow.'

She leaned her head on my shoulder, and all three of us sat under fluorescence in the greenroom listening to the sound of a pedestal fan.

•

Dad drove Tully, Zoe and me home. Kids in the back, Dad in the front; a giant, open box of 'Afro Good Times' flyers sitting on the passenger seat.

Nobody said anything the whole ride home.

We drove up the hill past Brindy, and then down the road with the vet that goes around the Reserve, and – just near the top of the hill that we turn down to get to mine and Tully's place – Zoe leaned across and kissed me on the cheek.

A soft, considered kiss that was just long enough to feel the breath from her nose against my skin. That warmth made me shiver.

Out the corner of my eye, I could see her smile, and I started beaming too. Smiling in the night, like the Cheshire cat.

I wound down my window, and gusts of wind swept through the car, sending Dad's flyers up and out in every direction, while he frantically tried to hold them down with his free hand.

'Mike, close that!'

But I didn't close it. I leaned my head out the window, and stared into the night, smiling.

I thought about seeing Mum in the morning.

I couldn't wait to tell her about Zoe.

I wondered whether she'd be proud of me.

And whether she'd remember my name.

CHAPTER EIGHTEEN

SUNDAY, 5TH APRIL 1998

I knew it was late because I'd woken up naturally; a hot, sweaty mess in last night's clothes, my forehead beading, my tongue like dust. A low, dull thud behind my eyes.

It wasn't just the headache, but the feeling. The feeling like I'd done something wrong. The feeling like I'd had a party and the neighbours were mad, except the party was just being myself, and the whole world was my neighbours.

But then a memory blasted through the fog like a ship's horn in the night.

The kiss. A peck.

An orange so big you'd mistake it for the sun, its zest probably shining through the blinds of Mum's hospital room window.

I suddenly felt stronger, and realised that today was the first morning where my downstairs didn't feel the size of a rockmelon. I was on the road to recovery. On the drive to the Dash.

And they don't lie when they say good things come in threes.

I was surveying my shrinking stitches when I found them ...

Three sparse, scraggly hairs, sitting in some kind of pubic Bermuda triangle, just above the base of my penis.

Only three hairs, but those hairs meant more to me than salt means to pepper. I wouldn't have swapped three bars of gold for those three hairs.

I just couldn't believe it. It had finally started. I was becoming a man.

I couldn't stop thinking about Zoe. And last night. And the kiss, even if we'd butted teeth. I had a sudden urge to tell Mum *everything*.

'Does kissing give you hair?' I asked, as we reversed out of our driveway.

Dad shook his head.

'What about this – you know how you have to wash the hair on your head? Do you have to shampoo other hairs on your body?'

'What?' Dad said. He hadn't talked much all morning.

I shot my dad a set of oily eyes. Two could play at that game, I thought. I wouldn't talk to him for the rest of the drive.

We drove past the Reserve, up past the vet clinic, onto City Road, past the school, and towards the hospital.

I stared out the window, and Dad had the air-conditioning on, but I wound my window down anyway. Dad looked at me, then turned the air-conditioning off. He wound his window down too, and shook his head.

I leaned my head almost right out the window and felt the wind thrashing at my hair.

We didn't even bother with the stupid old routine of lapping the nearby streets, trying to nab a freebie. Dad just drove straight into the hospital carpark.

'Finally,' I smirked, as we waited for the boom gates to raise.

'Finally what?' he asked.

'You've finally realised that superstitions aren't real.'

We found a spot immediately, and Dad didn't dare catch my glare as I sat smiling cockily in the passenger seat.

Dad turned the car off, and waited, staring ahead, barely blinking.

'Think of all the time we could've saved,' I said.

When we walked out of the lift on Mum's floor, I went ahead while Dad went looking for doctors. In fact, I'm embarrassed to say that I skipped.

I skipped down the hall, like I was Julie Andrews in *The Sound of Music*.

I couldn't help but let the happiness of Zoe's kiss bubble up and out of me like a champagne bottle on the winner's podium, though to be honest I really couldn't bear the thought of booze right now. I actually looked up this time, as I walked down the hallway, happy to let my eyes take in the sickness around me. The sadness and the sorry of the dying. Not to be smug, but to share my love. To share my oranges.

Oranges for everyone.

I could feel that things were looking up.

Feel Mum getting better. Stronger.

That I was finally growing up.

That this could be my year.

•

The door was closed.

When I arrived at Mum's room, the door was *closed*.

It had never been closed before.

A group of doctors and nurses approached, laughing, and I smiled at them, expecting them to provide some kind of answer, but they stepped around me.

'Excuse me,' I said.

One of the nurses stopped, 'What's going on, dear?'

I recognised her. The nurse that had filled in the day that Gretchen had been away. The one who hadn't bothered to introduce herself.

'My mum was in this room, but the door is closed. Do you know where she is?'

'Oh dear, I'm so sorry, I don't know. She may have been moved to a different room. Are you here with anyone?'

'My dad is here. He's asking the desk,' I said.

'Oh good, well, they'll be able to tell you what's going on, I'm sure.' And then she patted me on the shoulder. Not a light pat. One where her fingers gripped my upper bicep just the tiniest bit.

I watched her walk away and re-join the group of doctors and nurses who had walked past me, and she looked back. Just quickly.

Just quick enough.

'Mike,' I heard, behind me.

It was my favourite face; my favourite other than Mum's, and Zoe's.

'Gretchen, guess what? Zoe kissed me!' I whispered, excitedly. I didn't want Mum to overhear me, wherever she was.

'Mike,' Gretchen said, again. 'I'm so sorry.'

'Don't be sorry. I kissed someone! Well, technically she kissed me, but it still counts, I think.' I didn't mean to brag, but you have to celebrate your wins with your losses.

Gretchen's face kept dropping, draining, suddenly looking sicker than Mum's.

'Mike.' She looked at me, her eyes welling up. She looked tired. Tired like Dad.

'Is it Mum?' I asked, suddenly feeling heavy and light-headed at the same time.

'Mike.' Dad's voice now, behind me.

Standing there, his face almost bizarrely white under his dark black West African skin. His patterned, olive-green shirt that resembled a Magic Eye poster, drooping off his frame. Had he lost weight in a day?

'Your mother,' he said.

I spun around and looked back at Gretchen, and saw that she was crying.

'My mother, what?' I asked, my breath suddenly feeling hot. 'Just tell me.'

But she couldn't.

She just nodded, and hugged me.

She hugged me like a child.

And I smelled her hair.

CHAPTER NINETEEN

'Oh, sorry, Mike, I had to close the door. I just needed a moment, you know?'

Linda was already inside when I opened the door of Mum's room. I closed it behind me. Just me, Linda and Mum. Gretchen and Dad stayed outside, speaking in hushed tones, her arm over his shoulder.

Linda wiped her eyes and dabbed at her nose with a tissue, her trusty handbag unhooked from the crook of her elbow, lying abandoned on the bedside visitor's chair.

'Three generations. Three very different people,' Linda said, pointing between me and Mum, forcing a smile.

I forced a smile back.

I walked forward, slowly, inhaling deeply with each step, the pounding of my pulse now up around my ears again; each cool zing of ice-cold hospital air almost fooling me into thinking I was at the Brindy Shopping Centre, except this zing was masking something.

It had never occurred to me that a person may shit themselves when they die, much less the mum you used to play astrology dice games next to and listen to Bruce Springsteen songs with on a Sunday. They don't teach you that in the movies.

Linda kept dabbing her cheeks, folding her tissue, putting it in her bag, pulling out a different, less-used tissue, and repeating.

Mum was just lying there, the white hospital sheets drawn all the way up to her chin so tightly that I could barely make out her figure below. A tiny part of me wondered whether she was even all there. Was it a fake head and a couple of pillows?

'Pretty obvious why people believe in the human soul, isn't it?' Linda said. 'She's just so blue.'

Blue, still and cold. All machines off. All plans cancelled.

'She's not there,' I nodded.

We both stood there for a moment, staring at Mum; her lips open, exposing her snaggle tooth.

'Married to a dentist for so many years,' Linda said, shaking her head. 'Why she never did something about that damn tooth is beyond me.'

Linda's sniffles were providing the high-hat to the light droning synth of the vented air-conditioning.

'Are you OK?' I asked.

Linda let out a sharp shot of laughter. 'Oh, you know. So many things I would do differently, but what can you do?'

She was shaking now. The tears coming thicker and faster.

'She's got you, Mike. That's the main thing. You're really a very capable young boy, you know? That's all she could have asked for,' Linda said, stuffing her tissue back in to her handbag. 'I just wish she'd fixed that silly tooth, you know?'

She reached out and tweaked Mum's toe, ever so lightly, and then took a big breath in, to compose herself.

She walked close to me, hesitated, then put her arms around me. She stroked my head gently, lovingly. 'You know, I've always wondered what your hair feels like,' she said. Then she gave me a final pat, reached for a cigarette from her handbag, and headed out the door.

And then it was just me and Mum.

I stared around the room that had become her home the past seventeen days. The small table was now cluttered with more cards and flowers. I picked one up and read it:

'Dear Anne, well this is one heck of a way to get off work! The office has just seemed so empty without your laughter these past few weeks –'

I snapped it closed.

Linda's magazine was now folded into the bin.

I turned around to face Mum.

'Hey, it's just us now,' I whispered. 'Just in case this is a joke. In case you're a spy. It's just us.'

Mum didn't move.

'I have so much to tell you,' I said. 'I … that girl, Zoe … she –'

I had to stop.

The air was ice-cold, but I felt so hot in the chest that I almost couldn't breathe.

The sheets were drawn so tightly. I couldn't make out her figure.

I couldn't tell if she still had them.

I reached over her chest, and paused, realising how much my hand was shaking.

I just wanted to know.

Then the door opened, and Dad entered. He could barely look at me.

'Mike.'

He walked over to hug me, but I pushed him off.

'You knew,' I said.

His eyes flared, he shook his head.

'I had no idea.' He was looking me straight in the eye.

'Why did you park in the carpark?'

'Mike, I'm tired –' His bottom lip shaking.

'Why did you park in the fucking carpark?'

'The concert last night. Looking after you. I'm tired too, Mike.' His red eyes didn't lie. His stubble didn't lie. His slumped shoulders didn't lie.

'This is your fucking fault. Your stupid superstition!' I screamed, hitting at his hips and sides with my hands. 'You shouldn't have parked in that stupid carpark!'

Dad scrambled backwards, holding his arms up, avoiding my flailing fists. He ran onto the other side of Mum, so we stood on either side of her.

'You knew,' I said again, louder this time.

'Mike, stop!'

'When did you find out?'

'Mike, I didn't know!'

'You're happy. You're fucking happy. Now you can just live with Sonja, and Pete can be your fucking son, I fucking hate you!' I screamed.

I ran around the bed and went to hit him again, but he wrapped his arms around me. It always surprised me how strong he was.

A Dad.

That's all I had now.

'You should've forced me to get in the car last night,' I said, starting to cry.

'I can't force you to do anything. You're a grown-up, Mike. That's what being a grown-up is,' he said.

And I sank a little bit in his arms.

I stepped away after a moment and walked over to Mum's bedside.

'I kissed someone last night,' I whispered. 'I'm growing up. I feel older now. I'm going to win the Dash, for you. Don't you know we're curing cancer?'

Then I kissed her on the cheek, and she felt cold.

There was a knock on the door, and Gretchen poked her head into the room.

'Sorry, Marvin, there are a few things we need to run over.'

Dad nodded. He looked at me, and took a big breath. 'It's just us now, OK, but we can do this. You can always rely on me for anything, and tell me anything. I'm here for you, OK?'

I nodded, feeling those stupid friggin' tears again on my face. Here were those tears I'd predicted back when I'd seen Skon in all that pain.

'I love you, Mike, and I'm proud of you, and I know you want to compete in the Dobson Dash. I just want to say ... I know you'll be drinking a lot of sports drinks,' he said, with all the seriousness in the world. 'I just need to remind you that those things are very bad for your teeth. You need to eat cheese to neutralise the acids.'

I couldn't help but laugh through my tears.

As if cheese could save the day.

•

Tully was sitting in the waiting room, head in her hands. When she looked up, I could see bright white palm marks pressed into her red cheeks; a channel of tears had etched its way down the sides of her nose, meeting the delta of mucus and dribble in the valley between her nose and lip.

I smiled, lightly, but she looked away.

Tully's mum was reading a *Woman's Day*. She stood up and straightened out her black denim shorts and white singlet. The single tattoos on her left wrist, forearm, and bicep exposed. A duck, a love heart, and the words 'Tully Louise Maxwell'.

'Mike, darl, life's fucked, you know? Pardon my French, but this is just awful,' she said, hugging me.

'How come you guys are here?' I asked, still looking at Tully.

Tully's mum looked around confused, the wet slap of chewed gum between her teeth smacking every second syllable. 'Oh. I think we're supposed to take you home, darl. Your dad's just asked us to do that.'

Tully still wouldn't look at me.

Her mum was still clutching the *Woman's Day*. Most of the front-page real estate belonged to Tiger Lily Hutchence's 'crackpot christening', but a small tile was dedicated to Diana, Princess of Wales. She'd died eight months earlier, in Paris after her driver crashed into the wall of a tunnel trying to avoid paparazzi. Mum and I had been sitting in the food court of Brindy when we heard the news. We were eating a bad Chinese buffet, trying to listen to reporters on the centre's small TVs, as drilling and construction of the Chill Zone happened around us. We went back to Mum's and she spent the whole afternoon crying and I learnt the lyrics to 'Mo Money Mo Problems' by pressing play, writing down some words, rewinding, then pressing play, writing down some words, and so on. Laborious tasks like that were what made me want the internet so bad.

'What's happening with Lady Di?' I asked Tully's Mum.

'Oh, it's just trash. All this talk about a cover-up in the tunnel. I feel for her two boys, honestly, losing their Mum like th —' she stopped mid-sentence like someone had erased her mouth. She looked to the floor. 'Fuck, I'm sorry, Mike. I didn't mean to … you know.' She threw the magazine facedown onto the table.

'It's fine,' I said. 'It's not the only thing we have in common, me and those boys. Apparently, I have some royal lineage too,'

Nobody laughed.

And I realised people were going to treat me a little different from now on.

●　　♦

People expect you to cry in these moments. It makes them feel better. Truth is, I didn't feel much like crying. I didn't feel much like anything, really.

As we drove along City Road, I felt guilty. Guilty because I was relieved. Relieved that I wouldn't have to do that drive again, or smell the plastic of the hospital water cups again, or hear those machines beeping, or walk the hallway with my head down and see all those sick strangers. I wouldn't be called home from Tully's again for 'close calls'. I wouldn't have to spend afternoons watching Mum sleep, and grunt, and choke on her own saliva, and forget my name and yell for no reason. Then, as we drove past Brindy Shopping Centre, I wondered what I must've done to deserve this. I wondered whether karma had been keeping a tab and I'd just gotten one hell of a bill, or whether maybe this wasn't even happening, that it was all a set-up. That the world was full of actors and everyone was playing a prank on me. Then, as we drove along the road that went past the Reserve, I felt an intense sense of rage towards Mum, contemplating how she could've known about a lump in her breast for four months and not done anything about it.

I realised that every one of those days was a lie. Every smile was a lie. Every laugh was a lie. I wondered how she'd slept those four months. I wondered at what point gross negligence of one's own health crosses the border into the land of self-harm or child neglect.

How dare she. How fucking dare she.

I didn't feel much like anything except all of that. If that's something.

'Stop that,' Tully said.

I'd been scratching at the fabric of the car seat with my index finger without realising, and had burnt my nail down to the quick.

'Shame she didn't die next week. It's Good Friday. She would've been back on Sunday!'

No laughs, though.

Tully's mum offered a sympathetic glance in her rear-view mirror, and back to the road.

Tully and I both went back to looking out our respective windows and when we got to Tully's place, Mrs Maxwell made us sandwiches.

•

After lunch, we were sitting on Tully's rumpus room floor, surrounded by stacks of the local newspaper, bowls of rubber bands, and plastic shopping bags.

FERRY DRIVER RECALLS MOTHER'S SCREAMS: 'I WAS JUST FOLLOWING PROCEDURE'

That was the headline of *The Brindy Chronicle*.

'This is fucked. Zoe doesn't deserve this, just like William and Harry don't deserve their mum being talked about in the gossip mags either,' I said.

I folded the paper so the headline was on the inside. The back was visible, showing an advertisement for Vic's Mowing. I wrapped a rubber band around it.

'This isn't gossip, it's news, and you're folding them wrong,' Tully said.

'How am I supposed to fold them? They're newspapers. I mean, I make a great paper plane if you're trying to fly them into people's yards – '

Tully snatched the paper from my hands, re-folded it into thirds, headlines on the outside, then wrapped it in a rubber band and threw it onto the 'done' pile.

'I just don't think Zoe should see that,' I said.

'There are more people in the world than Zoe, Mike.' She glared.

We went back to folding the papers in silence for a bit.

'I bet you're pissed you can't see Danny today,' I said, before I felt a hot sting to my cheek.

I thought I'd been slapped.

Tully grabbed another folded up newspaper from her 'done' pile, and threw it at me. It clocked me right in the neck.

'Hey, what the fuck are you doing?' I reeled backwards.

She threw another paper at me that got me in the stomach.

'Hey, watch it! I've had an operation down there.'

'You didn't tell me! I can't believe you didn't tell me!' She yelled, throwing more papers. I was really dodging them now because that first one really scorched.

I felt a newspaper scone me on the top of my shoulder. I was scuttling around Tully's rumpus room, dodging the headlines, until the edge of the brown couch got me. I tripped over, tumbling backwards and ending up inches away from bashing my head against the glass corner of the sliding door.

I held my hands up as Tully stood over me, daring me to stand up and fight.

'Tully!' Tully's mum yelled from upstairs. 'Phone call!'

Tully paused. The onslaught had stopped.

I was wrong.

As I lowered my arms, I felt another blow come crashing down onto my nose, and I could somehow taste the black-and-white print.

A fully folded copy of *The Brindy Chronicle* had smashed me right in the face.

Tully was panting.

'You had me working this whole time trying to get Zoe to like you, but you just wanted a distraction,' she said.

'A distraction from what?' I asked.

'From your mum. You tried to pretend it wasn't happening.'

'No, I didn't,' I said. 'I like Zoe.'

'It was happening, Mike,' Tully said.

'I didn't know how to tell you,' I said, my nose suddenly trickling with blood.

'Tully!' Tully's mum yelled again. 'It's Danny!'

'I'll be up in a minute!' Tully called back.

'You're just angry because you had to come pick me up instead of going to see Danny.'

Tully's mouth dropped open. 'Mike, I'm angry because you didn't tell me this was happening. How could you not tell me?' Tears rose to the surface of Tully's eyelids, spilling over in translucent lava-lamp blobs, only floating down though, no coming back up. 'And the whole time this awful thing was happening. I could've helped.'

'You could've helped? Helped how? By bitching about Boobs and Danny? By making me eat shit off the ground or steal things for you when all I wanted was a tiny bit of help? Face it, Tully, you don't care about anyone else but yourself.'

Tully's mouth dropped open. 'Why are you turning on me?'

'Go and talk to your boyfriend.'

'Mike, your mum's just died,' she said.

'Tell him what happened last night,' I said. 'Let him know how you've changed.'

'What's that supposed to mean?'

I shrugged. 'You're a slut, Tully. That's what everyone thinks.'

A small whimper jumped from her lips as her eyes turned a brighter red.

'You're awful,' she said.

She walked over to the window and grabbed the phone that was dangling outside.

I watched her for a second, holding my nose, then I walked out the sliding glass door that led to the backyard area, down the little makeshift path to Dad's house, and I walked inside.

Dad still wasn't home.

I grabbed our phone.

It rang, and rang, and then ticked over to a recorded message.

'Hi, you've reached Graham, Denise, Zoe and Georgia! We're the Inghams. Please leave a message, after the beep.'

Beeeeeeeep!

'Hey, umm. It's Mike. I just wanted to say hi to –'

'Haha! That was a fake beep. Here's the real one!' Georgia's voice.

Beep.

I paused. 'Hey, ummm. It's Mike –'

Click. The phone picked up.

'Hello?' the voice was barely decipherable. A woman's voice. Mrs Ingham.

'Oh, I didn't mean to wake you up, I'm sorry,' I said, looking around the room for a clock. Was it really that early?

'Who do you want to speak with?'

'Zoe,' I said.

'If this is a media request, then I ask that you please leave our family alone.'

'Oh, umm … No. My name is Mike,' I said. 'We've met, at the shopping centre? I was very wet. And at the supermarket. You had your shoes on wrong. And again at the dental van. I was eating the peas.'

'Oh, did we?' Mrs Ingham paused. 'I don't remember much these days. But I'm sorry, Zoe's gone to be with her sister.'

'Gone to be with her sister?' I was confused, what did she mean by *with her sister*?

'Where we lost her.' The phone hung up.

Scratching. Scratching in the kitchen. I opened the small French wooden doors to the laundry.

There it was. A stupid little baby crab, in a bucket in the laundry. All tied up. No pincers.

I picked up the crab and ran to the Swamp.

It probably missed its Mum too.

•

Zoe was sitting at the end of the Jetty, her white legs swinging out over the edge, the sparkles of sunlight bouncing across the water creating a moving frame around her.

I cautiously manoeuvred myself down next to her, holding my little crab, and my fragile family jewels. The swelling was going down, but a boy can't be too careful.

'I know why they say drinking's bad,' she said. 'I really vomited a lot this morning. So gross. It just kept coming. There was stuff in there that I haven't eaten in weeks.' She smiled and looked at me.

I wanted to laugh. I did. But god made humans with the laugh and cry buttons right next to each other, and I couldn't trust my aim on a day like this.

'My mum died,' I said.

Zoe's smile fell like a wall painting off a broken hook. She turned back and stared at the water.

'I thought you said she was getting bet—'

'Yeh, I think I was imagining things. I do that sometimes,' I said.

'I don't know what I'd do if I lost my mum,' Zoe said. 'She's only just started coming back to life, you know?'

'Yeh, I don't really know what I'll do. I guess you just keep on living,' I said.

The crab in my hands started moving; even though it had no pincers, it gave a mighty wriggle. I held it out, over the water, just in case.

'I run through what happened out here every single day in my head,' Zoe said, watching the crab wriggle. 'Georgia just wanted the coin so much. That one I picked off your head. From the fountain.'

It's good luck if you throw them in …

'That's what she was doing. I kept pulling it up, just above her reach, and she kept jumping, trying to grab it off me, and she just slipped.'

The memories were holding on to a doorframe, Zoe's voice was dragging them out, pulling with a measured strength.

'Dad went to dive in, but the ferry banked right up to the Jetty. It closed the gap. We kept screaming for the driver to reverse out, but he couldn't figure out what we were saying. He thought he wasn't close enough for us to get on, so he kept revving the engines, you know, just trying to get closer, but he was already on the wood,' Zoe closed her eyes, swallowed hard. 'I just remember the noises. Everyone screaming, and the boat just kept chugging, louder and louder, and that smell of smoke, of exhaust.'

I stared at the water.

The crab was really starting to wriggle now, and I could see the paper towel I'd wrapped around it loosen. I threw the little crab out over the water, and it belly-flopped into the river. It started sinking slowly, when a giant, clear jellyfish floated up to it, and engulfed the whole thing, its blooms pulsing around it, swallowing it.

We sat in awe, the baby crab struggling inside the translucent organ, suspended just below the surface of the water, then gradually falling asleep in its grasp. Just when the crab finally stopped moving, the jellyfish, and the crab, disappeared to the depths of the Swamp.

'Did you see that?' Zoe said.

I did.

'You know cancer is the Latin word for crab?' I said.

'Mike, I'm in your class, and I actually listen. So yes, I know that,' Zoe said.

I laughed.

'This whole time, I had no idea my greatest fear was the thing that could actually beat it,' I said.

Zoe smiled. 'Hey look at us, Adjetey and Adjeley on a jetty watching jellies.'

I looked down at Zoe's hand next to mine. I reached across ever so slightly, and touched her pinky finger with mine. She moved her hand away.

'Mike, about last night,' Zoe said, taking a second to really figure out her words. 'I don't like you like that.'

It hit me like a sledgehammer. I jerked my hand away from hers like she'd told me she was actually made of Irukandji.

'I'm really sorry, Mike. I am. Because I think you're great. But, I'm really ... I'm still so sad, you know?'

My brain was processing each word that went into my ears, just to make sure I was hearing it right.

'You never seem sad,' I said, my heart really sinking. A baby crab of love suffocated by a jellyfish of rejection. 'You're always so cool about everything.'

'So are you, Mike,' she said. 'Maybe that's our problem.'

We stood up and started walking back towards the dirt carpark. When we got to the start of the Jetty, Zoe stopped.

She turned, and we both looked back at the Swamp. At the murky ripples of the river.

Full, and ebbing, and pulsing with life.

'Jump with me,' Zoe said, her eyes staring intently out at the water.

'What?' I said.

'We need to face our fears,' Zoe said.

'But ...'

'But what?' she said.

And then she started running.

Running down the Jetty.

Running towards the Irukandji.

And so I started running too.

Towards my greatest fear.

And we both jumped into the river.

I resurfaced from the water with a splashing gasp, immediately checking my sack for evidence of my balls. Thankfully, I'd protected the area with my legs a bit better this time, so everything felt fine, although I started questioning just how safe 'brackish' water was for 'blackish' testicle wounds.

I was facing the big open bay of the Swamp, the vast expanse of Brindlewood River reaching out in both directions diagonally in front of me, treading water, and looking to my right, waiting for Zoe to resurface, but after a few seconds, she wasn't there.

'Zoe?!' I screamed.

I took a big breath and quickly dived under the water, waving my arms in the hope I'd make contact, and scanning with my eyes, but the water was too murky.

I went back to the surface, puffing frantically, and it was only after the water had drained from my ears that I heard it.

Laughter.

Coming from the Jetty.

I wiped my eyes clear and turned around. There she was.

Zoe Ingham.

As dry as a bowl of Weet-bix with no milk.

Laughing at me.

'You didn't jump,' I said.

'Not in this white T-shirt, no way,' she smiled, pointing to her top. 'I've gotta have dinner with my parents tonight. They'd kill me.'

'Well, congratulations, you got me,' I said.

'Congratulations? I was too scared, Mike. I'm always scared, but you're not. You're never anyone but yourself, and that's what I like about you,' she said. 'Your mum made a really cool human, Mike.'

I couldn't really smile because I was using all my energy to tread water, but I tell you what, my head got so big from that compliment that I probably could've floated without even trying.

'I did it to impress you,' I said, laughing.

'You impressed me way before this, Mike,' she said.

I was feeling on top of the world, but then my smile dropped.

'What's wrong? Have you been stung?' she asked, looking around me for jellyfish.

I shook my head, suddenly scrambling frantically towards the jetty.

'I just remembered there are bullsharks in here!' I said.

And that made Zoe really laugh.

'Oh my god, quick, get out! We need you healthy for the Dash!' She reached out to grab my hand, and then we both lost it, laughing, as she struggled to help me out of the water.

'If that leap was anything to go by, I reckon you're going to win the triple jump for sure,' she said.

I scrambled back onto the Jetty and lay soaked on the wood, under the sun, smiling.

It was one hell of a jump.

I jumped into the Swamp that day, and I fell in love.

And even though she didn't jump, I wondered if Zoe fell a bit too.

Just a bit.

CHAPTER TWENTY

MONDAY, 6TH APRIL 1998

It's not the passing of loved ones that gets you down. It's the space people give you. All you do is think, and that really kills your spirit; thinking about the first time Mum showed me how to walk home down the Goat Track, or the day she'd packed her little black leather couch into the big moving van and moved to her apartment. All the nights spent listening to Bruce Springsteen, all the games of 'Stars and Dice'.

So much time to think.

The only silver lining is that you get a few days off school, not that I'd been there much lately. Weirdly I was starting to miss Ms Harris' clopping heels and Mr Bortey's lame jokes. Dad took the days off too, but he spent most of the time on the phone, and running errands. Dying requires a surprising amount of work.

Tully wasn't around either, so it wasn't very fun. Every day I wrote the word 'SORRY' on a small origami square of paper, and slid it through Tully's bedroom window, but every morning I woke up to a small origami square of paper sitting scrunched up on our front lawn. By Wednesday, Tully had closed her window.

I spent my days watching Kerri-Anne Kennerly entertain pensioners, and the loveable TV chef, Huey, cook whatever dish needed three kilos of butter. I spent a lot of time thinking about Zoe too, and occasionally I'd stare at our phone hanging on the wall and I'd try to make it ring with my mind. Sometimes hoping to hear from Zoe, other times wishing that Mum would have a message for me on the other end. Just something short and simple.

I'm in St Petersburg. They're coming to get you. One day.

My groin was almost completely back to normal, and I counted down the days to the Dobson Dash. I'd get to see Zoe, I'd get to compete, and I'd get to win.

We were running to cure cancer. Better late than never.

•

By Wednesday, I'd walked down to the cricket oval at the Reserve a few times, and I'd practiced sprints – running until I couldn't breathe anymore, until the hot autumn air buzzed painfully in my lungs like tear gas, and the sun scorched my forehead like a grill burning cheese on toast.

When I wasn't running, then it felt like the hour hand was crawling around the clock, and that's no way to train for a race.

Dad and I would sit at home, barely speaking. I would be watching him from the couch, poking away at my nuggets and chips, in front of the TV, wondering when he was planning to touch the semolina and stew he'd served himself. But he always just seemed to be sitting on the stairs, phone to his ear, delivering bad news to people in his little black address book.

'Hello, it's Marvin Amon, could I speak to Florence Bartley please? Oh. Oh, OK. The same Florence Bartley that used to work at the bank? Oh. Well, I'm very sorry to hear that.' Then he would listen. 'Oh no, I had bad news also, so it's good that she doesn't hear it. I mean, it's not good, obviously. An old friend of hers has passed away too, but I'm very sorry for your loss.'

Dad would hang up, and turn the page.

I'd feel down, and change the channel.

'What's the name of your Year Eight co-ordinator?' Dad asked.

'Mr Bortey,' I said, distracted by the 2pm episode of *The Teletubbies*. I honestly had no idea what those blobby freaks were talking about, but gosh damn I could not look away.

'Thank you,' Dad said, the sound of phone directory pages being rifled, catching my ear.

I snapped out of my Teletubbie tele-bubble. Dad was flipping through the Yellow Pages phone directory. 'Why?' I asked, suddenly alarmed.

Dad stood up and started dialing a number into the phone. He waited, then after a moment, 'Hello, I'd like to speak to Mr –'

Click.

Silence.

He looked into the phone's handset and then up, to find me, standing by the phone socket on the wall, its plug dangling loosely from my fist.

'Mike, what are you doing? I'm using the phone –'

'Don't. You. Dare.' I said, my fist clenching tightly around the phone's cord.

Dad sighed. 'Your teachers need to know, Mike.' One side of his button-up shirt was untucked out of his old light blue jeans. No shoes. His usually-well-rounded afro looked scrappy.

'So they can treat me different to everyone else?' My eyebrow cocked.

'No. They just need to know …' He was searching for the right words, so I finished off his sentence.

'So they can treat me different.'

Dad's shoulders slunk. 'Being treated different isn't a bad thing, Mike. These are extraordinary circumstances.'

I paused a moment, then nodded. I plugged the cord back into the wall.

'Thank you,' Dad said. He checked for a ringtone on the phone again, and started to dial.

'Just know,' I stepped towards him, as he cocked the handset between his shoulder and ear. 'That if you call the school right now, before the holidays, before I get to be a normal kid one last time and run the Dash, then I'm going to call my friend Dot at the radio studio. I'm going to tell her everything. That my dad, Dr Amon, the school dentist, makes me put those posters up all over town. That he always tells me how much the police are fucking bastards. That after going on the radio and saying fishing is more important that the lives of our children, he then forced me onto the Jetty at midnight that very night, and I ended up almost losing my testicles, because of his negligence.'

Dad's jaw was clenched so tight I thought he might need to check his own teeth after this.

'Oh, and I'll also tell everyone that I put my dick in the dental hose thing.'

Dad's shoulders slumped. 'Jesus, Mike, you didn't need to add that last bit.'

'Athletics is the only oranges I have. That, and seeing Zoe.'

I pretended to give him a karate chop, and he just stood there. Then, eventually, he sighed. 'It's good to see your mum is still with us.'

He hung up the handset, and went into the kitchen to reheat his stew.

•

THURSDAY, 9TH APRIL 1998

Finally, Thursday – the day of the Dash – arrived. I hopped so excitedly out of bed that officials could've considered it a practice jump. I'd been off school for four days and I was definitely starting to get over being at home. Turns out you get addicted to the rush of outsmarting bullies like Skon every day. Skydivers and bungee-jumpers would save a lot more money if they replaced expensive extreme sports with just being a dork.

Dad knocked on my bedroom door. I whipped it open, and shocked him with the sprightly grin on my face. He looked scruffy and tired; his stocky but lean, middle-aged, Ghanaian frame being held together by a pair of old blue Kmart undies. His rich, dark skin shining in the morning light, beaming through my bedroom window.

'Oh, I was about to wake you up,' he mumbled.

'Wow, you really don't have much hair on you,' I said, genuinely intrigued. It was the first time I'd really noticed.

'Mike, you need to get ready. We're going soon,' he said.

'Sure thing, skinbag!' I said, all chipper-and-that.

'What?' He said, confused.

'Ha! You're such an old man.'

I closed my bedroom door and started my ritual.

It went like this: bike pants, followed by my navy-blue Brindlewood State High shorts. Deodorant. Then nice, thick, white shin-high sports socks. I donned my navy and maroon

Brindlewood High athletics singlet, followed by our more casual polo sports shirt. Then, I whacked my old pair of warm-up sneakers on, followed by a Brindy High baseball cap.

There was one last thing though.

I scurried around the pile of dirty clothes that I had sitting in my bedroom corner, and found the shirt I'd been kicking around in a few days earlier. I took what I needed and stood in front of my wardrobe mirror.

The badge. It read, GO FOR IT, and I promised myself I would. I would 'go for it' no matter what it took. I felt good. For the first time in a while, I felt happy.

Dad knocked again. 'Mike, we need to leave,' he called through the door.

'Ready!' I yelled back.

And I was.

I was ready.

I was ready to win.

Ready to win for Mum, and for Georgia, and for Zoe, and for me.

I opened the door.

'Gee, you're looking a bit fancy for work,' I said, picking up my bag and walking past him.

Dad was in a full black suit, complete with black tie, and even a white flower attached to his pocket. 'What are you doing? You're not ready. You need to get ready.'

I kept strutting. 'Gee, I know you're not quite as encouraging as Mum, but you can at least appreciate me wanting to feel and look good before a competition. Now – I never thought I'd say this but – let's go to school!'

I was smiling.

Dad wasn't.

He looked awkward.

'Mike, we're not going to school today,' he said, quietly. 'Today is the funeral.'

He was right. I wasn't ready.

•

The problem with funeral homes is that they're designed for old people. The colour schemes, the coffee, the biscuits – they feel old. But most of their customers are old. So, really, they're right. I'm the wrong one. Shame on me for being a kid.

We took Mum to the Mt Kartha Memorial Centre, at the base of the mountain, on Dad's side of town.

Outside, there were gardens, lush, but manicured, with wooden two-seater park benches spaced evenly around a sprouting fountain, which would've been nice if people did literally anything other than sit and be sad on them. In my head I saw a woman in a cream suit, walking around a bare block of land, with a group of hard-hatted tradies in tow, saying things like, 'OK, now make sure the seats under the pergola aren't facing west; tear-drenched cheeks look awful under sunset.'

The building itself looked like it would've belonged on the junior campus of Brindy High. An old orange-brick number, with a light green A-frame roof that poked so disproportionately high in the middle that I wondered if the deceased were meant to scale their own way up it to heaven.

There was a small meeting area out front with tables of refreshments, where Dad and I said hello to a lot of people that we both only vaguely remembered. There was coffee and tea, and water, and a selection of soft drinks. I was pouring myself a creaming soda.

'Creaming soda, huh?' Dad said.

'Cream's healthy, right?' I said.

Dad shook his head. He handed me a small plastic packet of cheddar that was sitting in a box next to some dry crackers.

'You know what to do,' he said.

Everyone commented on how 'sharp' I looked in my suit, but the truth was that this was the first time I'd ever worn one. I'd borrowed one of Dad's ties, and Dad had gotten a suit jacket off Sonja, who had taken it from Pete's wardrobe.

As the ceremony commenced, we bumped into Kenny just outside the building.

'Good day, Mike,' he said, 'Looking like a scholar, I see. How good. Such unfortunate circumstances. I'm very sorry.'

I looked to his lap. There it was, the ship in a bottle. 'You brought the ship.'

He looked at it. 'Oh, yes. Well, really, this was hers,' he said.

'When did your mother start liking ships and bottles?' Dad whispered.

'Kenny, this is my dad,' I said, feeling awkward knowing that they'd never really spoken before. I hoped Mum's funeral would be the only time that would ever happen.

All three of us walked towards the entrance to the funeral home.

'Mike, my father passed away when I was only ten years old. His death taught me how to be a man. This will be the most difficult yet defining event in your life. Don't be afraid. Don't let emotions control your decisions. When my father died, I realised that –'

'Thanks, Kenny,' I said.

We walked on, Kenny trailing behind us.

'Mike, give me the strength to deal with that man over the next two hours,' Dad whispered. 'He is as tolerable as acid.'

I whipped out the square of cheese. 'You need this, Dad?'

A guilty smile in a funeral home. I slapped Dad on the back.

A shocking smash cut through the sombre hush. Behind us.

It was Kenny. 'No!'

Shards of glass littered the floor. The ship in a bottle was no longer a ship, nor was it in bottle.

Dad and I knelt down, risking our fingertips to clean up the mess.

Big chunks. Little chunks. Long chunks. Flat chunks. All going into my cupped palm.

'Don't cut yourself, Mike. We need to give that jacket back.'

Little chunk. Little chunk. Piece that looks like a sail. Big chunk. Stern. Stick that could've been a mast. Ring. Long Chunk. Little –

Ring?

I stopped. Sitting in the middle of my hand. A silver ring. Tiny diamonds lining its shoulders, flanking a shiny centre stone that was so dazzling it could've guided ships to shore.

'No, Mike,' Kenny wheeled forward, crunching across broken glass. 'Please, give me that.'

I looked at Dad. He was sweeping up shards with the side of his palm now, the world's most dare-devilish dustpan and brush.

I put the ring into Kenny's top pocket, and patted it.

'Thank you,' he said, and wheeled on.

During the ceremony, I sat in the long bench seating, staring at the fern-green walls, or looking around at the people crying, wondering who most of them were. I was seated with Linda and Dad on my left, and Uncle Greg on my right. At one point, during the speeches, Greg leaned over to me and whispered.

'Mike! Check it out.' He held out a small postcard with a picture of the guards out front of Buckingham Palace. 'I told you she'd write back.'

'Who'd write back?' I asked.

'The Queen, Mike. She sent me here.'

I took the card.

'Dear Greg, thank you for your letters. Everything is fine here. Be good to your mother, From Lizzie'

And I'll be damned if I hadn't seen the same handwriting on a few of my birthday cards over the years ...

Most of the ceremony was a blur.

'We call on you now to say goodbye to Anne Mary Amon, before we close the casket,' the funeral director said, her beige suit swapped for black today, though she still wore the blonde shoulder-length perm I'd imagined.

Various people took the opportunity to look at Mum.

Linda and Dad stood up and walked over to the open casket, whispering things, and shedding tears.

When Dad arrived back at our pew, he sat back down next to me. 'Are you going to say goodbye?' he asked.

I shook my head.

'You should, Mike. This is your last chance.'

'I don't want to,' I said.

'Why not?' he asked.

If I don't see her with my eyes, there's still a chance that it's not real. That none of this is real.

In the hospital we'd been all alone, no onlookers, she could have been asleep. Here, everyone was watching, staring. *Looking* at me.

'Mike, you should say goodbye to –'

I didn't let him finish. I just nodded, stood up, and started walking to the end of the pew, towards the aisle, except when I got to the end, instead of turning right towards Mum and her coffin, I turned left. Left towards the exit.

'Mike!' Dad shout-whispered.

I started walking faster.

'Mike, the ceremony's not finished!' Dad yelled across the room at me, as people started turning and watching me walk out.

I didn't turn back, I just kept walking, faster and faster.

'Where are you going, Mike?' Kenny asked, wheeling past me towards the front, face and beard damp, ring in hand, ready to say goodbye.

But that made me go faster.

I started running.

Running out of the big suburban block that housed the funeral home, out onto the road.

Running down from the vet, past Dad's house. Running right through the Reserve and across the cricket oval.

Running along the boardwalk that framed the north edge of the Swamp, past the Jetty where Georgia fell in, and where me and Zoe faced our fears.

Running over the little wooden bridge that crossed the Creek.

I ran up the Goat Track as quickly as I could, finally making it out of the Reserve and across the road to Brindy Shopping Centre.

Ran through the Chill Zone and past the fountain, under the watchful eye of the gods.

Ran out along main roads, and service lanes, and back streets of Brindlewood East, past Mum's apartment and the radio studios that were killing our women.

I didn't stop running until I got to The Showgrounds.

I ran for an hour, until my face leaked sweat and my cheeks roasted in the midday sun.

At one point, I took off the small round badge I had on my tie, and ran with it in my hand, looking at it any time I thought about stopping.

GO FOR IT.

So I did.

I ran.

Until I couldn't run anymore.

And the whole time I didn't cry.

Four months later I would get a letter from my mum's friend, Siobhan, telling me how she'd wept, spying me through the crowd at the funeral, introducing myself to Mum's old friends, smiling and putting on a show. She told me I didn't need to act so macho like that, hiding my tears from strangers.

It really made me mad. I wasn't hiding my tears from strangers. I was hiding them from *life itself*. I've heard it has a way of kicking you when you're down.

CHAPTER TWENTY-ONE

The Brindy Show smelled like a pet shop. The combination of saw dust, and animal droppings, and woodchips and hay, met with hamburgers and hot dogs, and candy and chocolate. A shoulder to bump at every step. Lost toddlers bawling. Cow shit. So much cow shit. Parents at breaking point. A sneeze. A cough. A ding. A bark. The squeal of a girl on the Gravitron. The green-faced silence of the boy next to her, who bit off more than he could chew.

I'd run through it all to get to the Dash.

'You're too late,' Mr Bortey said. Words like a dagger.

I collapsed onto the blue tartan run-up lane that led to the triple jump pit.

'No … please … you don't understand,' I was gasping desperately for air in between each word.

Mr Bortey squatted down and put his hand on my shoulder.

'Mike, you can't be absent from training for two weeks and expect to just walk back into the team. That's just not how life works. Skon jumped in the triple. I'm sorry.'

'Please, I've been sick,' I said.

'Then you probably shouldn't exert yourself, Mike.' He patted me on the arm and stood up. 'All the events have happened already, anyway. The only thing left is the relay, and I've given your spot to Gabe McCormack.'

I dropped to my knees and started begging. 'Please, Mr Bortey, I need to run. I really need this.'

'And I needed a story on my desk by the last day of term, and it's the last day of term, so even if there was a place in the relay team, it wouldn't be going to you.'

He went to turn and walk away, and I just felt my whole life slipping away. My world was collapsing.

'What about this,' I said. 'What about a story about a little kid, who just wants a girl to like him. And he doesn't think she likes him. And then his mum gets sick, and she goes to hospital. And she's dying. It's really obvious she's dying. But he just keeps pretending it's not happening, because he doesn't want to believe that something that bad could happen. And the girl he likes, she goes out with him. They go on a date. And on the date, the boy's dad calls him and tells him he needs to see his mum. It'll be the last time he'll ever see her. But he doesn't want to go, because he loves the girl too much. He really loves this girl. She's the only thing that makes him happy anymore, because his life has gotten so cloudy. But the next time he visits his mum in hospital she's not alive anymore. And the boy feels really bad. Because he kicked a crab, just like Hercules, but the crab didn't fly into space, it just flew out of the hospital, and the boy isn't Hercules. He's just a stupid little boy who misses his mum. And he feels like he's to blame, because when the mum was looking at all the treatment options, and they said they might cut off her boobs, the mum said she didn't want that to happen, and the boy – the boy thought, "Yeh, that's right. Don't let them do that to you. Because if they do that …"'

Tears arrived in my eyes, destined for the funeral, but fashionably late.

'… because if they take away your breasts, you won't be a woman. And now the boy feels really bad. So very, very bad. Because she'd be a woman no matter what. She was a mum. The best mum in the whole world.' I'd never felt so desperate before, kneeling there, begging for a chance.

'That's my story,' I said.

Mr Bortey took a handkerchief from his back pocket and dabbed the corners of his eyes, and sniffed, lightly. He cleared his throat.

'You said your mum went to hospital when we did the trials.'

'Seventeen days ago,' I said.

'Something like that. How is she?'

I thought about it all, as I kneeled on the tartan, staring up at Coach, watching the clouds float past, and the birds circle above us.

I thought about the way I felt whenever I saw the little gap in Zoe's front teef.

I thought about the lights of the emergency room and the constant beeping of machines every time we visited Mum.

And I thought about the tray of chicken nuggets defrosting on Dad's kitchen bench every night, and the unfinished game of 'Stars and Dice' sitting on Mum's coffee table, waiting for her fate to finally be dealt.

'It was just a bug,' I said, finally. 'She's fine.'

Mr Bortey smiled, and gave his eyes one final dab with his hanky. 'See? You need to look after yourself, otherwise these things can run you down.' He patted me on the back. 'That was a good story, Mike,' he said. 'I'll give you a pass, but you still can't run. I'm sorry.' Then he walked back to the centre of the oval, to oversee all the action of the Brindy Schools Cup.

I couldn't say anything at that point. I just collapsed back onto the ground, my eyes closed, panting.

Around me, various Year Eight triple jumpers wearing different school uniforms were packing up their shoes and icing up their sore spots.

Skon was slapping people on the back, and joking around. He wore the grin of a winner as he took off his socks to change into the shoes he wore for sprinting.

I unpinned the badge Zoe had given me, and just stared at it, remembering that day under the Bridge, when I thought the words printed on it meant something.

I felt so tired. I couldn't do it. I flung it away, onto the ground. That's when I heard the scream.

'FARRRRK!'

'Skon, no swearing!' Mr Bortey said.

But Skon had every right to swear.

He grasped his ankle, almost white in the face at the sight of an inch-long badge pin sticking right into his foot. He fell to the ground.

Mr Bortey rushed over and held Skon's leg up. The words GO FOR IT, stuck right into the sole of his foot.

'Get it out!' Skon screamed.

I lay watching on, quiet, as Mr Bortey raced around for medical assistance.

The school nurse arrived and crouched down next to Skon with a first-aid kit.

Zoe and Tully came down from the grandstand and stood near the commotion while the nurse disinfected the wound, and bound up Skon's foot.

'You need to recover,' I overheard the nurse saying.

'I can still run the relay!' Skon was yelling.

'Listen to the nurse,' Mr Bortey said.

Zoe and Mr Bortey helped Skon struggle to his feet, and then he tried to step on it, and he buckled again immediately.

'I'm sorry, Skon. We need to replace you,' Mr Bortey said.

And suddenly my hand was up.

Lying there on the tartan, exhausted.

'I can run!' I said.

Tully turned and stared at me.

'My heart's telling you to piss off, Mike,' she said, ice-cold. 'But my hair's telling me to forgive you.' She ripped her headband off, and her curly blonde hair flopped out onto her shoulders with a width that matched her forgiving smile. 'Can you actually run though? With your twisted "you know what"?'

'I can run!' I said again.

'Are you sure?' Zoe asked.

I looked Zoe right in her green eyes, like I was looking for the edge of the universe, and I nodded, then got to my feet.

Of course, I couldn't run.

Not after sprinting across town.

My balls were on fire.

I could barely walk.

'I can run,' I said.

•

I didn't have time to get changed. I was running in my funeral pants, rolled up above my knees so that they didn't get in my way.

I put my hand in the back pocket and immediately felt the goo, the grease.

The cheese.

I'd run across town with it grinding against my posterior and it had now almost completely liquified. When I pulled my hand out of my pocket, it looked oilier than an eighties sun-tanner.

'Good luck, Mike,' Moses Matakefu strode past in his pristine Sunshine River School athletics uniform.

'Thanks, Moses,' I said, trying to wipe my hands on my funeral pants.

'Nah, cuz, I should be thanking you. I needed to provide an example of my abilities by providing a story for my scholarship application. So I submitted a story about a certain farting life-saver,' Moses giggled. 'I provided them with an example of my ability to rub your name out and replace it with mine. Cheers, sole!'

I couldn't help but smile. At least someone had appreciated my genius.

We shook hands.

'Oh, gross, what the hell is that?' Moses whined, yanking his hand away, as though I'd forced him to hold a toad. He held it up to the light and the sun glistened off it.

'It's just cheese,' I said.

He looked at me suss, furiously wiping his hand on his shirt. 'It's all slippery,' he said.

Behind me, Sonja's Pete walked towards his start. He looked shaky. A ghost of the cocky athlete I'd seen the Saturday before, he belched out a loud, honking, wet cough.

'You sick, Pete?' I asked. 'You should get some rest.'

He pointed to his throat. 'Your friend gave me her cold,' he croaked. 'It's all up in my head.' He kept opening and closing his jaw, like he were trying to make his ears pop on a plane.

All the racers were in place. Down the opposite end of the 100m track, at the finishing line, I could see Zoe and Tully, shaking out their limbs to stay warm. They hugged.

In front of me, ready to run second, Gabe McCormack turned around. 'Do you want to hug too?'

'Sure,' I said.

Hugs all round.

I stood behind Gabe and looked up to my right. In the distance was the hospital, and I imagined Gretchen standing at one of those windows. Trying to find me. Hoping I could do what I promised.

I was here to beat cancer.

I was running for Mum.

I was picking all the oranges.

When the gun went off, it was like I woke up from a dream, the cheers from the grandstand hitting me head-on, like a wave that tailgates the one you ducked under.

Zoe was our first runner. When the announcer had said that she'd be leading the way for the Brindy High Harriers, it felt like the whole city erupted. Everyone knew Zoe now, after what had happened. She screamed out of the blocks, our shiny magenta relay baton flashing past her calves as she sprinted towards Gabe and me with ferocity and fire. She had a determination that you only ever saw in the eyes of Hollywood heroes, and the stadium's cheers matched the explosions they were always running from.

Zoe crossed the line first, handing the baton off to Gabe McCormack, and then flopped onto the track behind me, dry-coughing and clutching for breaths.

'You killed it,' I said.

'It killed me,' she panted, her face matching the red of her hair.

Gabe had set off on his usual steadfast shuffle and had been caught in a flash. We were now running second, then third, then fourth, then fifth.

'Come on, Gabe!' Zoe screamed.

'COME ON, GABE!' I backed up.

'Copycat,' she smiled, and I wondered how I'd run on two sticks of jelly.

Gabe had slid back to sixth now, calmly holding the baton up for Tully.

'Fucking get here, Gabriel!' She was screaming at him. 'Don't you fucking slow down!'

It was definitely Tully, but she looked different. Something not quite right.

She was standing right next to Boobs of Brindle Grammar and Brindy Bus Stop fame. Tully's face was like a pitbull's, staring fiercely at the approaching Gabe.

'What's Tully wearing?' I asked Zoe, who was upright now, standing right over my shoulder.

I took a long hard look, as Tully beckoned for Gabe to get the baton to her, the lace trim of a blue, satin bra poking out the top and sides of her athletics singlet.

'Wait – is that Serwaa's bra?' I said. 'From the concert?'

Zoe nodded, squinting harder to see. 'Yeh, but what's in it?'

Tully received the baton, just after Boobs. We were running eighth. Last.

Tully started charging towards me and Zoe, her chest heaving, and wobbling, with each bound.

'Where did Tully get those boobs from?' Zoe asked.

'A storeroom at the hospital,' I said. At least she was putting my thievery to good use. She was screaming towards us, jellyfish bobbling.

Bouncing out of control.

And then they bounced right out. Two crystal clear jellyfish bobbled up over the lip of Tully's singlet neck, and almost hit her square in the chin as they flew from her top and out, bouncing each and every way onto the track.

It was like she didn't even notice; she just kept running, that look of determination on her face as she did everything she could to match, and finally catch, Boobs with only ten metres to go. She'd only clawed back one spot, but it was the most important spot.

We were coming seventh. Second last.

Sixth in line to the throne.

Ten metres to me.

'COME ON, Tully! Run!' I heard Zoe scream. 'We can beat this!'

Beat this.

I thought about Mum. Whether they were burning her yet. What her face would look like as it was swallowed by fire. Reduced to a pile of ash. Her hair, burnt. Her skin, burnt. Her smile, burnt. Her snaggle tooth, the only thing left, waiting to be crushed by a crematorium technician in the aftermath, like Dad with his chillies in the mortar and pestle.

We weren't beating 'them'. We were beating 'this'. The thing that gives cancer to vegetarians who don't drink. The thing that drags girls under boats and feeds the ice-cream in their stomach to mud crabs.

I saw my competition on their marks to the left of me: Moses from Sunshine, Gus Hasty from GW Lutheran College, and next to me, in lane three, was Tully's Danny.

'How does it feel, Mike? Knowing my dad pays your school fees?' Danny whispered, showing off post-braces perfection with

291

a smug grin, his brown fringe hanging just low enough to clip his eyebrows.

'He also pays for you to not live with him, Danny,' I replied. 'How does that feel?'

To my right were four more boys. I saw Pete, Sonja's son, standing four lanes over, in lane eight. He looked uncomfortable, standing with his head cocked to the left, bouncing up and down like he was draining water.

'You been swimming, Pete?' I asked, cupping my mouth so that the jibe would carry across the lanes.

'Swimming in glory,' he smirked. Then he coughed, real loud, real wet again.

'Don't think about him, Mike,' Zoe encouraged 'He's fast, but you're smart.'

Was I?

I'd got my dick stuck in a dental vacuum.

I'd made a homemade merkin from my curly cut-offs.

I'd written a story about a lifesaver who does mouth-to-mouth with his butt.

Maybe I wasn't smart. But I was determined to win. I knew that.

Out in the eighth lane, Pete was the first of the final runners to receive the baton, and made his usual strides ahead, except he seemed shaky. Wobbly. He took about five healthy strides forward, but he started leaning, completely off balance, like how the whole world must look to the Tower of Pisa. He kept running and kept leaning, and eventually crashed all the way into the jump sandpit that ran adjacent.

I'm fifth in line to the throne.

I was waiting for Tully, waiting for Tully, waiting for –

And then a sharp noise to my side.

Clinking like an empty vodka bottle.

I looked to my left. Lane one. Moses. He'd dropped the baton.

'The damn cheese!' He screamed. 'My hands are so oily!'

Fourth in line to the throne.

Pete was lying in a sandpit out to the side, and Moses had dropped his chances.

Tully handed me the baton, and I was ready – ready to be the greatest. Ready for the papers. Ready to beat this.

Then I took my first step and squealed.

I couldn't believe the pain. I thought maybe someone had put a crab in my pants because I literally buckled over.

'Come on, Mike, you fucking pussy!' Skon barked from the grassy hill beside the grandstand, his foot bandaged in white.

I was limping. I had to grab my scrotum. I hobbled pathetically, with one hand clutching the baton and the other hand clutching *my* baton.

I was Alanis Morissette. One hand in my pocket, the other hand was running a relay.

I was running for Mum, and I was losing. I pushed through the pain, hobbling past the twenty- and thirty-metre marks, the cords in my neck flexing between my jaw and shoulders like the strings of a double bass.

I could hear families and classmates cheering as other racers caught up to me, and I felt like a loser, as I held the two runners behind me at bay, but saw the three leading racers streaking even further ahead.

'Get 'em, Mike, you big slut!' Tully screamed.

And I smiled. I smiled as I ran.

And then something happened that made me wonder whether there actually is a god.

It happened to Phillip first. He was from Mt Kartha Private School. He was in lane six, two over from me, about ten metres ahead of the pack when he got hit. At first, I thought bombs had been dropped, the way he went down.

A jet-black missile, coming straight out of the sky, aimed directly at poor Phillip's head. This missile sconed him fair dinkum in the back of the neck and poor Phillip dropped like a sack of shit. He squealed and fell across the lane next to him, which made the guy running third, Terrence Martin from Grammar, topple over him, falling in a body-folding heap right into the second lane up ahead.

The whole debacle caused the boy running fourth, Gus Hasty, to scream. He stopped dead in his tracks, and started crouching in fear.

But I kept running. Hobbling. Past Gus who had started ducking, scared about how he might meet his own fate.

Third in line.

Danny, was running first, and took a quick glance behind himself to measure his lead. He saw bodies down, Gus screaming, and me hobbling towards him like I had a firework in my crotch.

'What the fuck –' was all he managed.

The speed it came down at was too fierce. It was like a shotput being dropped from a plane.

Danny was facing us, so he saw it. His fate. Another missile. Black. It struck him straight in the face, and then careered directly into Tully's other fake breast that was lying on the blue tarmac of the running track.

I'd seen the debris explode off Danny's face, and then the ground.

It was feathers.

The missiles weren't missiles.

They were birds.

The blue track. Tully's clear fake boobs.

The track was water. They were catching jellyfish.

'Run, Mike!' I heard Zoe scream.

'Come on, skinbag!' Skon was shouting from the hill.

'You can do it, fuckchops!' Tully was yelling behind me.

Even Mr Bortey was slamming his hands together; thrusting his fists from the sidelines.

As I reached the twenty-metre mark, and then the fifteen-metre mark, I felt dampness in my shorts and I realised that I was probably bleeding. I didn't care.

I had three bodies lying directly in my path, with about eleven metres between me and the line.

Eleven metres. My PB.

I could hear the cheers.

I could see the line.

I had a chance.

All I had to do was do what I did best.

What I'd been training my whole life to do.

I triple jumped.

Planting my left foot in front of Phillip's face, his body sprawled right across my lane, I 'hopped' up and over him like he were nothing more than a stone-filled hopscotch square.

My left foot came down again, between Phillip and Terrence, who was grabbing his nastily grazed thigh from his fall. I launched off my left foot, 'stepping' over Terrence, sailing gloriously through the air with my leading leg at a perfect 90-degree bend, landing on my right foot just in front of Danny, who was desperately trying to crawl back to his feet, scrambling the final five metres after being slogged by a diving bird.

With all my strength, and the cheers from the crowd – and I swear Mum was watching from somewhere, wherever – I 'jumped' over Danny, doing a full-blown bicycle kick through the sky, before finally landing, stretching every muscle in my body, and crashing down onto the tartan.

As the whole city cheered me on. I'd made it.

I'd cured cancer.

•

'Ten centimetres, Mum. Ten centimetres. Can you believe it?'

I was standing at the fountain of Brindy Shopping Centre, a coin in my hand, poised to flick. 'That's how far away I was from the finish line.'

The truth is, you don't just make personal bests by wishing for them.

The truth is, I'd hopped heroically over Phillip, I'd stepped graciously over Terrance, and with everything in my tank, I'd jumped over Danny, and I'd landed perfectly. It was just ten centimetres short of the finish line.

I think I was in shock. My eyes were closed, and I'd heard all the cheers, and then I heard footsteps overtake me as the trailing runners ran past, and the fallen athletes either ran or crawled across the line.

When I opened my eyes, I realised it was just me.

Last.

Ten stupid centimetres from the finish line.

The team from Mount St Catherine's College ended up winning. They were raising money for Red Nose Day, which was good, I guess. I didn't really understand what Red Nose Day was for, but I still respected it.

'You should've seen it, Mum. Everyone laughed, and all my teammates ran down and jumped on me,' I said, feeling a bit bummed that I was talking to a fountain instead of the real deal. But it was better than nothing. 'Skon really gave me a hell of a dead arm, and called me a bunch of names, but that's just him. He's an idiot.'

'You're not talking about me, are you?' I spun around to see Tully, walking towards me. 'You're the bozo who can't jump eleven metres yet.'

I looked up through the eye of the gods, and I flicked my coin into the fountain.

'What did you wish for?'

'Nothing,' I replied.

'I bet your wish is over there,' Tully said, and pointed to Zoe, who was sitting on a bench in the Chill Zone next to Skon, who still had his white bandage wrapped around his foot, a set of crutches leaning against his thighs.

'I hate how well you know me,' I said. 'What happened with Danny?'

'Danny's not coming,' Tully said. 'After he saw what happened at the Brindy Schools Cup, he said he can't respect people who are so superficial.'

'What does superficial mean?' I asked.

'I don't know!' She said. 'He said his dad's a plastic surgeon and he thought that was the only reason why I was trying to get with him.'

'Serious?' I asked.

'Serious,' she said. 'I can't believe my taxes help pay for his education.'

The food court was absolutely pumping.

It's as close to a music festival as you can get when you're almost thirteen years old.

'Oi, come take a seat, Mike!' Zoe yelled, waving me and Tully over to the collection of bean bags they had set up.

I looked around, then hesitated, panicked suddenly by this public display.

'Go on, you loser,' Tully prodded me in my back.

When I sat down, Zoe put her arm around me. 'Ten centimetres, Mike. Have you ever wanted ten extra centimetres more in your life?'

I smiled. *You have no idea,* I thought.

Skon nudged me with his elbow. 'What's news, Mike? Why you missed so much training recently?'

'My mum died,' I said.

There was a beat. Awkward. Tully and Zoe both looked to the ground.

'What? Serious?' Skon asked.

Tully nodded, and Zoe looked away.

The whole group just sat there, until …

'Did she see your performance at the Brindy Schools Cup? Is that what did it?' Skon said, a smile forming on his face.

I didn't really know what to do. It was the first time someone had treated me normally since it had happened.

'You know, Skon, when you treat life like one big joke, you sometimes don't realise that the people closest to you aren't laughing.' But then my steely-face broke, and I started to smile. 'But I have to admit, that was fucking funny.'

It *actually* made me smile.

Skon jumped up onto his good foot. He wrapped the crook of his elbow around my neck and gave me a noogie. 'Truth is, I've lost my dad too, Mike. Pancreatic cancer. Jokes are the only thing getting me through. Maybe we should hang out properly some time? Compare notes.'

I smiled. 'Let's do it. Orphans crew.'

'Welcome to the club,' Zoe said. She jumped up from the bench and hugged me too.

'Can I join? I've never met my dad!' Tully said, and joined in.

I stood there and took it, and I'm not going to lie, I felt my throat constrict, my eyes start to prickle with oncoming tears. It was just nice to feel close to people again.

'So, you losers wanna see a movie, or what?' Tully asked. 'It's on me. My first and, probably, last newspaper paycheck is burning a hole in my pocket!'

'Um, nah. I should probably get home,' I said. 'I need to see a dentist.'

I watched them ride up the escalators to the Hoyts cinema upstairs, feeling like actual friends now.

It was real nice.

Sad.

But nice.

•

You can't miss your mum's funeral without some explaining to do.

I stood nervously outside the front door, figuring out how I'd justify what I'd done.

My hands shook as I got my house keys out, and turned the lock, trying to remember word-for-word the exact reasoning I'd scripted in my head. It was time to talk it out.

I needed to jump, Dad. Jumping is life.

The sandpit was calling me.

I was doing it for someone I love. Isn't that what most people do most of the things in their life for?

When I walked in the door, and I saw Dad standing in the lounge room with Sonja, my plans of redemption flew out the window as I felt my facial fahrenheit skyrocketing.

'What's she doing here?' I said.

'Mike, I know this looks bad, but your father asked me to be here.' Sonja had her arms up like I had a gun.

I looked at Dad. 'I know I shouldn't have run away from the funeral. You can ground me or whatever, but –'

'Mike –' Dad tried to interrupt me.

'You talk about me needing to respect people and yet you invite her here the same day as Mum's funeral?' I was really at boiling point.

'Mike! Calm down. It's not what you think. I only just got home too,' Dad said, then turned to Sonja. 'Did it all work out?'

Sonja nodded, and then stepped away. 'I'll go.'

'OK,' Dad said. 'I will see you back in the dental van. After the holidays.'

Sonja nodded, and slipped out the front door.

I was really angry. I glared at Dad with my lip curled up.

The fact he had this stupid, goofy smile on his face as he stood there, obviously trying to hide something from me, made me even more angry.

'What is going on?' I asked, crankily.

Dad's smile didn't waver. He just stepped to the side and proudly showed it off.

A box, sitting idly under the big, bulky TV we had on the old wooden TV stand, gathering dust, in the corner of the lounge room. He bent down and fiddled around with a few buttons on the screen, and then stepped back, his arms wide, proud as punch.

It was just Dad and I, standing in that old dusty room. Silly old Dad, standing there, beaming like an idiot, looking at me as the analogue crackle of white noise fuzzed away, and then suddenly clicked to black. The box below the TV whizzed and whirred, and then finally a super-imposition came up on the screen.

It said, 'WELCOME TO FOXTEL'.

'The man came over while I was out sorting out some stuff. That's why Sonja was here. I thought it'd be nice to have when you got home today,' Dad said.

'There's 104 channels, Mike. You can watch sport, or there might even be a really great movie on!'

'I already saw a movie today,' I said. 'With my friends.'

It felt good saying that.

Dad picked up the new remote from the old wicker coffee table, sat down on the couch, and started surfing through the program guide.

'You don't even need the TV guide with this, because it tells you what's going to be on TV soon,' he said, pressing all sorts of buttons at random. We watched as various teletext boxes popped up all over the screen.

'I like the TV guide,' I said.

Dad nodded. 'You can still use the TV guide, Mike. You just don't have to,' he said.

Then a tear dropped down his cheek.

'Are you OK?' I asked. I'd never seen him cry before. Properly, like this. Maybe I was being too mean.

'I'm fine,' he said, wiping his face with his white shirt sleeve. 'It's just very hot.'

I kept looking at him. Studying. Realising I didn't really know him very much.

'Chicken nuggets OK?' he asked.

I sighed. 'No offence, but can't you cook something else for once?'

He raised and dropped his shoulders. 'You could always have what I'm having? There's goat stew with black-eyed beans, but I'm also going to cook some fish. It's deep fried in lots of herbs and spices. It's like Kentucky Fried Chicken, but –'

'Ghanaian Fried Fish?' I asked.

Dad smiled through tears seasoned with their own secret blend of hope and relief. 'It was my Dad's secret recipe in our village just out of Accra. He used to make it for me when I was your age. I guess I'm the colonel now.'

My eyes rolled. He was always so lame. But it suddenly hit me that I didn't really know my dad. Not as a person. 'What was it like in Ghana?'

'When?' he replied, wiping furiously at the tears that kept coming from his eyes.

'When you were my age?' I asked.

He thought. 'I was waking up every morning at 3am, and helping the fishermen bring in their catch. That's how I made money. Then I went to school. Then some afternoons I helped my family on the farm.'

'You say that like it's a run-of-the-mill kinda day,' I said.

Dad shrugged. 'It was.'

'Was it like when you go fishing down at the Swamp?' I asked.

Even though he was crying, he let out a laugh. 'Oh, Mike. It was nothing like this. Where I grew up it was actual poverty. I'll take you one day, and show you where I grew up. You'll see. Ten people sleeping in the one room,' he said.

I tried to imagine ten people lying around in the lounge room we were in right now. I wouldn't have lasted ten seconds.

'Now it's just you and me,' I said.

He shrugged. 'I don't need anyone else.'

That made me smile. Not on the outside, but on the inside.

Dad looked around the house. 'Your mother and I built this house. We were living in an apartment, near where your mother lives ... lived now.'

'Why did you move?' I asked.

'You lived there too. You don't remember. You used to run and jump everywhere, so we had to move. Mike, you should've seen when they gave us the keys when we first moved into this place. Your mother was just so excited. We had stairs. You know Linda? And where your mother grew up? And where I'm from? I mean, we had *stairs*, Mike. People who had stairs were rich.'

'Now you and I could have a level each,' I said.

Dad let out a small laugh. 'Anyway, that was back then. What are you going to watch tonight?' Dad asked.

I shrugged.

'I don't really feel like watching anything to be honest. I just feel like lying down,' I sighed.

'Oh, OK. It was good chatting,' he said, as he walked out, then he turned back around to face me.

'Maybe tomorrow we can have crab?' he said. 'I'm going to head out, but I have to go right up the Creek. Find a new spot. They're closing the Swamp ... which is a good thing, I guess. You can come if you'd like?'

'No thanks, Dad. I don't really feel like crabbing right now,' I said.

He sighed, then went to leave, and stopped.

'Can I ask you something?' he said.

'Dad!' I moaned. 'I'm not in the mood, please, just leave me alone.'

He didn't though. He just stood there, standing at the bottom of the steps, between the lounge room and the kitchen, his white button-up funeral shirt untucked and unbuttoned, his little belly poking out over his black slacks.

'We need to move out of your mother's place tomorrow,' he said.

Then he walked into the kitchen. Pretty soon afterwards I heard the 'psst' of a beer and the sizzling from the stove, and the smell of chicken nuggets wafted through the house.

CHAPTER TWENTY-TWO

GOOD FRIDAY, 10TH APRIL 1998

The first thing we noticed were the flies.

There were flies all through the place.

As soon as Dad and I opened the front door of Mum's apartment, I noticed a fly on the wall, and suddenly we realised they were everywhere. On the old stupid chandelier. On the TV unit. On the cardboard box of 'Stars and Dice'. Some were really slow too, just crawling desperately up the old canvas wallpaper.

Dad had collected the mail from the garden letterbox too, so he had a plastic shopping bag full of letters and leaflets bulging out of his fist. With his other hand he grabbed a copy of *The Brindy Chronicle*, rolled perfectly into thirds, the headline folded outside, which read: COUNCIL TO BUILD NEW FERRY TERMINAL PRECINCT.

'Tully's been here!' I said.

'What?' Dad was too busy whacking flies.

We slapped at flies for five minutes at least, until I finally took a seat on the leather two-seater in the lounge room, puffing away from the exertion as Dad kept slapping around in the kitchen.

The ceiling fan in the room was spinning, its blades droning with the consistent hum of an old fridge motor. I couldn't help but wonder how much energy it had used over the past few weeks. What the bill would be? Who would pay for it?

I stared at the half-finished game of 'Stars and Dice' that sat on the coffee table in front of me.

I couldn't believe she never found out her fate.

Then I noticed the little white thing wriggling on the carpet just underneath the table.

I got down on my hands and knees.

'Dad!' I yelled. 'Is this a worm?'

Dad came out of the kitchen, holding a *Brindy Chronicle*, sweating. He knelt down next to it.

'Could you use it for bait?'

'That's a maggot,' he said.

And then we looked up, and like some sort of wriggling Magic Eye picture, the lightly coloured, grey carpet seemed to almost be moving.

Everywhere my eyes looked, there seemed to be tiny, crawling maggots. All across the floor. I couldn't believe how many there were.

I jumped off the couch and walked against their flow.

'Where are they coming from?'

It was a chicken bone in the kitchen bin, crawling with larvae, with flies sitting on top of it, flying away, and then landing back on it.

Dad held his breath, and his head to the side, as he picked up the small bin under the sink. He tied up the handles of the bin liner.

A buzzing sound cut through the apartment.

'What's that?' Dad asked.

'Come on, old man. It's the door bell,' I said.

'I've never been here,' he said, then walked out, down the hall to answer the intercom. I walked into the bathroom and looked around.

It was so weird.

When you get in the shower, you don't ever expect it to be the last time, you know?

There was underwear lying on the floor next to the shower mat, her pyjamas, draped over the towel railing. Her sky-blue towel, hung loosely on the hook behind the door. A cream jar left open on the en suite vanity that had crusted over.

I walked into Mum's room and thought about how many conversations we'd had there. Mum, lying patiently on her bed, a book splayed open across her chest, just waiting to be finished, while I yapped away about the latest happenings on TV. The origami cranes I made her staring from the dresser.

I'd never had to say goodbye to a home before.

It's so hard realising that everything is 'definite'. You're never coming back.

I opened up the drawer on her bedside table cabinet and there were a bunch of magazines. I'd seen them before because some of the times Mum had gone out with her friends, or to Kenny's house, I'd snuck into her room and looked through those mags, hoping I could find something resembling a porno.

One of the magazines had a picture of a naked woman, but it was kind of medical, so it always made me feel a bit uncomfortable. Like the old Italian man in that movie that day.

I picked up Mum's magazines and threw them in the big black garbage bag Dad had left me.

God, it was all so sad.

Underneath the magazines was a book.

Mum's diary.

I picked it up and felt a sharp pang of guilt as I undid the rubber band, holding its covers closed.

I opened it.

Was Mum watching? Was I allowed to read her thoughts yet?

I put the diary down on her bed.

I couldn't. It wasn't for me.

I suddenly tasted shame in my throat and I looked out her bedroom window, as if to check whether someone had been peeking in.

I walked back out of her room, towards the lounge room, then turned back.

Should I read it?

I felt so sad. I didn't know if I wanted to know.

I thought about the day we'd moved in and there was no furniture in the whole place, and Mom and I had played this game where we rolled all over the carpet, and I kept rolling over the top of her, and she'd groaned and said I was getting too big, and I just laughed. I think I laughed for three hours straight that day.

I remember thinking it was just me and her that day. Me and Mum, taking on the world.

Now it was me and Dad, taking on some bugs.

·

Dad and I sprayed the bathroom and hallway. Cleaning up dead insects, wiping up the mess, sanitising what was left of Mum's existence in this home.

Dad held the bathroom rubbish bag out at full length. 'I'm going to take this out,' he said.

'OK,' I said.

He left, and I walked out into the lounge room and looked again at the game of 'Stars and Dice' on the table.

I couldn't help but think about what the final spin would've been.

What Mum's fate might've been if she hadn't died.

I picked up the die, and threw it into the little plastic package octagon that contained the dice's random bouncing fury.

It was a '2'.

I checked the book.

A deep secret will shortly be revealed to you. It will bring you great joy. You will discover that someone you cherish cares for you in return. Be careful. Don't do anything to extinguish this burning flame.

There was more to this.

I knew it.

Mum didn't just leave me.

There had to be a reason.

For Georgia, for Mum, for all of it.

There had to be a reason.

I ran back to Mum's bedroom and picked up the journal. I opened it on the first page.

New Year's Day. 1998.

Her handwriting was always terrible, scrawled every-which-way-and-that, ramblings, surrounded by hand-drawn pictures of flowers. It filled me with the same sense of uncertainty that fills me when the phone rings and you're not expecting a call.

I agreed with myself that if I saw something that was too much, I would stop. I wouldn't even show Dad. I would just throw it away, throw it in the bag with all the other needless pieces that creep into your space over the life of a home.

But until then, I would read it.

I'm sure there would be a clue in all of this.

A hint. A wink. A tap of the nose.

Something telling me where she *really* was. Why she had to lie to everyone. To pretend to die. *I'm in Saint Petersburg. They're coming to get you. One day.*

I would be the only person to figure it all out.

I didn't even get a chance to read the first line when the phone rang, echoing down the hall, towards me in the bedroom. That perfect run-up of a hallway. Jumping into the lounge room sandpit.

I was busted.

Mum was watching. That's the sort of technology that spies have.

The phone bleated down the hall and I stood there, pausing for a moment, part of me realising that I should savour the feeling of loss, because I'd learn from it one day.

One day.

Soon enough I'd be lying with Mum again, on a beach, laughing.

Of course it was Mum calling. Who else would be calling this number? She knew. She knew that Dad and I would be here. Now that the Inghams had forced the council into admitting their guilt, we could all get real again. It was all a set-up. A mission from the government using Mum and Georgia as insurgents to unseat an unruly council. I'd pick up the phone and Mum would explain everything.

Where to meet. How to get there. Who to call.

I put the journal back where I found it.

I probably took too long to walk down the hallway.

Ring ring.

I was just in a daze.

Ring ring.

I imagined my little feet, scrubbing along the carpet in this hallway, growing with each step. From being the size six that they were when we moved in, to being the big size ten they were now.

Ring ring.

I hopped.

Ring ring.

I stepped.

I need it to be Mum.

Ring ring.

I jumped.

I plunge into the sandpit.

Ring ring.

And then I answered.

'Hello?' I asked, the way I always did. Looking across the apartment lounge room, looking out over the Brindle River, trying to spot whether maybe there was someone in an apartment across the water, someone holding something up. A sign. A torch.

'Hello.'

'It's me,' I said, my heart pounding.

'Who is this?' the voice said. The reception was crackly.

'It's Mike!' I said.

A pause.

'Mr Mike. I would like to offer you a better phone plan.' The voice sounded Indian. Maybe Sri Lankan. I didn't know.

I didn't care.

I ached.

The shame submerging me like water in a sinking ship.

I'd believed for a second, for a moment, long enough to watch the tide flow out and to take a walk along the sands.

I dropped the phone and watched it dangle on the wall by its cord. I fell to my knees on the floor.

I couldn't help it.

Jesus Christ, I tried everything to stop, but I just couldn't. They came pouring out. The tears. The guttural moan of the wounded, of those who've forgotten their words.

I cried so hard. I felt like the universe was falling apart while still holding onto my heart, pulling it in every direction.

The totality of never. Never again. I would never see my mum. I would never run down this hall and burst through her bedroom door to update her on my day at school. I would never feel her hugs or hear her voice or see her grey hairs disappear overnight, a box of hair dye discarded in the kitchen bin in the morning. I would never feel this carpet, I would never hear the air-con, I would never laugh with her, she would never see me raise my children, never see me fall in love, never see me picking oranges.

'Mike, who was that?' Dad walked through the front door, looking tired. So sweaty. He had masking tape stuck to his stupid, curly hair, and he was wearing rubber dental gloves for some reason.

He stood opposite me, as I bawled my eyes out, so embarrassed, weeping tears that burned like acid.

'Hey, come on. It'll be OK,' he said.

He hugged me, just as two big Tongan-looking guys, around twenty-five years old, strode in through the front door, bright orange muscle-tees clinging to their hefty frames, small navy stubbies wrapped around their tree-trunk calves. Sneakers with either small or no socks.

'Any room in particular you'd like us to start with?' The bigger one said. Then they spotted me, sitting like a little kid, bawling my eyes out.

'Hey, get it out, little man,' the bigger one said. 'Whatever it is, it's better out than in.'

'Of course he thinks that,' said the smaller one. 'He's a removalist!'

They both giggled, and walked up the hallway. 'We'll start in the bedroom first, uō.'

Then it was just me and Dad.

In Mum's lounge room.

Trying to plant some oranges.

ACKNOWLEDGEMENTS

I'd like to acknowledge my partner, Belinda, who was unwavering in her support as I undertook this project, an incredible mother, who took care of our beautiful daughter Sofia while I typed away at my keyboard at all hours of the day and night, who was the first person to read this, and whose encouragement brightened me up, week in, week out.

I'd like to thank my writing agent, Pippa Masson, who first approached me to write a book and consistently approached it with positivity and excitement.

I'd like to thank my management at Century Entertainment for supporting me throughout my career no matter what endeavours I choose to embark on.

Huge thanks goes to everyone in the team at Hachette Australia who guided me through this experience, in particular Robert Watkins, who showed immediate faith in me, my editor, Brigid Mullane, and CEO, Louise Sherwin-Stark.

Shout-out to my family: Michelle, Levi, William, Dawn, Russell, Seth, Linda, Nii, Tetteh, Naa, Sammy, Alejandra, Maya, Safia, Sahara, Isaac, Nico, and Janice.

To my sister, Rachel, thank you for being the best. Always supportive, always generous, guiding me through life at every turn when Mum couldn't.

To my Dad, the Daddy Mack, the one and only. We went through this together. I've learnt so much from you over the years, and I couldn't hope for a better friend, father and role model.

And finally, to my Mum, Roslyn Ann Okine, I love you and miss you every day. Thank you for making me who I am today.

I hope you all enjoy reading this.

x